Out There

To my wonderful Uncle David,
This book was completely
inspired by your lecture
over the summer about
how all men are pigs ☺
Thank you for the wise
words. Your niece,

Simi Prasad

Out there

Simi Prasad

Out There

First published in 2013 by
Anoma Press Ltd
48 St Vincent Drive, St Albans, Herts, AL1 5SJ UK

info@anomapress.com
www.anomapress.com

Cover design by Michael Inns
Artwork by Karen Gladwell

Printed on acid-free paper from managed forests.
This book is printed on demand to fulfill orders,
so no copies will be remaindered or pulped.

ISBN 978-1-908746-77-1

This book is available online and in all good bookstores.

Prologue

"Ava!" I yelled up the stairs even though I knew it was in vain; she was still missing. "Where is that girl?"

I rubbed my forehead and wandered into the kitchen. My whole body was exhausted, with fatigue, but also worry. I hadn't had a wink of sleep because I knew that finding Ava was my top priority. I walked over to the sink and poured myself a glass of water.

Inside I was terrified; I knew there weren't many places to go, as our city was only so big with barely five hundred people in it, but I could only imagine that she must have fallen and banged her head and was lying unconscious somewhere. The mere thought almost made me drop my glass.

Pull it together. I drained my glass and tried to brainstorm all of the possible places Ava could have been. She wasn't at her friends' houses; I had already gone to each one. That was another strange thing: they all said that they hadn't seen Ava outside school in weeks, and they used to spend every minute together. As soon as the bell rang, they said, she would be gone, as if she dropped off the face of the earth. At least she was attending.

I checked the clock: 2:20 a.m. I sighed, knowing that I had to leave for work soon, but couldn't because I had to wait for Ava to come home safely. The best thing to do was wait, she would return soon enough, and if not then I would know something was wrong. So, I busied myself organising the kitchen once, twice, and even then I wasn't happy with it.

I rearranged the closet and made sure the living room was neat before going upstairs and into my bathroom. After cleaning it thoroughly, I caught the reflection of myself in the mirror and sighed. It was unbearably obvious that I hadn't had any sleep or peace of mind. So, I took to freshening up; I washed my face three times and combed through the tangles in my hair. I thought back to the days when I put on make-up every morning and had to remind myself that those days didn't exist any more. Sometimes I wished they did.

I used to live in a time where the world was limitless and people came from all over. But my world was destroyed, and so were all the little pieces of it. I waved goodbye to trivial things like make-up and mobile phones. Not to mention something far more important.

Traces of daylight were filtering in, so I went downstairs to the kitchen to prepare breakfast, when I realised my hunger had been consumed by my worry. So instead I just sat at the counter and waited.

And in my wait, my mind wandered to other places. Often I thought about my life and what I had become: a woman with greying hair with a daughter slipping through her fingers. It was only months ago that Ava was the closest person in the world to me. Of course, it was obvious what had pulled us apart.

Then I heard something. It was the door opening. *Please be her.* I sat up straighter and waited.

She walked into the kitchen and I was so relieved to see her breathing with blood pumping through her veins that I almost leapt out of my seat and held her in my arms telling her that I loved her. But then I saw the cheesy, smiley and completely carefree expression on her face and I snapped. She had no idea that I hadn't slept or eaten or done anything but worry about her and she just waltzed in like everything was going to be OK.

My expression fixed into an icy glare and her face fell. "Welcome back Ava," was all that came out of my taut lips.

"M-mother why are you up so early?" She looked like a deer caught in the headlights.

"This is the time I normally leave, Ava. But, truth be told, I have actually been up since four a.m. yesterday." Yet at that moment I didn't feel tired. "Do you know why?"

"I can't imagine." She was holding something back and it was so obvious.

"Well, I came home from work yesterday, early in fact, and my daughter was nowhere to be found."

"I stayed over at Lexi's house. I'm sorry I forgot to tell you." I stared at her, waiting for her to tell me the truth. No such luck.

"Oh well, that makes sense," I continued. "I did actually personally visit the O'Connell's and the Samuels' and the Naumann's homes at one this morning after my daughter never turned up."

I saw her gulp. And I so badly wanted to run over and hold her close. But, I couldn't.

"You want to know what every single one of those girls told me?" I just kept pushing. "They said that they haven't seen you in weeks, except for school, and even then you're in your own world. Just what world exactly is that, Ava?"

She just stood there with no comprehension of how worried I was.

"What world is it?!"

"I've just had a lot on my mind."

I sighed and walked over to her. "Ava, you need to rest. Your surgery is days away." I began to stress the importance of her being rested so that the surgery would run smoothly, when she interrupted, "What, do you want me to sit in my room all day?"

Why was she raising her voice?

I tried to reason with her, but she just exploded, yelling at me about complete nonsense. She went off on a tangent about how I was never there for her, when I specifically remembered her acknowledging that I would be very busy if I got my new job. I pointed out that I was there for her and she knew I was, yet she still continued to stress that I wasn't. Was she making excuses to hide the fact that she was gone all night?

"Why don't you tell everyone the truth about men, huh?" she yelled out of nowhere.

"The what?!"

"They did more than oppress and hate and destroy and you know it!"

I stared at her like she'd lost her mind. "Where did you get such horrific ideas? Men were evil and nothing less!" It was of the utmost importance that she understood that, otherwise the consequences would have been disastrous. Nothing good came of men. That's why they all died out.

"What's your proof?!"

I couldn't believe she was still on that. "Look around you! Our world was almost destroyed because all men wanted was power and money and land."

"That's a lie! Stop lying to me! I am much older and smarter than you think and I know that men were more than that – some were, but not all."

Of course I knew she was mature, but some things were just better kept hidden. Ava's utter curiosity and strong-mindedness about everything always made it so much harder to get anything through to her. I knew that of all the girls her age, she would be the one that would never understand.

Then she pulled something out of her pocket and shoved it in my face. I knew exactly what it was.

I snatched it from her, completely speechless. Holding it in my hands caused a wave of sadness and regret to flood through my body, washing away all the barriers that I had built up to withstand the raging storm I had battled so many years ago. For a moment I thought I would crumble under the memories, but instead something inside me snapped.

"HOW DARE YOU! How dare you jump to conclusions! And go through my private things!" She had no idea what it was like; she had no right to judge me. Ava hadn't even the tiniest image of the sacrifices I made for her. Her behaviour was appalling. "And how dare you try to justify men when they almost cost you everything! Brave women fought for you to be alive and this is how you repay them!"

Her disrespect towards her liberators, who fought and fought to achieve survival during The Great Wars of the X Years, was shameful. It made me shudder and I thought back to how terrifying it was to be alive during the Wars. Everyone turning on each other, people fleeing to any sanctuary possible, and leaving nothing for anyone else. She had no idea how fortunate she was that several women joined together in the Movement and created our city. The last city. Otherwise we would all have been dead too.

"And what about Katelyn, Mother? Did you lie about her too?!"

Then I realised why she was so upset. I tried to comfort her, but she went off again about Katelyn and started yelling that it was my fault. If only I could tell her the truth. I wanted to protect Ava so badly, but I couldn't make exceptions for her because she was my daughter. I felt so torn, and she had no idea what I was going through.

"I don't want to have the surgery." I almost missed her say it.

"You what?"

"I'm not going to do it."

Then the yelling started again. She threw crazy statements at me about how I didn't see the real her or hear what she was saying. If only she knew that all I wanted was to keep her safe, even if it meant distancing myself. She could never know all that I knew; it was too much for her to understand.

Then she said the one thing that a mother should never have to hear her daughter say, "You don't love me! You love what you want me to be!"

I was stung. "Ava, of course I love you."

"How can I believe you again when all you do is lie?!"

I tried to show her that I cared, but she wouldn't stop for a minute to let me speak. Finally I had enough and even though grounding didn't exist any more either, I did it anyway.

"You, young lady, are not leaving this house, do you hear me? I will walk you to school and pick you up afterwards, apart from that you remain here. End of discussion."

"Oh, but this is not the end of the discussion."

She flew up the stairs in a rage and I ran after her, about to apologise, when she whipped round and said, "You know what?" Her eyes were full of hatred. "I blame you." Then without another word she vanished into her room and slammed the door.

I stood there shocked. Slowly I walked up the stairs myself. Suddenly all my emotions welled up and I felt so awful for keeping the truth from her. But she couldn't know about my sacrifices, for Ava wouldn't ever see them my way. She'd never understand as much as she believed she would.

I stumbled into my room as all these heavy feelings thundered through me. For a second I stood there, trying to be the strong woman everyone expected and needed me to be. But, in the end, I couldn't hold it any longer. I fell to my bed and for the first time in years, I cried.

Chapter One

Ava, Five Months Earlier

October 3rd Year 17 was one of the most important days of my life. Everything would be determined within the next ten minutes. I held my breath, clenched my hands and stared at the stage, paralysed. People in the crowd drifted around me and I picked out familiar faces. Of course every face was familiar in some way; no one there was new to me. The buzz of the audience was building yet I only heard a muffled sound.

The announcer began to take her place on stage and the sound filtered out, leaving only the thump of my heartbeat in my ears. She carried in her hand a perfect white envelope that dictated my fate. Well, perhaps not *my* fate exactly, but the effect on me was greater than that on most of the people there.

She strolled up to the microphone, another familiar face, and leaning in close she said, "Welcome everyone to the seventh Election for Leader of the Council." The audience applauded and she continued, "Today we will be announcing the results of the votes that have been tallied here today and we thank you all for participating."

The campaign of a candidate lasted a total of three days in Emiscyra, our city. On the first day, candidates had to declare that they were interested in running by presenting their principles to the current Council who then decided if they would back them or not. If a candidate had the support of the Council, they would speak at the school and try to win votes from the under-eighteens. They then each spoke at the Election so the rest of the community could decide whom to vote for. Every member of the community then voted thirty minutes later.

Once the voting began, and the under-eighteens were called first, I appeared at the desk in a flash, giving my name before they even asked. Taking the touchpad in my hands, there was not a single moment of hesitation as I typed in *candidate 7B*. After that, all I could do was hope that my one little vote was not alone.

The announcer continued, "Whoever is elected Leader today will hold the great responsibility of supporting our community and leading it through whatever may come. They will hold one of the highest honours and shall be respected by all of us for their commitment and effort. They will follow a long line of Leaders who all played a tremendous role in shaping our community. So now please join with me in welcoming our candidates."

The knot in my stomach grew as the three candidates took their places on stage. The first on was Meredith Dale. She seemed very warm and committed to the job, yet I couldn't help but feel she didn't quite grasp how great the responsibility was. She had served on the Council for the past three years as Leader of Education, voted for by the students only. She smiled and waved as she walked forward and the audience applauded.

Next on came Donna Hart. Her face was etched with wisdom, yet she had not a single wrinkle. Her speech earlier was golden and she was one of the most talented speakers I'd seen. She had served on the Council for the past twelve years in roles ranging from Member for Produce Production to Leader of Interrelations. She walked on confidently and elegantly.

The third on was Fiona Turner. Her speech was well delivered and she had many great ideas, yet her enthusiasm lacked. She had no history on the Council and had only just graduated, specialising in politics. However, her mother was the fifth Leader and did a fabulous job. Everyone expected Fiona to follow in her mother's footsteps. She walked on to the stage; her youth compared to the others was glaring.

The announcer applauded the candidates, thanking them for volunteering for such an overwhelming yet rewarding task.

Silence.

She gently opened the envelope. For a moment everything stopped. No movement. No sound. Just that rapid thumping of my heart. When I looked back, I was thankful it didn't burst out of me altogether.

She slipped out a tiny piece of paper. *How could something so small hold something so big?* She waved it in the air and the audience laughed.

Couldn't laugh, couldn't think, couldn't breathe.

She took a deep breath and opened the folded paper.

Two words. Just two words meant everything.

"And the seventh Council Leader is…"

The pause. The painful pause that made me dizzy with nerves. The silence was too great. I wanted to scream to destroy it. But then she opened her mouth…

"…Donna Hart!"

Cheers escaped the crowd and the silence was gone. It took a moment for the words to reach me. Then I heard them loud and clear: "Donna Hart, Donna Hart." I let out a wild cheer, screaming and clapping until my throat was sore and my hands numb. Donna was grinning from ear to ear as she hugged each candidate in turn and received their congratulations. She strolled up to the stage and hugged the announcer too, then went over to the microphone.

"Thank you all."

The crowd cheered her more and I could barely feel my hands. I was sure my cheers could be heard over every other sound.

Donna leant into the mic. "I want to thank you all for giving me this honour and I intend to make sure your support is not in vain. First I want to applaud Meredith and Fiona for their gallant efforts, which I hope don't go unsung. And thank you for all the support I have received as it means the world to me. Also a special thanks to my own daughter Ava, who has stood by me through all the late-night speech writing and re-writing sessions, the nerves and excitement, and for saying 'I understand' every time I told her how much winning would change things. Ava, thank you." She reached her hand out into the crowd as a symbol of appreciation.

Just as she said that, a bright light entered my vision and I could barely see anything. Confused, I lifted my hand to cover my eyes and to my surprise everyone in the crowd was applauding me. Donna was smiling at me and she mouthed, "Thank you, Ava." The spotlight was shining down on me and I mouthed back, "You're welcome, Mother."

The audience turned back to the stage as my mother continued, "You have my word that under my leadership our community will flourish, and your needs will be fulfilled. My determination is strong, but our community is stronger, and I have no doubt in my mind that we shall continue to develop so that our children's children can lead lives as fortunate as ours and be free of the poor judgment that once plagued our city. And on that note, I could not be more thrilled that I shall be leading us into the most highly anticipated phase of our development." The crowd cheered. "From the Analysis Phase and Re-Organisation Phase initiated by the First Leader, to the Infrastructure Development Phase, to the Education and Motivation Phase, to the Community Strengthening Phase, to now. Now I am proud to lead us in the Repopulation Phase."

The audience cheered and people turned to their neighbours to chatter about their excitement. A warm sense of pride filled me to know I might be part of it.

"This honour I have been dreaming of for many years now and to know it is finally here brings me great pride. So, thank you all again and as you have put your faith in me, I shall do everything I can to fulfil your expectations. Thank you."

The audience applauded her and the announcer stepped forward and said, "Now we shall transfer Leadership with The Oath, written by our liberators as a promise for us all to keep." The sixth Leader, Jemima Hewitt, walked on to the stage and shook hands with my mother. She then walked over to the microphone.

Silence again. This time it was for respect, and maybe secretly for a chance to breathe in the moment, a moment of history.

Jemima began, "I, Council Leader, can rightfully say that my duties to my community have been fulfilled. I have followed through with my promises, represented my city with honour, and helped us to prosper. I have been fair, I have been honest, I have been thoughtful, I have been a good example, and I have been true. I now hand over my responsibility to my successor, Donna Hart." She stood to the side and Donna came forward.

More silence. However, I felt it growing on me. Once a state of waiting, then a state of knowing something wonderful was to come.

Mother said with a strong voice, "I, Donna Hart, promise that I will fulfil my duties to my community. I will follow through with my promises, represent my city with honour, and help us to prosper. I will be fair, I will be honest, I will be thoughtful, I will be a good example, and I will be true. I now accept responsibility from my predecessor, Jemima Hewitt."

The announcer then walked forward and indicated for us all to repeat our section of The Oath. A collective body and a collective voice rang out, "We, the people, promise that we will fulfil our duties to our community and support our Leader as long as she obeys her Oath. We will represent our city with honour. We will be fair, we will be honest, we will be thoughtful, we will be kind, and we will be true. We promise this in honour of our liberators, who fought to keep our race and our gender alive when we were threatened by the faults of men. Long live the women of Emiscyra."

The Oath was thought to have supernatural powers. Whenever it was said, it bound people together and they instantly felt connected to each other. In that moment, I honestly believed that it was powerful, as the strong energy vibrated through the air.

All the faces – so familiar, so united – applauded as our new Leader descended from the stage and everyone dispersed to enjoy the celebrations.

The Town Hall was beautifully decorated for the occasion. Elections always brought on an excuse to add a little sparkle to the plain wooden walls. The most extreme decorations always came on Liberation Day, once a year. Truth be told, decorations were rare, because in Emiscyra we lived simple lives and never bought anything that was not a necessity or for a special occasion.

So the bright glittering lights and colourful banners were always a surprise to everyone at first. But the members of the community understood that they would be packed away that night and left to collect dust in a cardboard box for another three years, so we all might as well enjoy them while they lasted.

I found myself scanning the walls for a different type of streamer from usual or a new addition to the collage of colour. It was my sixth Election, and my first I attended at the age of two. The layout was always the same: same decorations, same entertainment, same food selection. Perhaps the fact that the same group of women always organised it had a part to play in the outcome. Nevertheless, it was a wonderful, perfect day. Giving up on finding anything new, except for the flowers, I decided to go and find my mother.

As I wound my way through the crowd, I was congratulated by a few familiar faces that must have recognised me from the blinding spotlight and special thank you. Finally, a flash of flawless jet-black hair caught my eye and I was soon right behind my mother, who spun round as I came up. She smiled at me and wrapped her strong thin arms around my waist and whispered in my ear, "We did good, sweetheart."

I hugged her back and said, "Congratulations Mother, I knew you could do it. I'm just so glad it's finally over, I didn't think I'd make it any longer before passing out."

"Oh darling, it's so comforting to know you care so much. What would I do without you?"

The group of ladies she was standing with smiled at us and I recognised Georgina O'Connell, my neighbour, and Sylvia Carter, Leader of Technology on the Council for the past seventeen years, among them.

"You must be very happy for your mother," one of the women said.

"Yes, I am. I'm Ava by the way."

"Oh yes, we all know how your mother has wanted this for some time and I can certainly say that her winning makes me very happy, don't you agree?" Sylvia said to me with her classic, serious, almost icy face.

"Of course, she deserves it more than anyone." I looked Sylvia right in the eye as I said this. She flicked a lock of grey hair off her shoulder and gave me her signature icy smile in return.

"Oh Ava, please," Mother sighed modestly.

"It's true though. There is no one better for the job than you and I'm so happy for you for getting what you've always wanted."

Mother smiled at me just as I spotted Jennifer Rose amongst the women.

"Jennifer," I said to her, "do you know where Katelyn is? I've been trying to find her, actually."

"I think she already went backstage to get ready," she replied warmly.

"Oh thanks. Mother, is it all right if I go? I'll catch up with you later."

"Yes, Ava, of course. In fact, I'll probably have a few things to do later so how about I meet you back at home after the celebration, OK?"

"OK. Congrats again," I said, walking towards the stage.

She waved me goodbye and turned back to her friends. Some women I recognised from the restaurant by school were already on stage, singing and playing a keyboard piano. Entering the backstage door, I soon spotted Katelyn. She wasn't hard to find with her signature blonde curls and rosy cheeks. Not to mention, she was probably one of the smallest people in the room. I watched as she carefully pulled out her precious guitar from its case and leant it against the wall. She stared at it with her hands on her hips – a sign I knew meant she was contemplating something.

Taking her pause as an opportunity to go over, I snuck up behind her and placed my hands over her eyes. "Guess who?" I teased.

"Ava," she said, giggling and turning round, "don't you think that's getting a bit old?"

"Whatever do you mean?"

"I'd know my best friend anywhere, silly."

"Oh right, I guess I forgot about that," I joked.

She playfully hit me on the arm and said, "Hey, help me with this will you?" She nodded at the guitar.

"Sure. What happened to it this time?"

"Well, I just got it back from repairs and it looks different to me, don't you think?"

I inspected the guitar for a second. "Oh, yeah, I can see it. There's a speck of dust on it, right there."

"Ava! Seriously, something's different."

"Katelyn, it looks fine, trust me."

"Well, OK. This is an antique so I just want to be sure. People don't play music like before, you know they once didn't have auto-tuners so they had to sit there and tune them themselves.

And they used to actually have people whose profession was to play music; it wasn't just a skill. And they…"

"Katelyn, I know, you've told me this a million times…"

"Oh sorry, it's just that…"

"…music is something that is going extinct and it's important to keep the culture alive," I finished.

"You know me too well."

"Wasn't that obvious before? So, are you on next?"

"Yeah, they asked me to play again this year, shocker. I feel like every Election and Liberation Day they have the same celebration."

"Well, you know how they like tradition."

"Yeah, but it makes the music boring. If you hear the same thing all the time then…"

"… you learn to hate it. You know you've said all this before, right?"

"Well, at least I know you were listening to me all this time."

"Hey, I can be a good listener too."

"Uh-huh. Oh, congrats for your mother by the way."

"Thanks, I was so relieved."

"Yeah, I know how much she wanted it, so I'm really happy for her."

"Well, now the hard work begins. She told me that if she won, it would be a big commitment."

"That makes sense; she does have the most important job in the whole city. But, if anyone can do it, it's Donna Hart."

"True, she is tough as a rock."

"Yeah, she's like you."

"You think?"

Mother and I shared the same glossy black hair – hers is straight, mine's wavy – and the same periwinkle blue eyes. Most people said we had the same nose and face shape too.

"Ava, no one is stronger than you," Katelyn said and her golden brown eyes lit up like they did whenever she smiled. "All right, time to go on."

"Good luck."

"Yeah, sure," she sighed. "Wait a minute, I have an idea."

"This better not involve me…"

"Come on *with* me!" she exclaimed.

"Oh no, remember last time we tried to sing together in public? Not pretty."

"Ava, that was like two years ago. It'll be fun! Please?"

"No, you're fabulous enough on your own."

"That's not the point, I want you to come with me. It'll be a hit, the Leader's daughter singing her heart out on stage!"

"No way, you didn't say anything about organs leaving the body."

"Ava! *Please.*"

I stared at her with my *no way can you change my mind* face, but it didn't work. Her puppy-dog eyes were impossible to resist. And before I knew it, my feet were firmly planted on the stage floor, mic in hand.

Suddenly silence wasn't comforting any more. I tried to push away the flutter in my stomach, but the butterflies seemed to have a mind of their own.

"Hi, I'm Ava and this is…" The lights turned on, blocking my vision once again. Squinting away the brightness, I continued, "Uh thanks. So like I was saying, I'm Ava and this is Katelyn." Katelyn waved. "And we're going to perform for you."

There was a moment of awkward silence, then the audience clapped. *Showtime.* I gave Katelyn my *you owe me* stare and adjusted the microphone in the stand. Taking a deep breath, I indicated to her that I was ready to start. She began to strum a melody and the gorgeous sound of Katelyn's old and precious guitar danced around the room.

The song was a classic from the early days of the city. Back then there was a woman named Naomi who wrote new music, as all records of old songs and tunes had been destroyed in The Great Wars. She created bright happy melodies with lyrics that told of our people's struggle for freedom and what our society had become. Then she became sick and passed away before the city's second anniversary. After that people only sang her songs – good thing there were dozens of them. She was also the last person in the city to die of a disease, said to have been a birth defect. Apart from her, and a woman who died of old age, everyone since the start of the city was still alive.

Katelyn was playing one of her favourites and I saw the crowd nod their heads before the lyrics even began. As my cue came, I opened my mouth and sang. I could barely hear myself over the thump of my heart, a very busy organ that day, and it took me a moment to realise that no one else could hear me either. I stopped and turned to Katelyn with wide eyes just as she stopped strumming her guitar. I looked out over the crowd of people all standing there expectantly and my face began to heat up.

I tapped the microphone. "Testing, testing." Some people in the front row seemed to understand, but beyond that there was pretty much silence. A few yawns, maybe a whisper or two.

"Katelyn!" I hissed. "It's not working!"

She didn't seem to have any ideas so I spun round and clutched the microphone between my sweaty hands. "Testing, testing. Hello?" I yelled out into the crowd, "Anyone know how to turn this on? Hello?" My last word suddenly sounded much louder and the audience began to cheer.

"It's working!" I turned to Katelyn.

"Start again?"

"Yeah, let's rock!"

She began to play once again and the people nodded their heads to the beat. With a bit more confidence the second time, I sang out the lyrics into the fully functional microphone. Then Katelyn joined in at the chorus and the crowd got really into it. Some began to cheer, others clapped with the beat until everyone was clapping along. Comforted by this, I continued singing and began to sway with the music, enjoying every note. As the chorus came around again I clapped my hands above my head and grabbed the microphone off the stand, dancing around the stage. I could feel Katelyn laughing, so I went all out. The crowd were laughing and dancing and singing along. As the last lyrics came I pointed the microphone into the crowd and they all leant in to sing. The last chord rang and the audience cheered us.

Laughing, I skipped over to Katelyn. "OK, I think I'm totally worn out now, your turn."

"All right, but you're coming on afterwards for the finale."

"If you insist." I flopped into her chair panting, as she walked up to the front of the stage.

Katelyn lowered the microphone and the audience chuckled as she moved it about a foot lower. Sitting on a stool, she began to pick a gentle melody, soft and slow, like a breeze that drifted through the room and stroked the heart of each person. She began to sing. Her voice was like that of an angel, the sweetest most beautiful sound that captured the attention of everyone there. The song was not well known, but I had heard my dear friend sing it all the time. She had said it was called *The Choice*. The audience was captivated as the oh-so-familiar lyrics rang out:

> *One choice may be safe,*
> *But in truth it brings pain,*
> *Live for what I love,*
> *Or live to gain?*

> *Would risking it all,*
> *Give me peace of mind?*
> *When defying the rules,*
> *Ends up costing my life.*

I liked to think of her voice as being as soft as rose petals. For when she sang, like a rose in full bloom, you couldn't help but stare. And as the song ended, it almost broke my heart to hear the sound of her voice fading. Then it was silent. A beautiful silence, though. A silence to appreciate and hold on to the last bit of something beautiful. Then the biggest cheer imaginable erupted from the audience and I saw Jennifer Rose smiling at Katelyn with love and pride. Right then, I would have been the proudest person in the world too if my daughter could create something as beautiful as that.

Katelyn came over. "Now, are you ready to wow them all?"

"Trust me, I don't think it's possible to wow them any more than that."

"Trust *me*, they won't believe their eyes when the dynamic duo take the stage."

"All right then, one more song."

That was an understatement. There were four more songs actually, each one louder and wilder and more exciting than the previous. Katelyn played that guitar until her fingers were red and both of us could barely speak as we stumbled off the stage laughing.

"That was incredible!" she exclaimed, clutching my shoulder for balance.

"Who knew we had so much talent?" I giggled, slumping on to the floor.

Katelyn mimed my dancing around the stage, flipping her hair and stomping her feet. She collapsed on to the floor laughing.

"Hey, I dance way better than that."

"Yeah, remember this." She stood up and slid across the floor on her knees with her hands in the air.

"Ha ha, very funny."

She laughed and fell back on the floor. "And you didn't want to come on."

"Don't give me an *I told you so* or I'll have to mimic you at the school party two years ago."

"Now that was some crazy dancing."

We took a moment to reminisce before I broke the silence. "Hey Kay, want to sleep over at my place?"

"Won't your mother want time with you?"

"Nah, she said she'd be out late, so it's fine. We can sleep in the yard…"

"You're so lucky, my house doesn't have a yard to sleep in."

"So, that's a yes?"

"Fine," she said, laughing.

I stood, holding my hand out to her and pulled her up. After her most precious belonging was packed away, we went outside and walked to the tram stop.

At my house, we went and gathered some blankets from the cupboard and laid them on the dry grass in the yard. Katelyn borrowed sleeping clothes and we climbed into our homemade outdoor beds.

Our sky in Emiscyra was always dark at night, projected by the Bubble. The Bubble was one of the many inventions of Sylvia Carter, designed to keep out harmful gases and wild animals that lived outside the city. It was a thin layer that spread across the city edges and curved above it. Sunlight triggered a clear blue sky to be projected, and darkness triggered a black night sky. This piece of pure genius was marvelled at and immediately promoted Sylvia Carter to the smartest woman in Emiscrya. She was practically an idol.

Sleeping in the yard meant that we could stare at the curved ceiling of the Bubble. It was always visible at night, never in the day.

"I wonder how that works," I said.

"How what works?" Katelyn asked, lying on the ground.

"The Bubble. How is it that you can see it at night, but not in the day?"

"I don't know," she puzzled. "You know before the Bubble people had to always be careful of looking into the sun. We're lucky that the Bubble doesn't show the sun but lets its rays through."

"What does the sun look like?"

"I think it's a glow in the sky. People are a moth to its flame, they can't not stare at it, but it hurts their eyes if they do." She turned to her side. "Are you excited for graduation?"

"It's like a year away, but yeah, I guess. I can't believe we're almost done, all fifteen years of school."

"I know, it's so strange. Before you know it we'll be assigned our own houses and intercoms and then we'll have to apply for a profession and receive income from the Council and everything!"

"We already get income, though."

"Yeah, but not adult-rate income. Hey, remember when our income went to our mothers to use to raise us and we didn't get to use it until age ten?"

"Who could forget? I mean I still give Mother a share of my income to buy food for me, but I know what you mean. And we get our eighteenth birthday bonuses soon!" I exclaimed, sitting up.

"Yeah, in like nine and a half months," she sighed.

"Still, we're almost eighteen! How weird!"

"I know. We're amongst the last people to graduate. After the year below us, that's it. No more kids."

"Well, I guess that's what the Repopulation Phase is for," I said, lying back down again.

"Do you think we'll be part of it?"

"I hope so, it would be a huge honour."

"Can you ask your mother?"

"She said that if she won, she wouldn't be able to tell me Council announcements before they tell the whole community."

"That makes sense."

The Bubble was so clear in the sky, like a covering over us. A protection. A mystery. In a way, it was a blindfold from the outside.

"What do you think it's like outside the Bubble?" I asked Katelyn.

"Full of wild animals and completely fogged up by gases. You know the robots that collect resources and build do it outside the Bubble."

"Imagine life before it. What do you think it was like?"

"You mean when men still existed?"

"Yeah, when there were two genders and no Bubble."

"Well, you know…"

And she was right, I knew all too well that men ruled with an iron fist and oppressed women. They were all evil and the world was a terrible place to live in. There was suffering, disease, cruelty, poverty, starvation and pollution. Then there were The Great Wars and the men almost killed the entire human race in their foolishness. I had heard it so many times that it practically recited itself inside my head. But for some reason I always asked anyway, maybe because some part of me didn't want to believe that such devastation could be possible.

"Yeah, I know." I wriggled in my sleeping bag. "Men equal evil."

"Well, it's true."

"Do you really think it's true?"

"Of course it is." She looked at me with a confused expression. "You don't?"

"Well, they did say history in the past had been exaggerated or changed and that's why they didn't preserve any of the old texts. So, I just thought…"

"You're crazy, Ava."

"I know."

Katelyn laughed. "I think we should sleep now, all that dancing took up all my energy."

"Hey, it was me that was doing the hard core dancing, so really I should call the shots about sleep time."

"Goodnight Ava." Katelyn giggled and rolled over.

"Night."

Soon her gentle snores could be heard in the silence of the night. I stared at the Bubble ceiling and removed it with my mind, trying to envision what it would have been like without it. But I realised a real night sky was something I had never seen and no matter how hard I imagined, I would never know what it was like outside.

Outside.

What was it like outside?

I used to think that question would never be answered.

Chapter Two

Ava, The Next Morning

Katelyn and I had forgotten something important about the following morning. One minute I was sleeping peacefully and the next I was trudging up the stairs to pick out an outfit for the day. In Emiscyra, everyone wore simple clothes as that came with the simple lifestyle. They taught us how people used to have to take ages picking out clothes to wear and spending a fortune to look right. I supposed that we were lucky that there was no term 'fashion' any more.

Soon we were down the street, standing outside the neighbour's door. Katelyn knocked and we waited until Georgina O'Connell opened it. She smiled at us. "Morning girls," she said in her warm Irish accent, "I guess you're here for Brianna."

"Yes, we are," Katelyn replied.

Georgina winked at us and went back into the house to call Bri.

"Good thing you remembered this morning." I turned to Katelyn.

"I know, imagine if we had forgotten?"

"Would've been madness."

Soon a figure appeared at the door, her fiery red curls were swept back into a ponytail and she tucked a loose strand behind her ear, opening the door wider as she did so.

"Surprise!" Katelyn and I shouted and ran over to hug our friend.

"Aw Ava, Katelyn." Bri smiled, hugging us back. "Thanks so much."

"Happy sixteenth!" Katelyn exclaimed.

"How do you feel?" I asked.

"Great!" Her baby-blue eyes lit up. "Finally I'm almost seventeen like you two."

I laughed. "Yeah, well, it's not easy, all that freedom and maturity…"

"Ava means to say happy birthday," Katelyn teased. "So, what do you want to do today?"

"I get to pick?" asked Bri, delighted at the rare opportunity to choose the day's activities.

"It *is* your birthday," Katelyn replied.

"Well…" She chewed on her lip. "How about we all meet at the café and decide together?"

Classic Bri – even when she got to choose for once, she passed it up to let it be a team effort. Every single bone in her body was benevolent. So, there wasn't much argument, and before I knew it, we were messaging everyone to meet us at the café.

Once they had something called a phone. Then Sylvia Carter, inventor extraordinaire, came up with the concept of intercoms. Each building had one and it allowed people to message each other through it. Most times everyone would intercom me asking what we should do that day and then I would decide on something and message everyone for feedback. They always agreed.

After getting yeses from Lexi and Jade, the three of us headed off to the café, our favourite place to eat.

"Hey girls, what can I get you? The usual?" asked the server, Roxanne, as we took our seats.

"For sure. Today is Bri's birthday," Katelyn replied.

"Happy birthday, honey."

Roxanne once told us she moved from America to escape The Great Wars and then helped out a bit with the Movement. Her accent was different from most people's and she said that's how everyone talked in America before it was destroyed. I found it strange that more women didn't come here like her, but she said it was almost impossible to leave and the whole place was on lockdown. She had to fake an extremely contagious disease so they would expel her from the country and she then snuck over the ocean from a place called Canada. We all found her story extremely exciting.

"Five milkshakes – two chocolate, one vanilla, one banana and one special coming up." She walked back to the kitchen to get our drinks.

"So, what's the special today, Ava?" Bri asked.

"I didn't check yet. But then again, the mystery is the whole reason I order it every time," I said, just as the other two walked in.

"Happy birthday Bri!" they shouted and ran over to hug her.

"Thanks," she said from inside the mass of bodies.

"Did you order already?" Lexi asked as she pulled up a chair.

"Yeah. So the birthday girl wanted us to choose what we do *together*," I teased.

"What! No Bri, today is your day," Lexi said.

"Well, seeing as it's my day, I decide that we should spend it doing something we all want to do," Bri replied firmly.

"Classic Bri," Jade said, rolling her eyes. We all laughed.

Then Roxanne came over with our milkshakes. "Here you go, girls. Chocolate for Lexi and Jade, vanilla for Katelyn, banana for the birthday girl and blueberry chocolate chip today for miss 'the special is always the most exciting'."

"Yeah, Ava, why *do* you always get the special?" Lexi nudged me with her elbow.

"Because she loves the unknown," Jade remarked, leaning back in her chair.

"No, it's because it's way more fun to try something different and unexpected every day than have the same thing," I replied.

"And because she loves the unknown," Katelyn joked and everyone laughed.

"I don't understand why. Change is so… unpredictable," said Jade, making a face as if change was the same thing as trash.

"That's exactly why! It's totally unpredictable!"
Lexi giggled beside me and Jade threw her hands in the air. "I give up."

Roxanne patted me on the shoulder. "And congratulations to your mother by the way Ava, beautiful speech."

"Oh thanks, I'll let her know."

"And I really enjoyed *your* little show too," she said, winking as she walked away.

The others laughed and Katelyn mimed my dance moves from the Election at me from across the table.

"Yeah, your mother must be so excited," Bri said.

"Oh yeah! Congrats to her, I can't believe she's our Leader," Lexi added.

"That practically makes you our superior." Jade exaggerated a gasping motion and they all pretended to fan me.

"*Please*," I said, brushing them aside with my hand, "today is all about Queen Brianna." I slurped up the last of my shake.

Just as I said that, Roxanne came over carrying a small cake with a lit candle on it. We all sang Happy Birthday, the one song that seemed to have survived from before the city, and Bri blew out her candle. We all cheered.

"This one's on me, girls," Roxanne stated as she sliced it into pieces.

For someone to pay for something out of her own share of income was rare and extremely kind. A business could not give anything out for free as all profits went to the Council. Roxanne was always generous to us, though.

"Oh Roxanne, you don't need to do that," Bri said.

"But I do! Now have a good birthday, little miss. I'll see y'all tomorrow," she said, taking away our glasses.

"She's the sweetest," Katelyn said.

"She's plain awesome," Jade stated and everyone laughed.

"Now Bri, what are we going to do today?" Lexi asked, leaning in.

"How about we go to the evening show?" I suggested and everyone agreed, of course.

"What about before that though?" Katelyn asked.

"The park?"

"The clothes store?"

"Someone's house?"

"Hey, what about the archives?" I suggested and the others all nodded in agreement.

We finished our cake and thanked Roxanne as we went to get on the tram.

The archives were open to anyone at any time and held artefacts preserved from before the Movement for people to see.

Usually they used the archives for educational purposes, but many times people just went to see what was there. The secret truth was that the members of the community found it amusing to see how barbarically people used to live. Maybe it made them feel better about the lives we led or maybe it gave them a reason to let out their anger against men for almost destroying our world. For me, the mystery, the discovery, the finding of something completely unimaginable or unthinkable was why the archives were my favourite place to go. Once I found a book of photographs of different wild animals, and it was incredible to see features that one would never have thought possible right there in front of you.

The tram stopped and we all walked over to the archives. Pausing for a moment, I took in all the mystery just overflowing from the shelves. Divided into dozens of sections, each part was either a set of perfect white shelves or a screen showing a movie clip or a display behind glass. Each year they closed it for a week to check everything and clean up the exhibits. I was always the first one in the door as soon as it opened.

"Where to?" Katelyn asked.

"Let's split up and meet back here in fifteen," Lexi decided and we all left to look at different exhibits.

Jade and Bri both went off to look at the documentaries playing and Katelyn went to the music exhibit, showing different instruments from before the Movement. Lexi followed me to the magazines and books section. There was something nice about the feel of a book. A portal to another world that you could hold in your hands and explore at will. There were no more books like that after the Movement. Everything at school was taught with touchpads and you never saw anything resembling paper.

"Hey, look at this," Lexi called, pulling one of the magazines off the rack.

She flipped through the pages to reveal photos of 'fashion' and women wearing different 'fashionable' clothes. We scanned the pages and laughed at one of the photos of a man and a woman with hair sprayed vertically to stand half a metre high.

"He's having a bad hair day today," said Lexi, pointing at the man.

"And look, it's contagious."

Lexi giggled, slapping her thighs. "Imagine getting your hair to look like that. You know how much work that would be?"

"And for what? Who were these people trying to impress?"

"Men. Men men men!" She threw her spare hand in the air. "Everything then was about getting men's approval. Here, look at this photo." She pointed at a woman drenched in water wearing a dress that only just covered her. "Does that look comfortable? Obviously not, nobody now would be caught dead looking like that. But for her that was acceptable because men liked it. That's justification enough."

I'd heard it all before yet I still asked, "Why did men like women dressing like that so much?"

"I asked my mother once, she said they wanted to demean them."

"And the women just went along with it?"

"Of course, they couldn't help it. They were pressured."

"All of them?" I asked, wondering how a gender so strong could all do something they didn't want to, solely based on pressure.

"That's what they said at school," Lexi said and shrugged her shoulders.

"I wonder if men ever did anything good."

"Unlikely," said Lexi. She flipped her glossy brown hair to the side and closed the magazine. "I just feel bad for our mothers, having to live in their shadows."

"Yeah, and how weird to think that almost two decades ago men walked on these streets."

"Gives me the shivers." She put back the magazine and flipped through some other ones. I did the same. There were pages after pages of arrogant men boasting their assets and women either having no recognition or being portrayed as the evil ones, when it was clearly the reverse.

"Look what I found," Lexi declared, waving a small leather book in the air.

"What?" I said, walking over.

"This has a list of all the leaders and how they got their role. Thought you might like to look at it," she said, handing it to me.

I skimmed it. "Wait, this is post-Movement."

"Oh yeah," she said, leaning over my shoulder, "I guess there must not have been many records so they improvised."

"They?"

"The community."

"They can do that?"

"Course they can," she stated matter-of-factly. "Half the artefacts here are copies of the real things because they were falling apart. Or they created books with information from old artefacts that they weren't able to preserve, or from memory."

"How come you know all this?"

"I specialise in Movement history, remember?"

"Oh yeah, sorry Lexi, it just slipped my mind."

She looked almost hurt for a second, then continued scanning through the books on the shelf. I felt bad; Lexi was one of the smartest and most confident people I knew, yet she always had a soft spot when it came to my friendship with her. She always agreed with what I said, took my side, asked for my opinion. Of course that didn't mean that she always took my advice, she was just sure to hear my side. She was beyond loyal, and expected me to be the same in return. That meant remembering basic facts about her.

I tried to steer clear of awkwardness by continuing, "So what profession are you going to apply for with that specialisation?"

"I want to go into History Preservation, have since age ten. You?"

"Well, with my specialisation in pre-Movement history I could work here. Which would be amazing, but I sort of want to do something different."

"Like what?"

"I don't know."

"Well, here's the book if you want to look at it," she said, handing me the little brown artefact.

"Thanks," I said, flipping through it.

There were lists of leaders of different cities and greater cities and photos to go with each one. It wasn't surprising that they were all men. I paused to read some of the bios. One read: *His female assistant wrote all his speeches and he was elected based on his way with words. Later he brought war and poverty on his people and when he wasn't re-elected, he said he had received all his advice from his assistant.* I recognised him from my studies. Then there was another one, which was a common pattern for a leader of that time: *He seized power through force and whenever he was questioned or challenged, he would kill ten of his people. He ruled for fifty years before dying a painless and easy death.* Classic.

And not a single woman. It wasn't surprising in the least, but a strange part of me always hoped that life wasn't always that horrible. I trusted everything I was taught, yet I sometimes felt like the only person who found it all so extreme.

"Can I help you?"

I turned round to find a woman wearing a white archive uniform smiling at me. She was familiar, of course, but she was new to the archives.

"Oh no, we were just looking. Are you new here? If you don't mind me asking."

"Yes, I just graduated actually, so I only started the job recently," she said.

"That's cool. I might apply here myself when I graduate."

"Well, it's a great profession. What's your specialisation?"

"Pre-Movement history. This is one of the only professions I can do."

"Well, there is this new programme opening, actually. It's called the archaeology profession. I wanted to apply myself, but there were only a few places for each year."

"Really? What is it?" I asked, curiosity building.

"They approve the applications of only a few people that show a strong interest and they send them off to increase the artefact collection."

"They send them where?"

"Outside."

"Outside the *Bubble*?" This was unbelievably shocking.

"Yes, it's a very unique programme. They send people overseas to the ruins of old cities."

"That's amazing! How do you apply?"

"Like any other profession, but you have to go through initiation first. I can get you an information pack if you like."

"Oh that would be great, thank you. I didn't catch your name."

"Hannah Peters – you?"

"Ava Hart."

"Oh, like Donna Hart?"

"Yeah."

"*That's* where I recognise you from. Congratulations," she said, walking away.

"Thanks, I'll pass it on."

Lexi strolled over. "Who was that?"

"She works here. She was explaining to me about this new profession."

"Cool. So did you find the book interesting?"

"Same old. Evil man takes over and makes women's lives miserable."

"Well, at least it's in the past. Hey, I'm going to go find the others and see when they want to leave. Can you put the book away? I'll be right back."

"Sure, Lexi."

"Thanks," she said, running off to the documentaries section.

I walked along the aisles, searching the section on politics. Soon I spotted the column of shelves dedicated to leadership, most often corrupt. I was slipping the book into a gap when I saw a tiny leaflet sticking out of the shelf opposite. It was perfectly held between two large books, even though it was only halfway in.

I inhaled the mystery of discovering something new and pulled it out. So tiny and fragile in my hands, I scanned the plain blue cover for a registration label.

Nothing.

It must have been a mistake. I was about to open the thin front page when…

"Ava!"

I jumped and saw Lexi and the others beckoning me over. Shoving the thin packet of mystery back on the shelf, I scrambled back over to my friends.

"Were we interrupting something?" Jade asked.

"No. You just caught me off guard," I replied with a straight face, but inside I was feeling a rush of excitement from almost opening the unregistered leaflet. The strange rare feeling that came with doing something you weren't supposed to was forming inside of me.

I must have just missed the label.

"So, ready for the show?" Katelyn asked.

"You betcha," I said, grinning, and we all walked out of the archives.

As we left, I peered over my shoulder one last time, as if looking back would reveal the answers of the mystery leaflet.

"Ava, are you OK?"

I looked over and saw Katelyn staring at me with her concerned expression.

"Yeah Kay, don't worry."

We boarded and departed the tram, leaving us at the theatre in the centre of town. Each of us stepped forward to purchase our tickets, and Bri bought hers using her birthday bonus.

"Hey, today's Comedy Wednesday, right?" Bri asked as we took our seats near the back.

"Oh yeah. We got lucky, Wednesdays are the best shows," Lexi said and the others nodded in agreement.

"Yeah, but the problem is that they often repeat the Wednesday shows several months later because they're the most popular," I stated, taking off my jacket.

"True. Fingers crossed it's a new one," Katelyn said.

Then the lights dimmed. Evening shows were always very exciting. The one source of entertainment handed to you on a silver platter and fed to you with a silver spoon. Anything else had to be created. Like the archives, they weren't that entertaining unless you knew how to make it that way.

The curtains parted to reveal several men sitting round a large table. Of course they weren't *real* men, simply women dressed as men. The classic man look being suits and beards. The audience laughed instantly.

I recognised most of them from earlier shows I had seen. My mind did a brief review: she was the blonde lady in the drama last Tuesday; she was the wild beast in the comedy three Wednesdays ago, etc.

All the 'men' were arguing over something, shouting at each other from across the table. I noticed there was a small flag in front of each of them, indicating they represented different countries. They kept shouting at each other as the audience laughed.

Finally one burst out, slamming his fists on the table, "I've had it! We'll never work this out."

"Well then, what do you suppose we do about it?" another asked.

"Hmm…" they all thought for a moment.

"Go to war!" they all declared in unison.

The audience cracked up. Lexi, Jade and Bri were almost doubled over in laughter and Jade was rolling on the floor at one point. Katelyn and I were giggling and making faces at each other to provoke the other to laugh even harder.

The actors then proceeded to show many different scenes where they blew each other to smithereens. They had one scene where there were two leaders sitting together and the messenger ran in shouting:

"Quick you must do something! All the troops are miserable and they won't last much longer!"

"What would happen if we took them out of the battle field?" the leader asked.

"We would lose, but our soldiers would be safe," the messenger replied.

The leaders looked at each other and laughed. "Tell them to toughen up!"

The show continued like that until most of the actors were lying on the ground dead and the cities were in ruins.

"Well, I say we call a truce," one of the survivors said.

"Good idea," the other agreed.

They looked around them and saw all the other dead and sighed, "Oh well. Guess it's just you and me."

The curtains closed and the actors took their bow. The crowd was laughing and cheering wildly. Clearly the actors were pleased at the positive response to their skit. I overheard people talking amongst themselves about particularly comical moments and recalling certain scenes. The five of us did the same as we gathered our things and left.

We were on the tram home when Katelyn asked Bri what she thought about her birthday celebrations.

"I had the best time. Thank you everyone." Bri smiled across at us.

"Do you have any plans for later?" I asked.

"Well, Mother and I are going to have dinner."

"That's nice," said Katelyn with a smile.

"Hey it's my stop," Lexi said standing up. "I'll see everyone tomorrow maybe?"

"Yeah sure," everyone agreed, waving goodbye as she got off the tram.

I leant my head on Katelyn's low shoulder and sighed, "I'm in the mood for one of your mother's famous red velvet cakes. Any chance I could stay over?"

"Ava, you're always in the mood for my mother's cake," she replied, laughing.

"Well, the fact that your mother is the best baker in town is the only reason we're friends you know," I joked.

"And the fact that your mother runs the whole city is the only reason we're friends, so I guess we're even," she said, smiling.

"So, I can stay over?"

"Don't you think you should spend some time with Donna? She did just win the biggest honour there is."

"No, I think I should spend some time in your kitchen."

Katelyn laughed. "Ava, you go home and I'll get you a cake tomorrow, deal?"

"As long as there will be cake in my stomach within the next twenty-four hours, I'm good."

"That's what I love about you."

"My ever-expanding appetite?"

"No, silly." She pointed at the tram door. "It's your stop."

I stood up with Bri. "So what is it you love about me then?"

"Night, Ava."

"My charm? My wit? My incredible sense of humour?" I asked, walking off the tram.

"Don't forget your modesty," Katelyn said and winked as the doors closed.

"Wait, I forgot to mention my other many virtues!" I exclaimed as the tram continued on the tracks.

Bri laughed next to me. "Come on, oh talented one, let's go home."

"I can tell *you* the list if you like."

"Ava, you are strange," she said as we walked to our houses.

"That wasn't on the list but I am open to suggestions."

Soon we were at our street and Bri hugged me goodnight. "Thanks again Ava."

"No problem, birthday girl," I replied, walking to my house next door.

Slipping through the front door, I switched on the lights and called out, "Mother?"

No answer. So much for spending time with my mother.

I threw my coat in the closet and went to check the intercom.

One message it read.

"Ava sweetheart, I'm going to be out late again tonight. Help yourself to dinner, and please try and eat some of the vegetables still in the fridge from four nights ago. By the way, it's Georgina's daughter's birthday today in case you forgot. Love you."

I sighed and wiped the intercom message bank clear.

No messages.

The vegetables were sitting on the fridge shelf right across from the milk and it only took a minute to vote cereal over bland greens. I poured myself a bowl and wandered around the kitchen for several minutes.

It was so strange not to have my mother around. She was always busy, but it was usually her sitting at the kitchen table, poring over her tablets and electronic documents with me giving appropriate feedback to her occasional questions. *Ava, would you rather give input to the Council if there were tablets outside the city hall or at school? Ava, does it make more sense to give speeches about progress weekly or monthly?*

But those were the days of her job as Leader of Interrelations. Things were different when she was the Leader of the entire Council. I hoped it wouldn't be like that forever.

Giving up on finding any source of entertainment in the lonely kitchen, I strolled into the yard and stared at the dark Bubble ceiling. Then the tiny sliver of blue came back into my memory. The leaflet. So perfectly placed in the shelf, as if I was meant to find it. The beautiful mystery of the missing registration label. It must have been on the inside cover.

But, what if it wasn't?

Then I remembered that I had completely forgotten about the information pack the lady at the archives was going to get for me about that new profession. My curiosity spiked and I knew I would have to go back to get it.

They send people Outside.

I was contemplating what that would entail when I saw something plastic contrasting against the grass. I bent over and picked it up then inspected the thin object. It looked like one of Katelyn's guitar picks so I pocketed it and made a mental note to return it to her later. Then I gazed back up at the sky.

There was something constricting about the Bubble, and even though at school they told us that we would experience needs to go against what we're told to do and not do, it was claustrophobic. My soul ached to know the answers of the other side.

Then there was a flash of light. Bright light zoomed across the Bubble ceiling. It was only there for a second but it was unlike anything I had ever seen before. I waited for what seemed like forever, but there was only darkness.

It felt like I had been handed an answer and then it was snatched away before I had time to read what it said.

I gave up and returned inside. It was probably nothing…

Chapter Three

Ava, The Next Morning

A loud bang woke me. I jumped with a start and stared around my room, clutching the blankets tightly. My head felt fuzzy and my throat was dry. I crawled out of bed slowly and peered around for anything that might make loud noises. The few items of furniture looked innocent enough and I wandered down to the kitchen in search of water.

"Morning Ava," Mother said as she shoved all her tablets into her workbag.

"Morning," I croaked as I took a glass out of the cupboard.

"Did you sleep well?"

"Meh," I opened the tap over my glass.

"There is this wonderful thing we use nowadays, it's called words."

The water seemed to take forever to fill up my empty glass. "My slumber was uneventful."

"Did you get my message about Brianna?"

"Yeah, but luckily Katelyn remembered anyway so we went over in the morning," I said while slurping down my much-needed drink.

"Oh, did you have fun?" she asked, zipping her bag shut.

"Yeah, we went to the show." I filled the cup again.

"That's nice, well I have to run, but I'll be back later."

"Already?"

"I'm sorry sweetie, I'm just so busy."

"Where were you last night? And the night before?"

"The Council has me working round the clock."

"But you just got the job."

"I know and remember what I said about things changing?"

I knew things would change, I really did. But some things could never be fully understood until they happened. And suddenly, change had waltzed through my door without even knocking. I missed coming home and recalling my day to Mother as she asked my opinion on whatever she was working on.

"Yeah, I understand," I sighed.

"Well, have a nice day, sweetheart. Enjoy your week off, it only comes once every two months," she said as she walked over and kissed my forehead.

"Thanks, I will."

"Oh, and you have some messages on the intercom by the way."

"I'll check them later."

"OK. Bye darling." She waved as she hurried out of the door.

"Bye," I sighed and gulped down the rest of my water, put the glass in the sink and strolled over to the intercom. *Three messages.* I scrolled through the names: Naumann, Rose, O'Connell. I decided to listen to Katelyn's first:

"Hey Ava. So, what's the plan for today? Should we get breakfast? Mother can bake us cake… I know you like nutritional sugar-filled breakfasts…"

I laughed and remembered my request for red velvet the night before. Then Lexi's voice came on:

"Ava girl, what are we doing today? I'm starving, feel like breakfast? Message me asap before I die of starvation."

I suddenly realised how hungry I was too. My stomach emitted a perfectly timed growl. "Be quiet, you," I said to it.

"Hi, Ava." It was Bri. "So I wanted to say thanks again for last night and are there any plans for today? Maybe we could all get something to eat. I wanted to say thanks again to Roxanne for the cake. Let me know, bye."

Well, it seemed unanimous. I found Katelyn under bookmarked intercoms and dialled.

"Hello?" she answered.

"Hey, it's me."

"Hey, did you get my message?"

"Yeah, so everyone else wants breakfast too."

"Perfect. Want to come over for cake? I was talking to Jade at the archives yesterday and she mentioned that she loves red velvet too."

The archives. I remembered in a flash: Me and Lexi laughing at magazines, the lady talking about the new profession, the unregistered leaflet.

"Hello? Ava?"

"Oh sorry," I said, coming back to the present, "what was I saying?"

"You weren't saying *anything*, that's exactly why I asked if you were still there."

"Oh right, I'm here."

"Are you OK?"

"Yeah, I was just thinking about something."

I heard the call of the mystery. The label must have been there, they didn't make mistakes. But, then again, if it was a mistake maybe it was my job to tell them. Either way, it would probably have been a good idea to go check just to make sure.

"So breakfast then?" Katelyn asked.

"Actually, I have to do something this morning. Could we meet for lunch?"

"Sure, but my mother has work later, so no cake."

It was a tough decision. Delicious velvety goodness or a gripping question to answer. Satisfy my appetite or my curiosity?

"Well, maybe some other time. Let's meet at the restaurant by school at say one?"

"OK sure, I'll just eat this cake all by myself…"

My stomach twisted in itself. "You are too cruel, Kay."

She laughed and said, "Yum yum."

I switched off the call and ran into the kitchen. Sorting through the fridge contents at rapid speed, I wasn't making much progress in the food department. Then I saw the vegetables from several days ago sitting on the shelf.

I groaned, "Why me?"

Sighing, I pulled them out of the fridge and put them in the microwave. My stomach was being very difficult that morning. The microwave beeped and I yanked the veggies out and began eating. It took a moment to realise I was eating with my hands.

After I had emptied the remains of the bowl and my stomach had settled down, I walked back to the intercom and called Lexi, Bri and Jade. They all agreed on lunch, but did complain about how their hunger might eat them alive first. Pun intended.

As soon as the messages were sent, I quickly changed and ran out of the door, propelled by the intrigue. Before I knew it, I was walking into the sea of perfect white shelves of mystery.

I made my way briskly to the magazines and books section and immediately started flipping through the artefacts. There seemed to be many more of them than from my memory and I couldn't for the life of me remember where I had put it. There were all sorts of books, old and new, but none that resembled the tiny blue leaflet.

I moved over to a different set of shelves, trying to recall where I had been standing when I found it. As I rushed through the collection and shoved the books from one side to another, I was about to give up when it happened.

The tiny sliver of blue caught my eye as it gently drifted to the ground and rested there, perfectly still. My old friend silence overwhelmed the room.

The blue mystery just sat there waiting. So still.

I quietly tiptoed over to it, afraid to disturb the peace, and picked it up carefully. It was just as fragile as I remembered. I held it in my hands and gently stroked the thin cover.

I didn't really know what it was exactly that I was looking for, or more importantly hoping for, but I had always felt the need for answers. Learning new information about something, anything, was what quenched my thirst. Every time I had the chance to experience something outside my world, I dived in headfirst. For a time I thought it was because I didn't belong in Emiscyra and I wanted to find out where I did belong. Later I thought maybe it was because my world was so small and I wanted to be part of something bigger, something out of my world.

Was the leaflet, which rested in my hand so perfectly, the turning point? Maybe. It *could* have been the moment everything changed, but then again, things would have changed anyway. I liked to think it was my desire for greater knowledge that was the thing that really altered everything. Maybe if I had been fine with everything as it was then life would not have taken such a dramatic turn. But, in that moment, with the leaflet in my hands, I had no idea what was to come.

Quickly, I checked over my shoulder to make sure I was not being watched. I steadied my hand and was about to lift open the cover, about to discover what made that leaflet unregistered, whether it was an accident or on purpose, about to know…

"Can I help you?"

The voice made me jump and I whipped round to find the woman from the day before standing there in her white archive uniform.

She smiled. "Oh, I know you don't I?"

"Uhhh…" I held the leaflet firmly behind my back, out of sight.

"Of course, you're Donna Hart's daughter. We were talking about professions yesterday. Am I right?"

"Yeah, that's me."

"What was your name again?"

"Ava."

"Oh right, now I remember you. Do you remember me? Otherwise this would be awkward," she said, laughing.

"Yeah, you were telling me about that new profession." I prayed she wouldn't notice the leaflet.

"Yes, the archaeology profession! I recall I was going to get you an information pack, but I completely forgot. I'm sorry. That must be why you're back here."

"Yeah, that's it," I said quickly before realising that wasn't exactly true.

"Well, I'll go and get it for you right now then. One second," she said as she walked back to the reception.

I let out a deep sigh and backed up against the wall. Taking in a deep breath, I held the leaflet out in front of me and was about to open it when…

"Here it is."

Once again I was caught off guard and shoved the leaflet behind my back.

The lady walked up to me. "I'm Hannah by the way, in case you forgot."

"No, I remember." Another exaggeration.

"So here is the information pack." She handed me an electronic document and I took it from her with my free hand.

She leant over and slid her finger across the screen to open it. I struggled to keep the leaflet out of sight.

"So, it basically tells you what the programme is about, and how to apply. They haven't sent anyone yet, they're still in training, but I think you'd really enjoy it if you like adventure and discovering new things."

My eyes lit up. "Yeah, I'll give it a look. Thank you."

"No problem. Do you want me to walk you through it?"

I was about to say yes when I realised that my priority was the tiny piece of paper that had my hand twisted in a knot and pressed against a wall to hide it. So instead I just said, "No thanks, I'll just look at it at home."

"OK. Can I help you with anything else?"

"No, I'm all right."

"Well, let me know." She turned to walk away.

"Wait," I said and she turned around. "All the artefacts here are registered, right?"

"Yes, that's how we sort them and help people find what they're looking for."

"So, what would an unregistered artefact mean?"

"There are no unregistered artefacts."

"But, just say there was."

She paused. "Well, it wouldn't be part of the exhibit, that's for sure. Maybe something someone left here by accident. We find lost bags and coats in the fashion section all the time and people mistake them for artefacts."

"Got it," I sighed.

"Why do you ask?"

"No reason," I said with as straight a face as possible.

She stared at me curiously for a moment then turned and walked away.

I sighed and untangled my arm from behind me then slid down the wall to sit on the floor. I hoped she didn't suspect anything.

Finally I was alone to read the leaflet that had caused so much anxiety. I stared at it and took in a deep breath. First I checked round the corner and I saw an older lady looking in my direction. Paranoid, I slid the leaflet under my leg and drummed my fingers on the floor, waiting for her to leave.

A few minutes later she was gone, but just as she left a few more women walked over to inspect the magazines section I was in. I snatched a book off the shelf and pretended to read it.

After what felt like forever, they left, but there were still several people milling around in the area. I was losing my mind over not knowing what the leaflet was. I tried to concentrate on the book I was holding, but it was just a story by a woman about how men had treated her and her children with cruelty when she asked for refuge.

The clock on the wall read 12:30 and I knew I had to leave to go to the café soon. I bit at my fingernail and peered around to see if anyone was looking. No one.

Excitement filled me and I placed the book back on the shelf and slid the leaflet out from under my leg. I held it in my hands and closed my fingers over the cover page when the loudspeaker beeped. I groaned as the voice rang out:

"Attention guests. Today we are closing early due to our weekly spot checks of the artefacts. Please be so kind as to put everything back where you found it and make your way to the exit in the next two minutes. Thank you."

Great. I looked around and saw people walking towards the exit. I began to panic and desperately wanted to open the leaflet, but feared someone would see. Reading it was like a forbidden act that I had to complete.

I considered putting it back on the shelf, but something in me didn't agree and, without thinking about it too hard, I shoved the leaflet in my bag, stood up, and made my way to the exit. My heart was thumping in my chest, harder than on the night of Mother's Election.

I was about to walk out of the door when I heard someone behind me say, "You dropped something."

I froze. I thought my heart froze too. Slowly I turned around and that lady – Hannah? – was bending down to pick something off the floor. It was concealed by her body, but I feared the worst.

"Here." She held it out to me.

I relaxed; it was just the electronic document she had given me about the archaeology profession.

"Thanks," I said, taking it from her.

"No problem, Ava."

I gave as calm a smile as I could manage and quickly walked out of the archives and towards the nearest tram stop. On the tram I sank into one of the seats and checked my bag to make sure the leaflet was still there. Thankfully, it was. I smiled to myself, but as I looked back up I saw a woman staring at me. There was no way she could have seen me take it, but I still felt a cold hand of fear run up my spine.

As I peered around the tram, it felt like everyone was staring at me. They all looked like those wild animals I had seen in a text at school once. They called them owls and they had huge eyes that stared right into you.

Finally the tram reached my stop and I jumped off and found myself running to the café. I screeched through the door and spotted the others sitting at a table. I rushed over to my seat and sat down, panting.

"Ava, what happened to you?" Lexi asked.

"What? Nothing. Sorry I'm late," I said while placing my jacket strategically over my bag.

"You look like you've been running," Bri said with a concerned face.

"Running?" I tried to stifle my panting. "No, I was just worried about making it here on time."

"You're only fifteen minutes late you know," Lexi said, pointing at the clock.

I looked up at it and she was right. "Oh right."

"So we were just talking about graduation," Jade said.

"Cool." I caught Katelyn's eye and she was looking at me with a concerned expression.

"Are you OK?" she mouthed.

I nodded at her and picked up one of the electronic menus. I slid my finger across the screen to open it and flipped through the list of dishes. Finally I decided on a tomato and mozzarella panini, something I hadn't tried before, and gave my order to the server.

"It's so unfair that you all graduate a year before me," Bri sighed.

"Don't worry Bri, we'll all come cheer you on when you graduate," Lexi said, squeezing her hand.

"But soon you'll all be receiving houses and applying for professions and I'll still be in school."

"It also means we get higher incomes," Jade said with a grin.

"Listen Bri, your last year of school is one of the most fun and you can laugh at us when we all get barely any weeks off compared to you," Katelyn said.

"I know and I'm really happy for you all, it's just such an exciting time and I wish I could be part of it with you."

"You are part of it." Katelyn reached over and hugged her.

The others continued to discuss graduation, but I was too fixated on the tiny blue corner poking out of my bag to hear exactly what they said. *What if someone saw me take it? What if it* was *registered and I had taken it when I shouldn't have? What would happen to me? What if it wasn't registered? Was it important? Or was it just a mistake?*

"Ava. *Ava?*"

"Yeah, what?" I turned back to the table.

"Has your mother said anything about the Repopulation Phase?" Lexi asked.

They all stared at me expectantly.

"Umm… no, not yet."

"Ava said her mother can't tell her anything before they announce it to the whole community," Katelyn explained to the others.

"That's a shame. I wanted to know if we would be part of it," Jade said sulkily.

"Yes, how wonderful would that be," Bri sighed dreamily.

"I just want to know what it would mean," Lexi stated. "Like how?"

"You're right, I do kind of want to know how it would work," Bri agreed.

"Everyone is super excited for it anyway," Katelyn said. "Mother said that it's exciting for the women that were alive pre-Movement because they never thought it would be possible until Sylvia Carter came around."

"She's a legend," Jade declared. "I plan to work in the technology field after graduation, like her."

"It's so weird to think back to the way things used to be and how different it is now," Lexi said.

"Like what would you do without the tram?"

"Or intercoms?"

"Or electronic documents?"

"Or the Bubble?"

Everyone nodded in agreement.

"All I can say is that without Sylvia Carter we would certainly be on the road to extinction," Jade stated, leaning back in her chair.

"Don't you agree, Ava?"

My head snapped up and I tried to find the voice that said my name. They were all giving me different looks: some puzzled, some expectant, others concerned.

"Yeah, I totally agree." I nodded at them all in general.

"Do you even know what I said?" Jade asked through narrowed eyes.

"Of course I do."

Jade raised her eyebrows. "What was it then?"

They all waited for my answer. I just stared at them.

"Here's your sandwich." The server bent down and placed the plate in front of me.

She went round handing everyone else their meals as well. Jade was still looking at me challengingly.

"Oh Jade, you have to let me try some of your soup," Katelyn said, taking Jade's attention elsewhere.

She turned. "Fine, but then I want in on your salad." She reached over to grab a forkful of greens.

The two of them began talking about something to do with food and Bri and Lexi were very engaged in a discussion about houses.

"I hope they give me one with a garden like yours and Ava's."

"I would love a cute little house like the one we pass on the way to school."

What if I lost the leaflet?

"What? No, vanilla over chocolate any day."

"You're crazy, chocolate is the best thing that ever happened to this place."

What if someone saw it fall out of my bag and they told the archives?

"And we can visit each other after work."

"And use our own intercoms."

Would I get in trouble?

"Seriously, your mother's chocolate cake is way better than her vanilla."

"No, vanilla! Either way her banana toffee is the best."

"I have to agree with you on that one."

Would my mother get in trouble?

"I just realised, soon Ava won't be my neighbour any more, because she'll have her own house."

"Yeah, but then you can visit her there."

"True."

Would they let me get my own house?

"Remember that time we had that cherry pie at your mother's bakery and we ate the whole thing?"

"How could I forget? I was so full at the end that my stomach was growling all through school."

Would my friends ever talk to me again?

"It's all so exciting, isn't it?"

"I know, we only have a few months left till we graduate."

Would they let me graduate?

"I remember you telling me that your teacher asked you to go calm your digestive system because it was so loud."

"Oh yeah, she did, didn't she?"

Maybe I should've taken it back.

"How strange that there are no years below us."

"I know we'll always be the youngest in the community."

"Not for long…"

But then I would never know what's in it.

"Whoa, you're eating all of my salad, get your own."

"But it's so good."

Maybe I should read it. Just in case.

"Do you think it'll work?"

"The Repopulation Phase?"

"Yeah."

"How could it not?"

I better read it fast too. Just in case someone saw something.

"Why don't you eat Ava's sandwich instead? She's barely touched it."

"Yeah, that's weird of her."

But, I couldn't read it here.

"Hey Lexi, can you tell Ava to pass down her sandwich if she doesn't want it?"

"Sure, wait, why hasn't she eaten any of it? That's weird."

I could read it at home.

"I thought she was always hungry."

"Me too. Ava, are you OK?"

But, I couldn't just leave.

"Ava? She looks pale."

"Ava, snap out of it."

Would they notice if I left?

"What's got her?"

"Someone splash water on her face."

"Jade! We can't do that!"

They might suspect something… maybe.

"Here, I'll do it. Pass the water."

"Anything to break her trance."

But, then again, I was very discreet.

"Thanks. Don't worry Ava, this is for your own good."

I did have nerves of steel, maybe if I…

Something cold and wet washed over my face. I gasped and rubbed my eyes trying to see past the blur. Everything sounded so much clearer than a second ago. It was so clear it almost hurt.

"Ava, what happened?"

Soon things looked almost normal, but my eyes felt sore.

"Ava, don't you make me splash you again."

I looked up. Jade was holding an empty glass of water and the others were all staring at me in shock. I stared down at my lap and saw I was completely drenched in water.

"What's with the water? You couldn't have just said I needed a shower, you had to go ahead and give me one yourself!"

Everyone sat back and sighed with relief.

"What?" I asked confused.

"At least you still have your sense of humour," replied Lexi with a laugh.

"Oh…" I stared down at the floor and saw the leaflet poking out of my bag.

Then I had an idea.

"So are you going to eat that?" Jade pointed to my untouched sandwich.

"Actually you can have it, I think I'll go home and dry off, if you all don't mind," I said, standing up to leave.

"Sorry about that," Jade said while leaning over to grab my plate.

"It's fine, I know you have trouble controlling your impulses, Jade." I picked up my bag and jacket. "I'll see you all soon, OK."

Everyone waved me goodbye. I strolled towards the door, but just as I reached out to grab the handle, I stopped and turned to walk back to the table.

Leaning over, I snatched my sandwich out of Jade's hands. "I think I'll keep it actually."

She stared at me with her mouth still open and about to bite. Then she laughed and said, "That's the Ava I know."

I turned and winked at her as I walked out of the door and towards the tram.

Throwing my bag on the ground, I ran up to my room and slammed the door shut behind me. I sat on the floor with my back against the wall and the leaflet in my hands. I was so close that I was beginning to feel faint.

So close to *what* though, I was still unsure. Something inside me was just screaming that I had figured it out. Figured *what* out, again I wasn't really sure. I partly thought that I had exaggerated the whole thing in my mind. Most people would probably have thought, *an unregistered leaflet, so what?* But, from my experience at the archives, I knew they never made mistakes. Our entire city never made mistakes. So when my inextinguishable curiosity, about anything and everything, was paired with an anomaly, which one would rarely encounter, I was a moth to the flame.

Taking in a deep breath, I slowly flipped the thin cover to reveal the first page. For a moment I didn't quite know what it was. There were several pictures with bios next to them all scattered around the three or four pages. As I flipped through, it suddenly dawned on me that maybe this leaflet was part of the book Lexi had given me and it had just fallen out when I was reading it.

I sighed and leant my head back against the wall. So much anticipation and worrying for nothing. I let out an exasperated laugh and threw the leaflet across the room. What I was unaware of was that paper couldn't move very far, so it just lifted up into the air and sailed back down again.

I stared at it. It almost felt as though it was mocking me, drifting through the air like that...

Or what if it was helping me, as strange as it seemed?

I suddenly remembered how I found it earlier in the archives. It just gracefully sailed off the shelf like a dream. But that made me remember how I found it the day before. It was held between those two books which, had they not been there, would have made the leaflet fall right out. So it must have been separate from the book Lexi gave me.

Hope rushed through my veins and I grabbed the leaflet off the ground and opened it again. I read a few of the bios. Some were of men and some were of women. The title at the top read: *The top twenty people that had the most positive effect on our planet.*

It was the most unusual thing I had ever seen: a leaflet about people that *helped* the world, with an equal representation from each gender. The most surprising part was that the authors were women, so it had to be genuine as everyone knew women were always true, even pre-Movement.

The sheer fact that women had written about the goodness in men was enough to make me feel dizzy. As I read it became clear that, if these records were correct, these people had actually done some important things. Like developing cures for deadly diseases, or saving lives, or creating movements against oppression, or working to save the planet from dying.

They never taught anyone anything like this before and I was stunned. The old joke was that the best thing men ever did for the planet was go extinct. I knew for certain that if what it said in the leaflet was true, which I was sure it was, then it had to be shared. It would have been a crime to hide away information from the community like that. Our Oath said that we would be honest and fair and true, so I felt it my duty to inform someone of my discovery.

The whole thing sounded crazy: *men doing good?* But as crazy as it was I decided to tell Mother about it and see if it was something worth sharing with the rest of the community. There were advantages to being the daughter of the Leader.

So, as soon as my mother walked through the door after work, I was all ready and waiting to tell her about everything I had found.

I was sitting on the sofa that faced the front door when she walked in.

Mother jumped when she saw me. "Ava what on earth are you doing up so late?"

I sprang off the sofa and rushed over to talk to her. "I wanted to ask you about something."

"Could you give me one second, darling? It's been a long day." She walked into the living room and put her bag down.

"Oh sure. How was work?"

"Fine, tiring. We had a lot to cover today." She took her coat off and put it in the closet.

"Like what?" I sat on the sofa where I was before.

"Ava, you know I can't tell you that."

"Really? But you could tell me before."

"Well, as Leader I cannot disclose any information to you before I do so to the whole community. You know that." She took a seat next to me on the sofa.

"Yeah, but why can't you just say what it was you were working on?"

"I guess I could tell you that. I just don't want to say too much by accident. It would be unfair. And I did promise the entire community a few nights ago that I would always be fair."

"I'll stop you if you say too much, promise."

She laughed lightly and put her hand on my knee. "Oh Ava, I have missed you."

"You didn't answer my question," I said teasingly.

"We were discussing the Repopulation Phase."

My eyes lit up. "Now I really want to know more."

"See, I told you it would be harder than if I just didn't say anything."

"But, Mother... please? For me?"

"You'll find out soon enough. What was it you wanted to talk to me about before?"

I remembered. "Oh, yeah. So I was at the archives today and I found this." I held out the leaflet.

She stared at me in shock. "Did you take this? You could have just told me there was something you wanted to show me and I would have gone to the archives with you."

"First of all, you would never have had time. And secondly, yes I took it only because it wasn't registered."

She blinked several times. "Are you sure?"

"Yes, I'm sure."

"But that's impossible."

"That's what I thought too, but then I read it. And I was completely shocked at what it said."

"What did it say?" She had a puzzled expression on her face.

"Well, it's called *the top twenty people that had the most positive effect on our planet* and it's about these men and women who did good things for their communities. And it's pre-Movement."

She just stared at me in shock, so I continued, "I know it's crazy and hard to believe, but it has some really amazing stuff in it and I was just so impressed. But I thought I should probably ask you what you thought about it first before I start assuming things."

Her face was tight and she said sharply, "Ava, I thought you knew that men often lied about themselves to seem better than they were. Haven't you ever seen artefacts about men boasting achievements that we all know they would never have had the character to achieve?"

"Well yes, but this one is different."

"How so?" Mother stood and walked over to the fireplace.

"It's written by women."

She turned with wide eyes. Slowly she turned back and pushed some of the buttons on the fireplace and it came on in full blaze.

"Ava, I need to tell you something." She walked over and sat next to me. "Now I know you have always been taught that men are the root of all evil. But the truth is, they were more than that."

I stared at her in awe, transfixed by what she would say next.

"Men were not only evil, they were also manipulative."

Some wisp of hope in me vanished.

"So much so that they had ways to get into people's heads and make them believe things that weren't true. Most women were in fact so mystified by the lies of men that they didn't even know what was happening to them. So, when the world was crashing down around them, they finally realised that they had been tricked all those years and they took action. And that is why we are so fortunate to be here today. Do you understand?"

"Not really."

"This leaflet," she said, snatching it out of my hands, "was a mistake. We don't like to give you children artefacts like this because it confuses you."

"How would it confuse me?"

"Don't you see? Men were so manipulative that for a moment you believed their lies, and you were only reading about it. These women that wrote this did it while under man's spell."

"But I don't get why you don't keep artefacts like these."

"Because even though it is something from pre-Movement, and we try to preserve everything we can, sometimes it is too hard for you to understand."

"Understand what?"

"Oh Ava, it's pretty pointless for me to try explaining this to you. But those of us that have lived through the times of men know their deceitfulness. Your mind is young and impressionable and the last thing we want is for you to get the wrong idea about men. They were all evil, it's as simple as that."

She stood up and walked back over to the fireplace, the little blue cover poking out of her hand.

"Mother, was my father evil?"

She whipped around. "Excuse me?"

"I know that everyone had a father because there was no other way to create children back then, but does that mean that even though you needed him to make me, he's evil too?"

Mother's eyes blazed stronger than the fire burning behind her, then they froze over like ice. "Your father was merely a necessity to get you, because a child is the most precious thing anyone can have. But, apart from that, he was pure evil, just like the rest of them."

She glanced at the leaflet in her hand then, with a flick of her wrist, threw it into the fire.

"Goodnight, Ava."

And as she walked away, I watched any hope of gaining a deeper understanding burn into nothing.

Chapter Four

Ava, Later That Night

"Katelyn, wake up."

"Five more minutes."

I shook her shoulder harder. "Kay it's me."

"Ava?"

"Yes," I whispered, "wake up girl."

She rolled over in her bed to face me. "What on earth are you doing in here?"

"I had an idea."

Katelyn groaned and buried her head under her blanket.

I yanked it off her and said gleefully, "It's a great idea."

"I'm sure it is, but can't it wait for later? Like when the sun is actually shining later?" She reached out for the blanket.

"No, not really."

She sat up and yawned. "What it is?"

"OK, so I was up tonight and I couldn't sleep because I was thinking about our discussion at the café earlier and how things were so different before because of Sylvia Carter, blah blah, and it gave me an idea."

"Wait, how did you even get in here?" She looked around trying to figure it out.

"I climbed through the window, but that's beside the point."

"Fine, let's hear your mastermind idea that couldn't have waited until the morning."

"If we want to know what's outside the Bubble then there's only one way to find out…"

"I don't see how this is related to our conversation at the café, but go on."

"We have to go outside!" I exclaimed, jumping slightly.

"Outside what?"

"The Bubble!"

"Are you crazy?"

"No! I'm totally serious."

"Maybe you didn't really wake me up, maybe this is all a dream."

"Katelyn, it's not funny, I mean it."

"What, you just want the two of us to waltz outside of the Bubble into the unknown because you're a little curious?"

"Well, not just the two of us, I thought Lexi, Jade and Bri might want to come too."

"You really are crazy. Who is going to want to go outside of the Bubble? Especially at this time of night."

"You?"

She snatched the blanket out of my hands. "I'm going to sleep."

"No!" I grabbed it back. "Please Katelyn, for me? Haven't you ever wondered what's out there?"

"How would we even *get* outside the Bubble? Have you thought of that?"

"Don't worry, I've got it all covered."

She stared at me for what felt like forever. I chewed my lip and waited for her to say something.

"Fine. But only because I have to make sure you don't do anything stupid."

I threw my arms around her tiny body. "Kay, you're the best."

"Uhuh, let's just go."

Soon she was changed and we were sneaking out of her window back on to the street. When we got there, Bri was huddled up in her thin jacket waiting for us.

"Wait, you already convinced Bri?" Katelyn said as she saw her.

"Well, did you expect me to get you then go back for her when she lives next door?"

Bri gave a little wave and said, "Hey Katelyn."

"Hey," Katelyn said and waved back. "So remind me again Bri, why are we friends with the crazy lady?"

I gave Katelyn a light shove. "Listen, when my idea works you'll all be eating your words."

"And when it doesn't work, you'll be getting your own cake." She linked arms with Bri. "Come on, let's go get the others."

Before I knew it, all five of us were on the tram heading towards the furthest part of the city. The carriage was completely deserted and the others were practically falling asleep on each other. When we reached our stop I had to peel them off the seats and almost carry them out of the tram.

We crossed the street and walked along the row of houses until we found an opening. It was a tiny alley, only big enough to walk through sideways. We slipped through one by one and I received several complaints from the others about the whole thing being unreasonable.

Behind the last row of houses was grass and a few trees scattered around. When I looked over my shoulder I noticed that there weren't any windows at the back of any of the houses.

Quietly, the five of us walked across the grass until we reached a thick row of hedges.

"You sure this is it?" Jade asked.

"Yeah, I can see the Bubble wall behind it." I pointed for them to look.

They all followed my finger and sure enough there was a glowing clear wall curving up from behind the hedge. I forced my way through the thick bushes and the others followed suit. On the other side was just grass for about two metres and one short but thick tree off to the left. The Bubble was very visible in the night, like holding up a piece of glass, yet it seemed to radiate a clear light. The only thing was that the other side appeared to be just darkness.

It was so close that it felt unreal and I lifted my hand out to stroke the clear glowing matter in front of me.

"Don't touch it!" Jade slapped my hand away. "How do you know it won't do something weird?"

"Like what? Explode?"

"I don't know…"

"How are we meant to get through it anyway?" Lexi asked.

"Ava said she had it all figured out." Katelyn turned to me. "Right, Ava?"

"See… the thing about that is…"

"You don't even know how to get through!" Lexi exclaimed.

"Well, I do." They were all staring at me. "I just don't at the same time."

They all groaned and sat on the floor.

"Can we go back to sleep now?" Jade yawned.

"Just give me a second."

I searched around the empty ring of grass that stretched for miles on both sides. I assumed that it probably looped around the entire edge of the Bubble, but this was one of the closest spots we could find to it. The other side of the city was all buildings for city robot storage.

Soon I spotted a small rock lying on the ground next to the tree. I picked it up and slowly turned it over in my hands. Then in flash I threw it at the Bubble wall with as much force as possible.

"Ava, no!"

But the little rock glided right through the Bubble without hesitation. The others all stared open-mouthed.

"So I'm thinking that maybe the Bubble isn't really meant to keep out wild animals," I said, grinning. "Come on, let's go."

I had to drag some of them off the ground, but soon we were all lined up facing the Bubble, our faces only centimetres away.

"So, who wants to go first?"

"I think that maybe you should go first, Ava, seeing as this was all your idea," Jade decided and the others nodded in agreement.

I looked over at them then back at the Bubble. "All right, here goes nothing."

Inhaling a deep breath, I closed my eyes and leapt. It felt like flying for a split second then I landed on solid ground. Opening my eyes, I just saw more grass and it stretched on in front of me for a few metres before reaching thick trees up ahead.

I turned and saw that the wall of the Bubble was similar to how it looked on the inside except it drifted between images of grass stretching on forever and my friends standing on the other side. Like a semi-transparent border. I saw their faces searching for something.

"It's OK, you can come through!" I yelled out to them.

Katelyn jumped. "I think I just heard Ava."

"Are you sure?"

"Yes, I'm OK! Come through!"

"There she is again. I think she's OK."

"Oh yeah, hi Ava!" Jade waved slightly to the right of me.

"Come through everyone!"

"Well, here I go." Katelyn jumped up and flew through the Bubble.

"Katelyn!" I ran over to her. "See? It worked!"

She looked around in shock. "Wow, I can't believe it."

Then Lexi came running out of the wall squealing with delight, "This is so cool!"

Jade and Bri popped out a moment later, linking arms. "Did we make it? Are we alive?" Jade still had her eyes squeezed shut.

"Yes, Jade, you're OK."

She opened her eyes and looked around. "This is not at all what I was expecting."

"Shall we continue?" I gestured to the trees in front of us.

"But how will we find our way back?" Bri bit at her nail.

"I've got it all figured out, trust me."

"Ava!" they all yelled.

"I do this time!" I exaggerated slightly.

"You better."

"All right, we came all the way here so let's just go." Katelyn began to walk towards the trees.

The others all followed her and I saw Lexi skipping around and laughing while Jade and Bri were practically tiptoeing. It was funny to see Jade looking so petrified when she had always put on the act of being fearless.

"Hey Jade, you OK?"

She whipped round, still clinging to Bri. "Geez Ava, don't creep up on me like that."

"Since when do you get scared?" I raised my eyebrows.

"Who said anything about scared?" And with that she stormed off, Bri in tow.

Once we reached the trees, our surroundings turned into dense forest with trees and moss overgrown around ruins of roads and collapsed buildings. We carefully manoeuvred around chunks of concrete and large fallen trees. It was a complete mess.

Lexi was running around with Katelyn, laughing and dancing around the trees. Soon Jade and Bri began to loosen up a bit too.

"How come this feels so liberating?" Lexi gasped through pants.

"Because you're doing something you shouldn't," I replied.

"Huh?"

"Don't you remember?"

She shook her head.

"Ages ago, before we specialised, they taught us that at a certain point we would have urges to do things we weren't supposed to."

"Why?"

"I don't know, they said it was just the way things work."

"So why don't we do this more often?"

"Because, Lex, our mothers don't want you to go against them obviously, so they encourage you not to."

"But this is so fun!" she yelped and did a little dance around Jade.

"Whoa, watch it," Jade said, shoving her to the side.

"Come on Jade, run with me!"

"I don't think that's such a good idea." But Lexi had already dragged her ahead.

After a while the ruins vanished and we were just wandering through masses of trees. Then something incredible happened.

"What was that?" Jade jumped.

"What was what?"

"I just felt something fall on me."

"Like what?"

"Like water…"

Soon little drops of water came falling from the sky. They landed with little splashes and each gave a sigh as it made contact with the earth. Some formed as tiny bubbles on the leaves and I felt them drip down my face and land in my hands. It was the most amazing thing I had ever seen.

"What is this?" I breathed.

"Is it dangerous?" Jade was brushing the droplet off her arms.

"I think it's OK," I said, spinning round.

The tiny beads of water fell on my face and hair. It was magical.

We all danced in it as it gradually became stronger and stronger until water was pouring from the sky like a giant shower. My hair was wet and clinging to my cheeks and my clothes were drenched as well.

"This is getting a bit strong," Katelyn said.

"Maybe we should get out of it."

"How?"

I looked around for a dry spot. "Let's stand under that tree over there."

The five of us ran and huddled under the protective branches of the tree. As we waited in silence I thought about the water that fell from the sky. How come I had never seen it before? It was amazing. Maybe it was a phenomenon only found in this special spot. Then I thought *how would we get home if it never ended?*

"I think the water stopped," Bri whispered.

I crept out from under the tree and sure enough the water was gone. There were pools of it on the grass and the dirt had turned sloppy.

"I suppose we should turn back now." Katelyn walked out from under the tree as well.

"OK," Lexi sighed in disappointment.

"Before we go, can we just rest for a moment?" Bri asked.

I looked over and saw her yawning. "Sure Bri, you can sit on this fallen tree."

She threw herself down and rested her head in her hands. Jade, Katelyn and Lexi followed suit. I looked out at where we were; it was dark, but light was peeking in on the horizon. I went over and sat next to Katelyn on the tree.

"That was incredible!" Lexi exclaimed, throwing her arms in the air.

"What do you think it was?" Bri asked, sitting up.

"I don't know, I've never seen water fall from the sky before," Jade replied, lying down on the grass.

"Well, whatever it was, it was amazing," I sighed, thinking back to the little drops.

"Yeah, but now I'm all wet," Jade groaned.

"I think we should mark the occasion." Katelyn stood up.

"How?"

She untied the thin pink ribbon from her hair and walked over to the tree. "I'm going to mark our tree so we never forget the place where water fell from the sky."

"Do you think it will ever come back?"

"Well, at least this way we know where it happened so we can celebrate." She reached up to thread the ribbon around the lowest branch.

"Celebrate being drenched in water?" Jade shivered as she spoke.

"No, celebrate doing something wild and crazy that turned out to be extremely fun." She tied it tight and stepped back to look at her handiwork.

"And this can be our spot!" Lexi exclaimed.

"Our *secret* spot. No one can know we came," I warned.

"Of course. Who knows what they would do to us if we told," Lexi agreed.

I looked over at the little pink ribbon swaying on the branch.

"So, will you all be willing to come back again?" I asked hopefully.

"Maybe at a reasonable hour," Katelyn teased.

I laughed and hugged her tight.

The light was beginning to filter in gradually and everyone's faces were becoming clearer. We all sat in silence, breathing in our surroundings. I thought I heard Jade snoring after a while.

"Honestly, I don't know why we can't come out here," Lexi broke the silence.

I scanned the endless masses of trees. "It looks safe to me."

"Well then, why would the city put up a big Bubble over us all? It must be for a reason," Katelyn added.

"Why?"

She shrugged. "Because the city never does anything without a reason."

"Like what?"

"Think about it. Everything in our lives is only there because we need it."

Lexi thought for a moment. "Well, what about the theatre? We don't *need* that."

"But we do," Katelyn said matter-of-factly.

"How? We would survive without going there, right?" Lexi turned to me and I nodded in agreement.

"Imagine a life without entertainment, you would get so bored that you wouldn't be able to keep your sanity."

"What about the archives?" Lexi was determined to prove her wrong.

"We need those too."

"Why do we need to look at old books and pieces of the past?"

"I need to!" I burst in.

Katelyn laughed. "Because if we forgot about our heritage and our past then how would we be able to move on in the future and learn from it?"

Lexi chewed her lip.

"And Lexi, you study Movement history, don't you of all people agree that we need to honour the women that brought on our freedom? If we destroyed the records of them then they would cease to be honoured."

"OK fine, but what about the Bubble? What's the point of that?"

"You know."

"Oh, but I don't." Lexi crossed her arms and pretended to look confused.

"To keep out toxic gases."

Lexi looked around, then gave a sly grin. "Well, if we need it to keep out toxic gases then how come we're still able to breathe out here?"

Katelyn's eyes widened and she looked around in shock. "Wow! I thought they said we would die if we lived outside the Bubble."

"So my point remains, we don't need it."

"Yes, we do, though."

Lexi let out an exasperated sigh. "In what way?"

"To keep out wild animals."

"Do you see any wild animals?"

Once again, Katelyn looked around her. I did too, but there was nothing there.

"All right, but there has to be a reason, I know it."

"What if they just haven't told anyone what the real reason is?" I interrupted.

They both turned to me and just stared in complete silence.

"They wouldn't do that."

"That would be breaking the Oath. They would never break it."

"Who's *they* anyway?" I asked, the thought suddenly occurring to me.

"The Council, of course."

"The people that set up the city."

Something inside me began to process. "Why do I feel like it's more than that?"

"What do you mean?" Katelyn leant in closer.

"Like maybe *they* is everyone."

"Everyone?" Lexi tilted her head to the side.

"Yeah, like everyone that was alive pre-Movement."

"But they don't call the shots."

"But don't you feel like everyone's running on the same clock? Like everyone has the same priorities?"

"I don't really know." Lexi thought about it for a while.

I hadn't really thought about it like that until that moment. Suddenly the pieces began to fit together. What if it was all some huge conspiracy? The Bubble, the forest. What if everyone was part of hiding a deeper truth? My dream had always been to leave the Bubble, and I did. But something in me felt that there was more. More to what I was seeking than a few trees. I knew what was outside, but maybe what I was looking for was inside.

Inside? I was beginning to sound crazy, probably from lack of sleep. "Whatever," I said shrugging my shoulders. "It's probably all in my head."

I looked up and saw Katelyn staring at me. But it was with some strange emotion across her face that I couldn't decipher. Like she had just realised something important and she was stunned about it.

"Hey, I think Jade fell asleep," Bri said, pointing at Jade lying on the ground.

I looked back at Katelyn, but she was walking over to Jade. We all gathered around her and stared at her. Then she let out a sort of grunt and we laughed.

"I guess we should wake her up."

"Hey, anyone have some water I can throw on her face?" I asked.

They all laughed. "Ava, just wake her."

I bent down and shook her tiny wet shoulder. She didn't budge.

"Guess she's really tired." Lexi shrugged.

"Listen, I don't give up so easily." I rolled back my sleeves and jumped on her, screaming, "Wake up Jade! It's an animal attack!"

She leapt up, sending me flying, and jumped on to the fallen tree. "Where is it?" she yelped frantically. "Did it eat someone?"

Bri helped me off the ground. "No Jade, Ava was just messing with you."

"Is this payback for the water? Because you really freaked me out."

I shrugged the dirt off my shoulders. "No, I just needed to wake you. But maybe I had ulterior motives…" I picked a leaf out of my black ringlet. "But there was no need to shove."

Lexi helped Jade move from standing on the log to sitting on it.

That's when I heard it.

A tiny rustling sound in the thick bushes. It was so quiet, but it echoed in my head. Then silence. "Did you hear that?"

"Hear what?"

Then it came again. But this time there was a darting of movement to go with it. I froze, straining my ears to hear something. "Did anyone hear that?"

"Can we just go home?" Jade whined.

There was a crunch. Or more of a snap. Like stepping on a twig. "Ssh! Please tell me you heard that."

"I did," Lexi said.

"Yeah…" Bri took a step backwards.

"You mean the snap?"

We all stood in silence, waiting. My heart thumping in my chest.

"Do you think it could be an animal?" Jade sucked in a raged breath.

Katelyn looked around her. "I don't know, I've never seen one."

More silence. So still it felt louder than anything.

"Maybe we should go."

"Yeah, let's get out of here."

We all started scrambling away when there was another rustle. I whipped round just as something shifted in the bushes. My voice caught in my throat yet I managed to get out a single warning: "Run."

And we ran.

Feet scraping the dirt causing it to fly into our faces. Clumsy dodging of trees with branches like claws. Faster and faster until eventually we were all screaming and running for our lives. I was jumping over fallen trees and narrowly dodging branches and thorny bushes. I felt like I was being followed. Chased. So I risked turning to look over my shoulder, but there was nothing there. A shadow danced across the grass from above the treetops. I almost tripped I was so distracted. I barely noticed that the sun was almost fully up.

"Ava, I take it back. This was a terrible idea!" Lexi yelled as she ran round the bushes.

"If we die, I just want to say I love you all!" Bri shouted over to us.

"We're not going to die!" I was intent on getting back.

We kept running and screaming until our feet were numb and our throats sore. Katelyn tripped over a root poking out of the ground and I skidded to a stop then turned and ran over to help her up.

"You OK?"

"Yeah." She clung to my jacket as I pulled her up. "Do you think it's still behind us?"

"I don't know." I stole another glance back.

"Ava, are we going to die?"

I looked at her for a moment. "Not on my watch."

We sprinted ahead and kept going until we were headed downhill and the trees thinned out.

"Are we at the Bubble yet?" someone yelled.

"Yeah Ava, what was your plan to find our way back?"

"That's the problem! I have no plan!"

"What!"

We kept running and I thought that maybe we would never make it in at all.

There were barely any trees left, but that only made it easier for us to get eaten. I was beginning to understand Katelyn's point about the Bubble.

"We're going to die!"

"Is it still chasing us?"

Then I saw the Bubble up ahead. The glistening clear walls that curved the opposite way from the inside, bending outwards.

"There's the Bubble!"

"Will we make it?"

"Only one way to find out." I narrowed my eyes and propelled myself forward at the Bubble wall. The distance was closing and just before I reached it I smiled with pride, closed my eyes and leapt.

And in my mind I imagined myself flying. But I never ended up flying. I smacked hard into the wall and collapsed on the ground. I looked up in shock.

It wouldn't let me in. We were stuck.

Chapter Five

Ava, Seconds Later

It wasn't possible. There was no way that we were all trapped right outside our home. I turned over my shoulder and saw the mass of trees, like claws reaching out to grab me. Would we be stuck there? Struggling to find food and water, living like savages?

"Ava, are you all right?" Katelyn ran over to me and knelt down.

"Why are you lying on the ground, Ava? Come on or we're going to get eaten!" Jade shouted as she came sprinting downhill.

"I'm fine Kay." I rubbed my throbbing head. "But we might have a problem."

"Yeah I saw, what happened?"

Jade ran over and tried to yank me off the ground. "Get up, quick!"

"Ouch, Jade stop!" I pulled back my arm. "It won't let me through."

"What! What do you mean it won't let you through?" She looked around frantically.

"The Bubble."

"Wait, so we're stuck here!"

Lexi and Bri ran up to us. "Did she just say we're stuck?"

My head was making a strange pounding noise and everything else sounded distant. Like I was standing miles away listening in.

"Are you sure you're OK, Ava?"

"Yeah, I'm fine," I replied as I gripped Katelyn's hand and tried to stand, but I stumbled.

"Here, you sit for a minute, " said Katelyn. She walked over to the Bubble and tilted her head to one side, inspecting it.

"What happened to you?" Lexi asked.

Her voice was coming closer.

"Well, I ran into it, but it wouldn't let me through."

Jade was pacing in circles. "You don't think it's still chasing us, do you?"

Lexi walked over and shook her by the shoulders. "Calm down Jade."

Jade took a deep breath. "OK, I'm calm."

"What are we going to do?" Bri asked nervously.

It was pretty much completely light by then and I was trying to guess how much time we had spent outside. My head was beginning to feel somewhat normal so I lifted myself to my feet. "I'll get us out, promise."

"But is that a promise you can keep?" Jade asked, with one hand on her hip.

Slowly I crept up to the Bubble wall. I lifted my finger and gently poked it. It was like poking plastic. I tried again and again, harder every time, but it was obviously not going to open.

"We're doomed!" Jade cried out.

I sighed and slumped to the ground, placing my head in my hands. Maybe we were doomed.

Katelyn looked over at us with concern. Then she paced back and forth thinking to herself.

"Wait, you can't be serious!" Lexi exclaimed. "Stuck? We're never going home?!"

"So much for graduation," Jade moaned.

"You know what, stop it, OK? I understand that we have a bit of a problem, but can you all just calm down and quit complaining so that I can find a solution?" I snapped. "Or better still, how about you all actually try and help out instead of always leaving it to me and Katelyn?"

Silence. They just stared at me in disbelief. Lexi looked wounded and turned her head away, yanking at the grass with her hands. Bri stared down at her lap, her cheeks burning.

Katelyn was giving me a strange look, like the one from earlier – a combination of understanding and accepting. Then she turned away, scanning the ground for something.

"Maybe there is a way out," said Bri and looked up. "Let's see…"

Out of the corner of my eye I saw Katelyn picking something off the ground and then walking over to us with it concealed in her palm.

"What if we all jump at once? Or maybe we could all…" Bri continued brainstorming.

Then Katelyn, in one swift movement, took the object from her hand and threw it hard at the Bubble. It sailed straight through. But it did something else too. The tiny object, as it vanished through the Bubble, left a thin gap. The gap was the same width as the object and it stretched from the bottom of whatever it was to the floor. But then it disappeared after a second.

I looked at her in shock. "What was that?"

"A rock."

"Did anyone else see the little gap it made directly beneath it?"

"Yeah," Bri exclaimed. "Katelyn, you're a genius!"

I stood and walked to where Katelyn was standing earlier. There were a few rocks scattered on the ground so I took three in my hands and joined the others. One by one, I threw them at the Bubble and they all went right through, leaving the same little gap. But when I ventured to put my hand in it, I couldn't even make a dent.

"I don't get it," Lexi said and came over to me. "How come rocks go through, but not people?"

Katelyn, who had walked away to collect more rocks, soon returned carrying other items as well. She handed me a thin twig. "Try this."

I took it from her and poked it at the Bubble. As I held it in place, the same gap appeared except much narrower, as the stick was thinner than the rock. All the leaves and dirt and rocks Katelyn brought over made it through. How come we didn't make the cut?

"This doesn't make sense," I sighed. "So we know anything here that's not alive has made it over, but anything that breathes hasn't."

"Well, we don't exactly know that, maybe animals would make it too."

"What's the connection?" I thought aloud.

I rubbed the rock in my hands, its smooth texture cooling my burning palms. "All I know is that inanimate objects get through and we don't."

"So how do we get in then?" Lexi asked.

I thought for a moment and scanned the grassland for something large enough for the plan I had in mind. Then I spotted a perfect thick tree a few metres away.

"Give me one second."

I ran over and walked round the trunk several times. It seemed like it would work, so I gripped my hands on a loose bit of bark and stripped it off. It was a large piece too, almost half my size. I held it under my arm and strolled back to the group.

Katelyn looked up as I walked over. "Did you take that off a tree?" she asked.

"No, it fell from the sky," I replied sarcastically.

She laughed. "You're crazy."

"That's for sure," Jade agreed.

"Prepare to see the craziest thing of all then." I winked and stepped forward to the Bubble.

It snickered at me like a challenge and I grinned at it because I knew I had won.

"Can I please have a volunteer?"

I waited for someone to come forward, but they all stared off into space as if they couldn't hear me.

"Fine, I'll do it," said Katelyn as she got up and stood next to me.

I gradually lifted the bark so that it was a bit over Katelyn's height and parallel to the ground. Then I held it in the Bubble and, lo and behold, a gap opened just big enough for Katelyn to fit through.

She gasped, "Ava, that's genius!"

"Go on, you can walk through it."

"You sure it's safe?" Jade asked cautiously.

"Yes, I'm sure."

"OK then, here I go."

Katelyn carefully walked through the little archway of a gap and made it to the other side. She spun in a circle and cried out, "It worked Ava! It worked!"

They all cheered and each of them took turns to walk through and come out on the other side. Then, as my turn came, I placed my hands flat under the bark, gripping it with my fingertips, and manoeuvred myself directly under it. Then I ran through, holding the bark over my head. I turned back just as I got through to see the Bubble sealing once again and the forest turning into nothing but darkness.

Everyone threw themselves at me and we all collapsed in a heap on the ground, laughing and exclaiming, "We made it!"

"And even though we were almost eaten, I still had fun," Jade said.

"Aw Jade!" I hugged her tight. "I'm sorry I almost had you eaten."

"It's OK, I guess we're even now."

"Look how light it is," Lexi gasped, "we should probably head back."

"Oh my mother is going to be so worried," Bri said, picking herself off the top of the heap.

"Mine too. My sister is so lucky she gets her own house." Lexi got up too.

"Let's go then." Katelyn stood and held out her hands to help me and Jade up.

The five of us quickly walked around the ring of grass until we saw the tree that we passed on the way in. I carefully leant my bark against it so we could use it if I was ever able to convince them to go back. Then we each crawled through the hedge and walked over to the ring of houses until we reached the alley between the buildings. Taking turns to slip through, we eventually made it to the tram stop and I had that same experience of thinking everyone was staring at me.

There were only a few people on the tram as it was pretty early, but still enough to freak me out. It was like all their eyes were trained on me suspiciously. No one else seemed to notice it and they were excitedly chatting about one thing or another. I prayed that no one would ever find out that we got out, for I had no idea what the consequences would be.

Soon Bri and I got off at our stop.

"Well, thanks for a great night, Ava. I mean it was a bit scary at times but it was cool to do something different,"

"Hey, I'm just glad we made it back in one piece."

"Yeah, well, goodnight. Or good morning I guess." She began to walk over to her house.

"Good morning." I waved and strolled up to my door.

Then I thought about Mother and how she would be worried sick about me. I imagined her pacing back and forth in the living room wondering where I was, thinking of all the places I could be and trying to figure out whom to call to confirm it.

Slowly I turned the doorknob and quietly let myself in. As I shut the door silently, I braced myself for Mother to come running out into the hallway to confront me. But she didn't.

I hung up my coat and walked into the kitchen to see if she was waiting in there. In my mind I saw her sitting at the table drinking coffee and, without looking up, saying, "Welcome home Ava" as I walked in, that blank expression on her face. But she wasn't in there.

"Mother?" I called out.

Nothing.

I walked over to the intercom and saw I had a message.

"Hi Ava, it's your mother. I'm sorry I had to run out to work early again. I hope you slept well, and get a good breakfast today, OK? I should be home regular time, sorry I didn't get to see you this morning, darling. Have a good last few days of break."

I sighed. Some part of me questioned whether it was a good thing or a bad thing. Yes, it was probably for the best that Mother never discovered I was gone, which would have saved me a lot of lying. But, then again, it almost made me sad that she didn't even realise I was gone all night. Did she even care?

I climbed the stairs to my room and saw it was exactly how I had left it. The pillows were still under the blanket to look like I was in my bed when I obviously wasn't. She hadn't even bothered to check on me like she always did before leaving. She just ran off to go to her precious job.

Maybe I was being selfish. She was probably just really busy and had to rush. I mean, she was the Leader, so what were my individual needs next to a whole community's needs?

I went back downstairs and suddenly discovered that I was starving. I began to prepare myself a sandwich and recalled in my mind all that had happened the night before. Then the intercom beeped.

Putting down my sandwich, I waited to see who was calling. Most likely it was Katelyn. But then I heard another voice altogether. It was Mother.

"Hello this is Donna Hart, seventh Leader of the Council."

It was surprising to hear her introduce herself when obviously I knew who she was. I took a bite of my sandwich and walked closer to the intercom so she could hear me better.

"Hi Mother, yes I did get a good breakfast if that's what you were going to…"

"And I am here today to talk to you about a very exciting time for every single one of us here in Emiscyra."

Why did she interrupt me? I looked at the intercom to check it was a call, not a message. The screen read: *Incoming call*, then it changed to: *Broadcast*, then back to *Incoming call*.

So, it wasn't Mother calling me, it was her calling every intercom in the entire city. She must have been giving out an important message, as that was the only real reason for broadcasts. She continued:

"I am here to discuss the Repopulation Phase."

The Repopulation Phase? I guess the time had finally come.

"And I am proud to announce that it will begin this week!"

This week?

"So now I shall explain the procedure, as I am sure many of you are very excited to know how this will all play out. Firstly, you will be part of the Phase if you were younger than age one on the first day of the city. That day being June 30th Year 1. Anyone older does not apply. Therefore fifty-seven girls in our community will be taking part. Congratulations on holding this honour.

"Everyone that is eligible will take part in rotation, from eldest to youngest. You must be eighteen to undergo the procedure, which I shall explain shortly, however it may not begin exactly on your eighteenth birthday but shortly after."

I took another bite of my sandwich and sat on the chair in the hallway. I turned one on July 6th Year 1 shortly after the city was founded. So wouldn't that have made me one of the first people to take part? It was an exciting yet scary thought. So I leant in closer, waiting to hear what Mother said next.

"The Repopulation Phase is the phase of our city's development in which we shall help our community to grow.

We have built this city and made it strong, but that would all be for nothing if we didn't have people to leave our legacy to. This phase is about creating future generations while also giving our children the responsibility and honour of leading the way.

"Now I know that to many of us the idea of having children without men seems impossible. But I am here today to tell you that it is not. Sylvia Carter, the woman we owe all our technology and innovation to, has created the solution. When the Movement started, she created billions of frozen fertilised eggs, each with an analysed and approved DNA sequence. All girls of course. So now our children can carry our grandchildren just like we have always dreamt they could. So ladies, it is possible. We have found a way to do the unthinkable, without men.

"And now to explain how this will work. Each girl who is eligible will give birth to two children, one at age eighteen and the other between twenty-one and twenty-five. We shall be sending the order of the applicants to every intercom within a few weeks. Then each girl will be notified about a week before she is due to begin treatment. On the day she is requested, she will go to our newly built Community Reproduction Centre. She will then undergo a short surgery that will consist of impregnating her with one checked and approved embryo. Then she will remain in the Centre during her pregnancy of nine months and will be monitored and cared for, to ensure a healthy pregnancy and birth. She will follow a regular schedule of exercise, healthy diet and sleep.

"Once the child is born, the mother will receive funding from the Council on behalf of the child. Then when the child turns ten she will gain control over her income. Each child will get the same education as their mother, for fifteen years from age three till eighteen, specialising for five years.

"All girls that have already graduated have received their own houses, and so will girls who still have to graduate that do not apply. However, girls that do apply, when they graduate, will not receive their own house but will continue to live with their mothers. This will allow their mothers to help them raise their children.

"The first girl has already been notified as she will begin treatment nine months before her birthday. This is so she can be monitored to ensure the process goes smoothly and so the second girl can begin on schedule. The first girl holds a great honour and we all owe her our gratitude for accepting to be the first to embark on this exciting journey.

"If this process is successful, then it will cycle through future generations for many years to come. I cannot express how excited I am and I hope you all share this excitement with me. Good luck to all of you."

The intercom stopped flashing and I was left to soak in the silence. I was eligible. It was the strangest feeling. I was going to be a mother. I had never really thought about it like that before. There would be little Avas running around. I mean they wouldn't really be little Avas seeing as they carried artificial DNA. But they would still be mine.

Mine.

I would be their role model, the person to guide them, to teach them about the world, to help them grow and develop and contribute to society. They would call me Mother. And I would get to name them. How would I ever come up with names? There were so many.

What would they look like? Probably not like Mother or me, with our rare periwinkle blue eyes and jet-black ringlets. I hoped they would have eyes like Katelyn – warm and caring and thoughtful. Or hair like Brianna – fiery red that sparkled gold in the sun. Or golden brown skin like Lexi and her older sister, Tatiana.

It was all so much. I felt like my world had opened up and it would suddenly be full of more than just me. There would be another me.

But then again, she wouldn't be me. She would be unique, with her own hopes and dreams and likes and dislikes. Would she always order the special like I did? Or would she ever ask me what lay outside the Bubble? If she did, I would take her there and show her how beautiful it was. It would be our secret. Me and my daughter exploring the unknown.

My daughter.

My daydream faded and I slowly gathered myself and returned to the kitchen. I also noticed that I had finished my sandwich even though I didn't remember doing so. I must have been so preoccupied with Mother's broadcast.

Then the idea of the procedure came into my mind. I would have to spend nine months in a centre with a child growing inside of me. Nine months? I had no idea how it worked. They never taught us how children were made.

I recalled a class, before specialisation, where I raised my hand I asked the teacher, "How do you make children?" I must have been eight. She looked at me for a moment with a puzzled expression then said, "Before the Movement you needed a man and a woman but now we have a new method, thanks to Sylvia Carter."

Back then no one knew about what the new method was, they just knew that it existed. The teacher never told me why you needed a man or what actually happened so I just assumed they had to build a child together, like from a kit. When I got older I figured that wouldn't make sense because a child grew inside a woman, but I still didn't really know. Every time I asked people they just said it didn't concern me and therefore me knowing or not wouldn't make a difference.

Hearing about the Repopulation Phase suddenly made me more curious and I took a moment to consider asking Mother. Then I realised she would never tell me anyway so there was no point.

After sitting in the kitchen for what felt like hours, I decided to intercom Katelyn to talk about the broadcast. I strolled over to the intercom and dialled her house.

"Hello?"

"Hi, it's Ava."

"Oh, hello Ava darling. Do you want to speak to Katelyn?"

"Hi Jennifer! I haven't seen you in ages, I miss your red velvet."

"I know, Katelyn told me you've been needing some cake. Well, drop by soon and I'll make you some."

"You're the best!"

She laughed. "Now I'll go and get Katelyn for you."

"OK, thank you."

Katelyn's mother left and the intercom read *On Hold*. I hoped she was serious about the cake.

"Ava?"

"Hey Kay. Did you hear the broadcast?"

"Yeah I did."

"So, any thoughts?"

"Your mother did great," she replied.

"Not about my mother! Thoughts on what she said."

"Oh, well, I thought it was really exciting but not really what I was expecting."

"Yeah I know. I thought the new method would mean skipping the actual pregnancy part or would make it shorter."

"Yeah, I don't even know what it entails," she sighed. "Mother tried to explain to me that you get a lump on your stomach or something but it didn't really make sense."

I tilted my head to the side. "A lump? Like a little bump?"

"No, like a big lump. Like on the back of those animals."

"Which animals?"

"You know, the ones in the sand, it begins with c."

"Caterpillar?"

"No, it lived in the desert."

"Camel?"

"Yes that's it! It had a lump on its back."

"We're going to get a camel hump?"

"No, just something like one, on our stomachs."

I imagined Katelyn and me walking around like camels and shivered. "Does it stay like that forever?"

"No, just for the nine months."

"What else happens?"

"She said your mood changes a lot and you get cravings and stuff."

"So like me with cake?"

"Yeah, but all the time."

I grinned. "I think I'm going to like this pregnancy thing."

"Fingers crossed."

"OK, but what I don't like is that we don't get our own houses."

"I know!" she exclaimed. "But then again, I don't know how to raise a child so maybe it would be good to have my mother there."

"I suppose, but come on, I think I'll figure it out."

"You?" I could practically hear her raising her eyebrows.

"Don't mock me, I've got it all under control."

"You? Under control?"

"Yes, me. It's like you think I never come prepared or something."

"Or something…"

"Ha ha, laugh all you want, but my child is going to be awesome."

"I have no doubt about that."

"Thank you very much. Oh, I forgot," I lowered my voice, "did your mother find out about…?"

"Oh no, she was upset but I told her I stayed over at your house and forgot to tell her."

"Good."

"What about yours?"

"She wasn't there when I got home and she didn't realise I was gone."

"Lucky you."

"Yeah… lucky me."

"I haven't heard from the others though."

"Lexi probably said she was at Tatiana's, and Bri's mother probably forgave her in an instant."

"True, who can stay mad at Bri?"

"And Jade most likely created a big extravagant cover-up."

"Yeah, something about sleepwalking probably."

"Or a threat to humanity."

Katelyn laughed. "Probably both!" She paused. "Ava, does this qualify as lying?" she whispered.

"Lying?" I hadn't thought of it like that. Suddenly a sense of guilt formed inside me. "Well… what else can we do?"

"But…"

"It's not lying. We're just leaving out the truth. Nothing wrong with that."

"If you say…"

"But I think we should go back soon anyway."

"Yeah, strangely I'd like to," she sighed, "but maybe not for a while."

"But it's calling me! I feel it in my bones."

"Oh Ava, you're so melodramatic."

"But that's why you love me, isn't it?"

"I love you because you are the only person in this world who can eat a whole red velvet cake without pausing for breath."

"Come on, there's got to be more to me than cake."

"OK, I love you because you can make the littlest thing into something completely out of this world and totally hilarious."

"True, true."

"And I love you because you are the most incredible person I know and you're so different from everything and everyone but you don't even see it."

"What do you mean?"

"You'll figure it out." I could hear her smiling through the intercom.

"And I love you because you say the deepest things but they're so deep that I don't get them and when I ask what they mean you always say that if I figure it out for myself it's better for me."

"You know me too well."

"Believe me Kay, I know you *way* too well."

She laughed and I could just see her tossing her curls back and letting out her amusement.

"Oh yeah." I just remembered something. "I wanted to ask you if you know when the order comes out."

"I think it's not till later this week."

"Oh, 'cause I think that we must be in the top few, seeing as we turned one right after the city was founded."

"About that…" her voice trailed off.

"Yeah?"

"You know how they said the first girl begins this week?"

"Yeah, because she's like the test dummy," I said, smirking.

"Well, I know who she is."

"Who? Do we know her?" I asked excitedly.

"Yeah we do."

"Then who is it?"

"Ava…"

"Yes…?"

"It's me."

Chapter Six

Ava, A Few Days Later

I squeezed Katelyn's hand tight as the three of us stood at the foot of her future. It was tall and all glass on the outside. The sun made the frosty panels look like clear ice. Strangely, it almost reminded me of the Bubble walls.

"Are you ready?" I asked her.

She inhaled deeply. "Yes," she said, "I am."

Together we walked up the thin glass steps that weren't even a centimetre off. Every step made a tiny sound but in my head it sounded louder. Each sound was in rhythm with my heartbeat. Soon we passed into the shade of the building and when I looked around, I realised it wasn't glass at all. The inside looked like regular white walls. Well, not regular, they were spotless and smelt new.

Everything in the large entry appeared to be made of perfect pieces of glass, yet I had a feeling that it was just another of Sylvia Carter's inventions. 'The glass that's not glass'. People would think of her as a genius. "*What will she do next?*" they would say.

"Katelyn! Welcome!"

I looked up from staring at the clear reception desk, at which sat one person, to see Mother scampering over with her arms outstretched. She embraced Katelyn, causing me to lose grip on her hand. "Oh, Katelyn, welcome to the Reproduction Centre!"

Then she turned to Jennifer Rose next to us and said, "Hello Jenny dear, it's been far too long."

"Oh, I've missed you too, D." And the two of them hugged as well.

"Hello Ava sweetheart, did you get a good breakfast?" Mother asked her usual question.

"Yes of course, Mother."

"I baked her a lemon tart," said Jennifer, leaning into Mother.

"Ava!"

"What? It had fruit in it…"

"It's fine." Mother turned to Katelyn and smiled. "Today is Katelyn's big day."

She curled the corners of her mouth slightly in return.

"So I'm glad you had a nice time at the Roses' last night and I'd love to hear all about it later, but what do you say we go and have a chat with Katelyn?"

I looked over at Katelyn and she nodded her head.

"Come, let's go to the waiting room. It has a beautiful view of Niagara Falls." Mother turned to the reception desk. "Louise, would you tell the doctor that Katelyn has arrived?"

"Of course, Donna."

"Thank you, darling. Now, follow me." Mother beckoned us to follow her down the hallway.

I held Katelyn's hand again and all of us made our way over to the waiting room. The view of Niagara Falls was incredible, but we all knew that it had crumbled years ago in the Wars.

The mere illusion was still peaceful though. We took our seats. Jennifer sat next to Donna, in the faux glass chairs, across from Katelyn and me.

"So Katelyn, firstly I'd just like to say congratulations on this honour. You have been chosen to lead your generation through this important phase for our community."

"Thank you for giving me this honour."

"No Katelyn, I should be thanking *you*. For what you are about to do is very brave and noble and I thank you for accepting this. For it may have wonderful outcomes but the road to get there is never straight."

"Katelyn is very excited about this, I can assure you," Jennifer said, putting her hand on her daughter's knee.

I looked over at Katelyn. When I had asked her the night before how she was feeling she said, "I'm ready to do this, I want to do this, I'm just worried."

"Worried about what?" I asked her.

"Worried if it will work."

"Of course it will," I assured her, "Sylvia Carter never fails."

"That's not what I meant."

Looking at her in that waiting room I still didn't understand what she meant. But I saw the emotion in her face. Katelyn once said nobody was stronger than me, but I knew she was wrong. Her face said it all; she was frightened, about what I was unsure, but she put that aside because she knew what she had to do. Maybe someone was stronger than me.

"This is what will happen next. You will undergo a quick surgery and then we shall give you your room. There you can rest and recuperate. You will remain there for the next nine months until the baby is born. That will allow us to monitor the process, as you are the first, and make sure you get enough exercise, sleep and food for you and the baby to be as healthy as possible. After your surgery I will talk to you about your schedule.

"You may have visitors, like Ava here, or your other friends if you wish. Be prepared for members of the community that you may not know so well turning up as we all want to wish you luck. Jenny will have her own room next door to you and she can either stay here full time or come and stay whenever she feels like it. The Council will also allow her to take five months off work during your pregnancy and she can choose when those months will be."

"I'll probably stay here full time, if that's OK with you, honey?"

"Of course Mother, I wouldn't want it any other way."

"And I will be visiting every day, twice a day," I added.

"You better." Katelyn hugged me tight. Tighter than usual.

"You will not have to attend school or do any work until the baby is born. Then you can finish your studies and graduate at the end of next year. But what happens afterwards is another story," said Mother, laughing. "Now Katelyn, are you ready to have your surgery?"

Katelyn took a deep breath and said, "I think so."

"All right, let me get the nurse and she'll do a few tests. Then the doctor will talk to you about the surgery. Wait here a moment." Mother stood up and left.

"Are you ready, sweetie?" Jennifer asked.

"I think I am, Mother."

"Oh I'm so proud of you. Thank you for coming too, Ava."

"No problem. Katelyn will do the same when it's my turn."

She turned to me and smiled. "You bet I will. And I'll bring Katelyn junior with me."

"It's so exciting! There will be two of you to tell me how much you love me!"

"Yeah, I guess there will be."

"Katelyn?" A lady in a light blue medical uniform was looking down at us.

"That's me."

"Hello, my name is Claire, I'll be prepping you for surgery."

"Oh, great."

"Now if you come with me I'll get you all ready and then, before you know it, it'll all be over."

"OK, give me one second." Katelyn turned to me and said, "I'll see you soon, Ava."

"Good luck, you'll do great, girl."

"I hope so."

She hugged me goodbye and then hugged her mother.

"Good luck, Katelyn honey."

"Thanks Mother."

She stood to leave and waved to us as the nurse led her down the hallway.

Then she was gone.

"Did the nurse get her?" Mother asked, walking over and taking her seat again.

"They just left."

"Oh good. This is just so exciting, isn't it?"

"I couldn't be happier," Jennifer beamed.

"Oh Jenny, I feel like I haven't seen you in years. I miss my best friend."

"I miss you too, D. But I understand that the life of a Leader is very demanding."

"You have no idea. One night I was there until eleven at night then I had to rush out again at three in the morning to prepare for my broadcast."

My head snapped up. That was the day I snuck outside the Bubble.

"Oh, that must have been so tiring. Did you sleep at all?"

"As soon as I got home, after talking to Ava, I passed out. Then I had to drag myself out of bed and I was almost late."

That was the conversation where she threw the leaflet into the fire and told me my father was evil. I wondered if she even remembered.

"Well, you sounded spot on in that broadcast."

"You think? I was so tired I almost fell asleep."

Jennifer laughed and said, "That sounds like the Donna I know," and turning to me said, "Did you know, Ava, that when I first met your mother she fell asleep halfway through our conversation?"

"I was very pregnant then," said Mother.

"So we were at birthing class, I know you've heard this many times before, and Donna was on the mat next to me. This was back when rumours about a bunch of women starting a rebellion were circling. So I said hello and we talked about pregnancy for ages but when I looked over Donna was asleep. And I thought she must think I'm so boring. So guess what I did?"

"What?" I asked, looking at my mother giggling and blushing next to her.

"I took my water and poured it over her head."

I flashed back to Jade drenching me in the café.

Mother laughed and said, "Tell her what you said after I woke up."

"Oh right, so your mother jumps with a start and she looks over at me and I said 'If you think I'm too intelligent for your tiny mind to comprehend then maybe you should sit somewhere else'."

The two of them burst out laughing.

"So your mother looks at me and says, 'I'll have you know it was actually that I have such superior intelligence to you that I couldn't stay awake to hear your idle chatter any longer'."

They kept laughing and their faces were beginning to turn red.

"And after that we became best friends," Mother said, laughing.

"The funniest part is that even our daughters became best friends," said Jennifer, smiling at me.

Suddenly I was filled with a warm sense of love for my best friend who must have been sitting in a little faux glass room, worrying herself out of her mind. Soon I missed her dreadfully even though all that stood between us was a glass wall.

"That's a great story. It actually sounds like something Katelyn and I would say to each other."

"How time flies, we must have been in our mid-twenties then," Jennifer recalled.

"And our doctor was a man! Look how much has changed."

I thought about what that must have been like, to have men around everywhere, for you not to recognise every face in your city. Anonymity. For me, even if I didn't know someone, I still had the sense that I had seen them before and that they were a fellow member of my community.

Jennifer and Mother continued to chat like teenage girls for the next few hours. I sat there and picked at my nails, hair, jeans – anything to distract me. Then the doctor came over.

"Hello, I'm Doctor Karen."

"Oh, hi Karen," Mother said, and stood to shake her hand. "So how did it go?"

We all stared at her, waiting.

"The surgery was very successful and Katelyn was a great sport. She's in her room resting now if you wish to see her."

"Yes please," I said immediately.

"Right this way."

We all followed her as she led us down another white walled hallway, up a flight of glass stairs, and over to a series of rooms, each with a glass door. She stopped at one and said, "Here she is."

I peered in through the glass and saw that Katelyn was turned to face the other way. Her blonde curls covered her face and I saw her tiny fragile body rise and fall as she breathed.

"Can we go in?" I asked the doctor.

"You can but be gentle with her."

I slowly opened the door and crept inside. Mother and Jennifer stood in the doorway as I tiptoed over to the side of the bed and looked at her rosy-cheeked face. Her eyelids were closed and she was deep in dreamland. She looked so peaceful I couldn't wake her. So I leant in and stroked her hair then I crept back out of the room to join the others.

"She's asleep," I announced.

"Oh good, she needs the rest," Mother said, closing the door carefully behind me.

"So is that it? What now?" Jennifer turned to the doctor.

"Well, now we wait. Katelyn will be having a lot of rest in the next few weeks and we will give her regular tests and check-ups to see how she's doing. Then in a week or two we will be able to tell whether the surgery was successful or not."

"I thought you said it was successful?"

"The first part was, but now we have to see if she does indeed become pregnant, or not."

"Why wouldn't she?"

"Sometimes it doesn't work exactly as planned but we have practised this many times and I can assure you that Katelyn will be fine."

"You're sure?"

"Yes I'm sure – was it Jennifer?"

"Yes, Jennifer."

"Don't worry Jenny, Katelyn is doing great. Better, even." Mother held Jennifer by the shoulders. "You have nothing to worry about. In fact, we should celebrate!"

"Is it OK to leave her?"

"Yes, there are many members of staff here to watch over her," Doctor Karen assured Jennifer. "She is our only patient so far."

Mother laughed lightly and said, "Come Jenny, let's go out for lunch. Ava, would you like to join us?"

I turned to her and replied, "Oh no Mother, I think I'll wait for Katelyn to wake up."

"Are you sure?"

"You should go, she won't wake up for hours," the doctor added.

"No really, I'm fine here."

"If you insist. I'll see you at home, sweetheart."

"OK, have fun."

"We will." Mother linked her arm through Jennifer's and they strolled out of the fake glass door.

So I looked around for a seat and planted myself there. And I waited.

School started again right before Katelyn's surgery, so I was back to my usual schedule. Things were picking up with graduation just around the corner. They started to introduce new classes for those that were eligible for the Repopulation Phase. That meant that everyone born on July 1st on the last of the X Years, the year before Year 1, and after, learnt all about raising children and being responsible role models.

The funny part was that there were girls in my year born only a few weeks before me that didn't apply. So their lives would follow the traditional pattern of getting a profession, a house and an income. But my life, and Katelyn's, would include two children.

While we had lessons about motherhood and what to teach our children, the other girls learnt about adulthood and how to contribute to society in a different way. Every time I spoke to someone in one of those classes they would always say how much they wanted to be like me.

The fifty-some of us that applied were like the golden ones, untouchable. I thought that the others were upset at first that they didn't get to have children and that's why they wouldn't speak to us often. But I later found out that they had been told in their classes that they had to take extra care around us because they didn't want anything to happen to a single one of us. Adults would be walking on eggshells around us, as if one word would make us lose confidence in ourselves and we wouldn't be able to carry children any more.

It wasn't like no one spoke to us, I still talked to some of the other girls in my year but I guessed that it was lucky that all five of us made the cut.

Another thing that was different when school started was that everyone would always ask me about Katelyn – my teachers, friends, acquaintances and even strangers.

I was buying a new coat for the winter approaching when the saleswoman came over. "Are you Ava Hart?" she asked.

"Uh yes, that's me," I replied. I was stunned.

"How is Katelyn Rose doing?"

"She's doing good, resting."

"Have you seen her?"

"Yes, I go every day after school."

"Do you think she would mind visits from people she doesn't know too well? I don't want to make her uncomfortable."

"I think she would love it, actually."

"Oh that's wonderful. Well, tell her I say congratulations anyway."

And then she was gone. It was the strangest thing; overnight I had become known around the community. People recognised my face from when Mother won the Election but it was nothing like Katelyn's pregnancy.

Mother's regular broadcasts did add to the matter. I would often be at school or at home when her voice would come on declaring that Katelyn Rose had made it through surgery, or Katelyn Rose had taken a nap, or Katelyn Rose had eaten a salad, or Katelyn Rose had sneezed. And then she went on to tell the entire community to drop by and say hello. I was sitting in my motherhood class at school when I heard her say over the school intercom:

"Good morning Emiscyra, Donna Hart here. Today is the third day after Katelyn Rose underwent surgery. She is doing well and would really appreciate visits from anyone who wants to say hello. You can drop by any time, or if that's too much of a trip you can ask her best friend and my daughter, Ava Hart, for updates. She looks just like me in case you don't know which one she is."

Everyone in the classroom turned to look at me and I felt the awkward feeling of discomfort. They all stared at me before bursting into a rapid fire of questions about Katelyn. Even the teacher stopped the class to make her enquiries. The constant attention started pretty much after that announcement.

True to my word though, I did visit Katelyn after school every day. They hadn't yet confirmed that her pregnancy was positive but she was treated like it was.

"Hey Katelyn, how're you doing today?" I waltzed through the door and parked myself in the chair next to her bed.

"I'm good, Ava bear. I was playing with the controls earlier, look what I can make the view do."

She picked up a thin remote and pressed a few buttons; the window transformed from bodies of water to deserts to mountain peaks.

"The world was once so beautiful," she sighed, staring at the frosty ice cavern.

"Yeah, and then men ruined it," I remarked, picking up the remote. "Here, let me try."

I pressed the button and the scene changed to a flock of trees, all green and tall. They were leaning towards the light, with their branches swaying lightly.

"Remind you of something?" she asked.

I turned to her and said, "When you said we might not be able to go back for a while, I didn't realise you meant not for nine months."

"I'm sorry Ava, you can go if you want."

"Without you? Never."

She reached over and switched the screen back to the regular window. "Hey, maybe we can take Katelyn junior with us next time."

"I think she would like that."

"Excuse me?" a voice called from the door.

We both looked up as the doctor walked in.

"Morning Karen," said Katelyn with a smile.

"Morning Katelyn, how are you feeling today?"

"I'm good. Ava and I were just testing out the window."

"They are great, aren't they?"

"Yes they are."

"So, I came to give you an update on your situation," said Doctor Karen as she walked over to the bedside.

"Am I OK?"

I reached over and held Katelyn's hand.

"I wanted to let you know that you are indeed pregnant with a healthy baby girl. Congratulations."

"I am?"

"Yes, you are," replied the doctor; it looked like tears were forming in her eyes.

Katelyn turned to me and exclaimed, "Ava, I'm having a baby!"

"Congratulations Kay!" I reached over and hugged her.

"Ava, it's happening!"

"I know, you're almost there."

"This is amazing!"

"This is beyond amazing!"

"I'm going to be a mother!"

"I know!"

We screamed with joy and rolled on the bed laughing.

"Careful, you might squish it."

"Katelyn, I don't think I can squish it."

"You never know, babies are very small and fragile."

"You're having a baby!"

"I know!"

I continued to visit her after school, and every day she was just glowing. Warm and friendly and sweet. I saw that she was beginning to understand the responsibility she had and how much she was doing for the community. Her room was always full of flowers and balloons.

One afternoon I walked in just as a bunch of ladies walked out, wishing Katelyn luck as they left.

"Who was that?" I asked.

"Those were the women from the theatre, they came and did a little skit for me personally. How sweet is that?"

"You're so lucky! What was it?" I sat next to her.

She scooted over slightly and said, "They did a skit about motherhood and it was really touching. It was about a daughter learning from her mother. Apparently the motherhood skits are very popular now."

"I heard."

"They said they're creating a Motherhood Monday which will feature skits about me. How strange is that?"

"I will definitely be seeing those. I think they should cast an Ava Hart as well, seeing as I am the most important figure in your life story."

"That's true, there is no story without Ava Hart."

"We should be called the dynamic duo. I can see it now: *Come see celebrities Katelyn Rose and Ava Hart describe their exciting adventures through motherhood!* It's going to be a smash hit."

Katelyn giggled. "Oh Ava."

"*Watch them demonstrate nappy folding, bathing and feeding right before your very eyes!*"

Katelyn clutched her stomach in laughter saying, "Don't make me laugh!"

I began to tickle her and she was laughing so hard the nurse had to come and tell me to stop. We sat perfectly still, stifling giggles.

"How're the girls?" she asked.

"Didn't they come in?"

"Yeah, but that was almost a week ago."

"Everyone misses you. I'm actually seeing them tomorrow, as it's Saturday."

"Oh, I wish I could join you."

"We could come here."

"No, I have to do a lot of tests tomorrow anyway. You have fun though."

"It won't be any fun without you, obviously, but I'll try."

The next day the four of us were all sitting around Lexi's kitchen table eating lunch, as planned.

"So how is she?" Lexi asked.

"She's resting. Yesterday they told her that her pregnancy is official. You should've seen her face, it was amazing," I said.

"Yeah, your mother told us all on the intercom."

"She sounded so happy I think she was tearing up," Bri added.

"Donna Hart cry?" I raised my eyebrows. "Never!"

"My intercom won't stop beeping these days. We get a message from the Council with updates like twice a day," Jade munched on her sandwich as she spoke.

"Why is everyone so happy all the time?" Bri asked.

"Yeah, today on the tram some woman asked me if I knew Katelyn Rose. When I told her I did, she hugged me." Lexi took another bite of her sandwich. "A perfect stranger."

"That happened to me too," Jade nodded.

"I think people are so happy because they never thought it would be possible," I said as I walked over to the cupboard to get another sandwich.

"She's become Emiscyra's sweetheart."

"I think people are just happy that she's OK," Bri said.

"No, I think they're all excited that there are going to be more people in the community, otherwise they're out of women to do the jobs," Jade remarked, picking at her crust.

"Well, I think Jade's almost right," I said turning to grab a pre-made sandwich from the cupboard and walked back to the table. "The whole point of the city was to prevent the human race from going extinct and I mean I think everyone thought that without men they wouldn't be able to keep the generations cycling. So Katelyn is like their hope, or their proof that they can do it without men." I sat back in my chair. "I mean Katelyn is basically fulfilling their original goal for the city, she's making kids."

"Clever," said Lexi, wagging her finger at me.

"I miss her though," Bri sighed forlornly.

"We all miss her," said Lexi, reaching over and wrapping her arms around Bri. "But think, we'll all be doing the same thing soon."

"We're going to be mothers!" Bri exclaimed.

"Yeah, my sister is so jealous that I'll get kids and she won't. She asked me if I could give her one," Lexi chuckled.

"Yeah, but Tatiana has her own house, I'll forever have to live with my mother," Jade scowled.

"Come on Jade, it won't be so bad," I said and nudged her.

"It's not the living with my mother that's annoying, it's the fact that I'll be stuck with the same creaky bed for the rest of my life."

"Why don't you take it in for repairs?"

"I'm too lazy."

We all laughed and Lexi said, "That's Jade for you."

"Don't worry, you have the rest of your life to take it in," I teased.

Jade groaned and ripped off a piece of sandwich.

Then there was a beep from the intercom.

"Hello, this is Donna Hart."

"Here we go again," said Jade and put her head in her hands.

"Katelyn Rose is doing well. She just completed a round of tests which all showed superb results. If you have time, do try to go and pay her a visit. It need not be long, but she does love hearing from you all. Thank you to everyone that has visited already or sent lovely gifts. Katelyn told me personally to tell everyone that they really brightened her day. And thank you also for leaving your kind wishes with some of her friends and family, they are much appreciated."

"You should see her room," I said, turning back to the table, "it's completely full of flowers and stuff."

"Yeah, and I was passing her house recently and there were all sorts of notes taped to her door," Lexi said.

Then the intercom continued, "I also wanted to inform everyone that the order for the rest of the girls has been sent to every family intercom. We will notify you a week before you are due to come in. Thank you."

We all looked at each other. Then we bolted towards the intercom, shoving each other out of the way.

"It's my intercom! Let me read it!"

"No Lexi, move over!"

Lexi opened the new message on the intercom and a list popped up. It had the names of every girl and their birthdays followed by the estimated date for surgery.

"Where are we, Lex?"

She scanned the list. "I'm number twelve!" She jumped up.

"That's so soon!" Bri exclaimed.

"I know!"

Jade shoved her out of the way and scrolled through the list. "Bri, I found you!"

"What am I?"

"You're fifty-one."

"That's almost last."

"That means you have plenty of time to prepare," I reassured her.

"I can't find my name," Jade said. "Oh wait, here it is. I'm thirty-five."

"Congrats Jade."

"My turn," I said as I moved to the front of the pack.

The list was in small print so I had to look through it several times.

"I can't find it."

Lexi came over. "Let me look."

She held her finger over the list, scanning the whole length of it twice then she pressed her finger to the screen and gasped, "Ava!"

"What? What am I? Is it good?"

"Oh my…"

"Lexi, just tell me what it is." I looked to where her finger was pointing.

I gasped and threw my hand to my mouth.

"Ava… you're number two."

Chapter Seven

Ava, Four Months Later

"Good morning Ava," the receptionist greeted me as I strolled in through the glass doors.

"Same to you, Louise. How's my girl today?"

"Good, she's waiting for you."

"Thanks Louise," I said and made my way up the flight of stairs and down the hall to Katelyn's room.

On the way I saw Mother, Jennifer and some Council members chatting in the sitting area outside her room.

"Hello Mother," I said as I hugged her briefly.

"Hello darling, would you like some coffee?"

"No, I already got some." I lifted my flask.

"Oh good. You can go in, she just finished her tests."

"Thanks. Oh, hi everyone," I said, waving to the Council members.

Some of them returned the gesture and I turned to go into Katelyn's room.

"Hi Ava."

She was sitting in bed rubbing the tiny bump that had formed on her stomach.

"How's the kid?"

"She keeps giving me a hard time."

"And to think she'll only get bigger!"

"Not funny."

I laughed and took a sip of coffee. "Remember that time when you told me that baby bumps were like camel humps? Hey, that rhymes!"

"When was that?"

"It was when they told us about the Repopulation Phase, remember?"

She thought for a moment. "Wait, so like four months ago?"

"Wow, I can't believe it's been that long."

"Almost halfway there."

I squeezed her hand. "You're doing great. So how were your tests?"

"Fine," she replied and turned her head and stared out of the window.

For the past few weeks, every time I came her window was set to regular and she would always be staring out at the street, watching the people walk by.

"Hey Katelyn, you're looking a little pale. You all right?"

She looked over at me. "Yeah, of course. So how was school?"

"I haven't gone yet, silly, but yesterday we learnt about the importance of changing nappies on a regular basis."

"I thought you already did that stuff."

"Well, apparently not in enough detail."

"It's better than what I have. The nurse comes in and teaches me everything personally, so there's no way to doze off in nappy training."

"Speaking of dozing off, you look tired."

"I'm fine."

"Kay, are you sure?"

"Yes Ava, I'm sure."

"Well, is there anything I can get you?"

"No Ava, I told you I'm fine," she snapped.

I sat there for a second looking at her then she rolled over to look out of the window again. Holding my coffee cup up to my mouth, I realised it was empty.

"I'm going to get a refill. Want some?"

She shook her head.

"OK…"

I stood and went outside to the coffee machine. Jennifer walked in as I left. After selecting my order I looked over and saw Mother and the Council members intense in discussion.

"Of course it will," Mother said firmly.

"These tests results don't show a positive sign, Donna."

"She's having an off day."

"Wouldn't that put her at a total of twelve off days?"

Mother chewed on her lip.

"You do realise what would happen if this procedure were to fail, right Donna?"

"Of course I know, and I completely assure you that will not happen."

"Well, what if it does?" another member asked.

"We have no back-ups," another replied. "It's this or bust."

"Sylvia can figure something out," Mother said confidently.

"I'm sure she can, but not in the small window of time we have."

The coffee machine beeped, but I continued listening.

"Margaret's right, Donna, soon all the girls will be too old to have children."

"And Sylvia may be a genius, but some things not even someone like her can do."

"Well, what do you suppose we do about it?" Mother asked challengingly.

"Do about what?" asked Jennifer, walking over to them from Katelyn's room. "Is Katelyn OK?"

"Of course she is, Jenny."

"It's just that she's barely eating or sleeping, she just stares out of that window. I'm worried about her."

Mother put her arm around Jennifer's shoulders and said reassuringly, "I promise you, Jenny, as your best friend, Katelyn is doing perfectly. We couldn't have asked for a better first girl."

The others nodded in agreement.

"And I know that if anyone is up for this job it's Katelyn. This phase is completely normal, give it time."

"OK D, I mean she is showing good tests results, right?" asked Jennifer.

Mother flinched for a second then replied, "Of course."

"Well, that's good to know."

That confused me; didn't the Council members just say the test results were bad? Had my mother lied?

"I don't know about you all, but I feel like some coffee," said Mother.

"Oh that sounds lovely, Donna."

They started to walk over to where I was standing so I quickly turned and ran towards the room, ducking behind the sofa so as not to be seen.

"I thought you went to get coffee," Katelyn said as I rushed through the door.

"What?" I spun round in a circle then looked down at my empty hands. "Oh right, changed my mind."

"Then what took you so long?"

"I had to pee."

"Oh."

I walked over to her bedside and snuggled up next to her. The two of us just stared around the room for a while. The walls opposite her bed were decorated with drawings of flowers and swirls of colour. The ceiling was littered with tiny lights that at night created a beautiful pattern. She had all sorts of remotes by her bed to call for the nurse, doctor, Jennifer, or whomever else she needed. She also once told me that she could ask for anything and they'd bring it: her guitar, tablets to draw on, electronic documents to read.

"Ava I'm sorry I snapped, maybe I am a little tired."

"Katelyn, it's totally fine."

"No it's not, I shouldn't make excuses but I just haven't been able to sleep much and it's pretty boring in here."

"Boring? But they bring you anything you want."

"But you know how often I go outside?"

"How often?"

"Maybe once a week."

"I'm sorry Kay, you can come with me if you want."

"Oh no, but that would be disturbing my schedule," she said sarcastically.

"You don't like it here?"

She sighed, "I do and you don't know how honoured and proud I am to be doing this. It's just…"

"Just what?"

"People tiptoe around me all the time, like walking on eggshells. They're all so afraid of saying something that might make the baby suddenly combust inside of me. I feel like people think I might break any second."

"It's a bit like that at school. The girls that aren't eligible barely talk to the ones that are because they're so afraid of us suddenly becoming unfit to do our duties. Like I would really be so scarred by something someone says."

"Yeah. I mean it's a wonderful feeling this whole baby thing. I just want some space."

"From people?"

"No."

"Then from what?"

"From their expectations."

Later that afternoon I was sitting in motherhood class once again when the intercom beeped.

"Hello, if you haven't already guessed, it's Donna Hart. Katelyn Rose just did a series of tests today, which she passed with flying colours and we look forward to submitting a photo of the foetus to every intercom soon so you can all take a look at the first baby girl. She's truly beautiful and all of our hearts are with Katelyn now. Have a good day."

All the girls turned to each other and started giggling about the baby and how exciting it was that there were going to be children running around. But I was completely stunned. Mother had just announced to the entire community that Katelyn had shown positive – no, perfect – test results when I knew for a fact that it was a lie. A lie. Lying went against the Oath. Lying was unheard of. Except for the occasional tiny stretches of the truth, that even I made, no one lied in our community ever. So why then?

Straight after school I hurried back to the Reproduction Centre to visit Katelyn again. She was jogging on the treadmill as I walked into her room.

"Hey, how was school?"

"OK," I said and threw my bag down on the chair. "Nice to see you getting some exercise."

"I do every day, it's just usually while you're at school."

"Right. How're you feeling?"

"Fine," she replied as she wiped some sweat off her forehead.

I looked over at my friend. She was rather skinny and very pale, not rosy-cheeked at all.

"So I was thinking about the forest today," she said over her shoulder.

"Oh really?" I got up and closed the door. "Go on."

"Well, we haven't been back in a while and I'd really like to go."

"You think they'll let you?"

"Of course not. I want you to sneak me out."

"Sneak you out! Are you crazy?"

"Come on Ava, it'll be fun."

"That's my line. I thought you found the forest too risky and dangerous and…"

"And adventurous! And exciting! Ava, I haven't left this room in four days. I haven't even gone across the hall!"

"How about we secretly go and take a walk in the park?"

"No! That's not the point."

"Please, enlighten me."

"You know how you always order the special?"

"Uhuh…"

"You do it because you want a taste of adventure or a chance to try something new, right? Well, that's what I want, to step out of my comfort zone."

"Personally, I think we should remain in our comfort zones. You know, for safety."

"Ava, you can't stop me."

"Oh great," I said and flopped on to her bed.

"So are you in?"

I sat up. "Why the sudden interest in the forest?"

"It's not the forest exactly, it's just that I feel like doing something exciting. It's so boring around here."

Honestly, I knew better than anyone what that was like. Were the fresh green treetops and breathtaking sky showers not calling my name too? Of course they were. But maybe it was the fact that I could almost see my dear friend's ribcage poking out through her shirt that held me back. Then again, maybe a change of scenery would help her stay strong. I groaned and fell back on the bed. "Fine! Because I'm such a great friend."

Katelyn leapt off the treadmill and ran over to hug me. "Thank you, thank you Ava!"

"Anything for you."

She smiled at me then her face twisted and she put one hand to her stomach and the other on the side of the bed to steady herself. She looked in pain as she bowed her head and moaned.

"Katelyn, are you all right?"

She waved her hand at me and said, "I'm fine."

"You don't look fine, maybe we shouldn't go."

"No. We're going. Just give me a second." Slowly she stood up straight, with one hand still on her stomach. "There," she said with a smile, "good as new. So when do we leave?"

Later that night, I was crouching behind the row of hedges in front of the Centre waiting for the lights on Katelyn's floor to go out. After about twenty minutes there was darkness and I slowly crawled out from my hiding spot and tiptoed over to the front door. I pulled on the handle but it was locked.

That was strange. No one ever locked their doors.

I peered round the corner but there were no other doors, only windows. *Windows!* One window was at the perfect height for me to reach and open slightly, so I walked over to it and gripped the ledge with my hands. Using all the force I could muster, I pushed myself up and locked my arms so my feet weren't touching the ground. Then I swung one leg over to bend on the ledge and rested my weight on it. After checking my balance, I slipped my hands underneath the open window and pushed it up to be fully open. I swung my other leg so it was in the dark room and jumped to land on the floor.

The place was completely deserted and almost pitch-black. Luckily I was used to it after sitting out in the dark for so long. After wandering down several random hallways, I eventually found the one that led to the staircase. I gripped the railing and followed it up until I was at the end of the hallway that led to Katelyn's room. Before I could take another step though, a light went on. I slammed myself against a pillar so as not to be seen. Jennifer Rose came scampering out of the lit room and ran over to check on her daughter next door. I let out a deep breath and noticed that my hand hurt a bit from the force of my movement.

After what felt like forever, Jennifer returned to her own room and turned off her light. I waited another ten minutes then slowly walked over to Katelyn's room while keeping my back pressed flat against the wall. Once I reached her door, I checked to see if her mother was asleep. Her snores echoed from her room acting as my cue to gently open Katelyn's door and sneak inside.

"Katelyn?" I whispered.

"Ava?"

I followed her voice and ducked behind her bed. "Where is everyone?"

"Some of them go home but many stay overnight in the staff rooms on the third floor."

"Oh. What did your mother want?"

"She does this every night," she sighed. "She comes in to see if I'm OK. Tonight she said she had a dream that I was falling."

"Falling from what?"

"I don't know."

"So are you ready to go?"

She whipped off the blankets to reveal that she was wearing her normal clothes. "Ready."

I giggled quietly and said, "This is so bad."

"What rebels we are!"

"Let's go, we need to sneak out of the window," I said as I helped her out of bed.

"What about the front door?" she asked.

I slowly opened the door to her room and we slipped into the hallway. "It was locked," I replied.

"Locked?" She stopped.

I grabbed her hand and dragged her out of sight from Jennifer's room. "Yes, locked."

"That's impossible."

"Well then, impossible has just been given a new definition."

We continued down the hallway and the stairs until we reached the room with the open window.

"So they locked me in?" Katelyn said with disgust.

"I'm sure it was for another reason," I said as I hoisted my legs over the windowsill.

"Like what? No one locks their doors; people did that before when there was a chance of being robbed. No one robs anyone any more."

"Maybe they don't want people trying to visit you in the night," I said. I jumped and landed on the ground below.

"That's not a good enough reason," she replied and looked out of the window down at where I was standing. "Wait, you want me to jump?"

"That's the plan."

"What if the baby gets squished?"

"It won't. Here, I'll catch you if that makes you feel better."

She nodded.

"You can do it, Katelyn."

Slowly she swung her legs so they were dangling out of the window. "Ready?"

"Ready."

Katelyn squeezed her eyes shut and jumped right into my arms. I stumbled a bit and then fell backwards with her on top of me. "Good thing you weigh nothing."

"Yeah, but technically I am two people," she said with a grin and got off me.

Katelyn held out her hand to me and soon we were both on our feet.

"Oh my goodness! We did it!" Katelyn threw her arms in the air and laughed.

"You bet we did!"

The two of us started to dance in a circle, squealing and laughing.

"Wait, someone will hear us," Katelyn said, throwing her hand over my mouth.

"Let's celebrate in silence." My voice sounded muffled through her hand.

"What?" She removed her hand.

"I said let's celebrate quietly."

"OK," she whispered.

And the dancing continued, minus the sound of course. Katelyn and me, laughing silently in the cool night air. It brought back memories of the night four months earlier when we sang at the Election. Katelyn's golden curls streaming from behind her as she danced,,belting out every note beautifully. It was one of those moments when I just felt this surge of undying love for my best friend. I knew in my heart that she was the most precious thing in the world to me and I would never let her go. I guessed that in that wonderful silent dance I formed a goal in my mind to hold her hand tighter during the next five months, to make her world even more exciting and vibrant, to find even more ways to make her laugh, to be her voice whenever she needed me. I made my own little oath to protect her with every bone, muscle and nerve in my body. Then right as I promised that to myself, the world shattered into a thousand pieces.

Even in the darkness I saw the colour drain from her face. She clutched her hand to her stomach and gripped my arm with so much strength I thought she punctured my jacket with her nails. It was all in slow motion. She stumbled to the ground, landing on her knees and dragging me down with her. Her whole body was shaking violently and I just stared at her, paralysed. Every breath was heavy and she gripped me so hard that I saw my own hand turn white.

Then she jolted like a wave of pain just ran up her body and let out an unbearable scream. She rolled on to the ground and curled herself up into a ball, breathing heavily.

"Katelyn! Katelyn say something!" I could barely hear my own voice my ears were pounding so hard.

"Please Katelyn, please!"

I looked around to see if anyone saw. "Hello! Help! Help!" I screamed.

No one answered and Katelyn kept shaking all over and groaning with pain. Then she looked up at me, her eyes were pouring tears and her face was ghostly. She gave me a look so innocent and helpless that it made my heart burst.

"Help me," she wheezed.

Then something clicked. I pulled myself to my feet and ran over to the window. There was a rush of energy in me and I leapt into the air and caught the ledge with both hands, pulling myself through the window.

"Help! Help!" I ran towards the stairs and kept running all the way to the third floor.

It was similar to the second, with rows of rooms each labelled with someone's name. I ran down the hall, skimming the names, until I saw 'Karen'. I banged hard on the door and shouted, "Open the door! Katelyn's in trouble!"

I kept slamming my fist at the wood until it opened and I almost fell inside.

"What's happening?" Doctor Karen appeared wearing sleeping clothes.

"It's Katelyn, she's outside."

"Outside?"

"By the side of the building."

She looked at me for a moment. "Wake the nurses," she ordered. She ran back into her room and came out carrying a small kit. Then she shoved her way past me and hurried to the stairs.

I followed her orders until every nurse was grabbing pieces of equipment and rushing outside. After the last one was on her way, I ran down to follow them and shoved my way through the front door, recently unlocked, until I was standing by the ring of women surrounding Katelyn.

I peered over their shoulders and saw her tiny body still shaking as they fed her liquids and pills and sips of oxygen. Her eyes were stained with tears and there were still traces of immense pain in them. I looked over at her and let the tears pour out of my own eyes. It felt like I had failed her. I was completely helpless as the nurses all treated her until she was breathing normally and the pain in her eyes had subsided.

They lifted her up and brought her back inside and up to her room.

"You have some explaining to do later," the doctor said as she walked past me.

If only I *could* explain.

I wasn't allowed to visit Katelyn for three days following the incident. After they had got Katelyn back into bed and run a series of tests on her, I was interviewed. There was no alternative but to lie, even though it went against everything our community stood for. I had found myself lying a lot at that time. I merely told the doctor that I went to visit Katelyn that night because I forgot my purse that had my electronic essays for school in it. Then she said she was feeling light-headed so we decided it would be best to get some fresh air and then she just…

They told me and everyone else that she had a bit of a fever but would most likely be back on her feet in no time. But the way she had been shaking all over with pain, it just didn't seem right. I had no choice but to hope that she would recover.

I didn't even get a chance to sustain my own oath because they didn't let anyone visit her. Mother was allowed to but that was it; not even Jennifer could see her. Every afternoon I asked Mother how Katelyn was doing.

"She's almost at the top of the mountain, darling, she'll be back to normal soon."

Then on the second day I spent every minute of it picking at my fingernails and sitting on my bed waiting. As soon as Mother walked in, I ran downstairs.

"How is she?"

"Give it time, she's doing better."

"Can I see her?"

"No Ava."

"Why not?"

"You don't want to see her like this, it'll break your heart," she replied and walked away.

The third day of being away from her was unbearable. I stayed in my room and drifted between restless sleep and painful reality. There was no place to hide from my feelings and Katelyn's face as she begged me to help her, so I forced myself into sleep, my refuge.

"Ava, wake up."

I opened my eyes and saw Mother looking down at me.

"What?" I croaked.

"It's Katelyn."

I sat bolt upright. "Yes?"

She smiled and said, "She's fully recovered and wants to see you tomorrow."

"She does?"

"Yes, darling."

"Oh Mother!" I pulled her into the tightest embrace I could muster.

"Ava, I can barely breathe."

"Oh sorry," I said and let her go.

"Now you sleep and tomorrow we'll go and see Katelyn."

And when the fourth day came I was there as soon as the sun rose. I ran up the stairs and over to Katelyn's room and burst through the door.

"Katelyn!"

"Ava!"

I ran over to her and held her so tight she too had to tell me to let go. I looked up at her face, it was warm and bright and rosy-cheeked. Her chocolate eyes sparkled and danced as she smiled.

"You look amazing," I gasped.

"The doctors said it was a pretty miraculous recovery."

"I agree. How are you?"

"I'm good," she said, smiling. "And you?"

"I've been pulling my hair out waiting to hear from you."

She squeezed my hand and said, "It's not your fault."

I looked into her eyes. "But if we had just been more careful…"

"No. It was my idea and you took the blame. I knew I was in no condition to exert myself that way but I still did because of pride. And I'm sorry I got you into trouble."

"Don't be sorry, I should've tried harder to stop you."

"You know nothing was going to change my mind," she said, laughing.

"Yeah, you became me."

Then the nurse came in. "Here's your breakfast, Katelyn. Can I get you anything else?"

"No, I'm fine."

The nurse placed the tray on the bedside table. "Is this OK? Do you want something else?"

"This is perfect, Claire, thank you."

The nurse walked back towards the door. "Are you sure you don't need anything else?"

"Yes, I'm sure."

"OK," said the nurse. She hesitated in the doorway then turned and left, shutting the door behind her.

"I just realised, we're going to be mothers together," I said.

"Oh yeah, you're number two."

"Imagine that, us raising children together," I sighed.

"They can play together and go to school together."

"And they'll be best friends just like our mothers and us."

"And we can help raise our granddaughters together."

"And maybe one day we could take them all to…"

"I almost forgot," the nurse interrupted me, coming back in. "You have your tests in ten minutes so Ava will have to leave now."

"OK, thank you."

The nurse nodded and left again.

"I guess I'll see you tomorrow," Katelyn sighed.

"Tomorrow? Girl, you'll be seeing me as soon as the first tram after school stops outside your door."

"I love you, Ava," she said as she leant over and held me tight.

"I love you too, Kay."

"Have a good day at school, perfect those nappies."

"Cross my heart, I shall be the best nappy folder in all the land!" I got up to leave.

"And don't forget about bathing."

"I shan't forget my superior bathing skills," I said as I waved and slipped out of the door.

"Bye, Ava bear," she called as the door shut behind me.

"Bye Kay."

School seemed to go on forever. The clock on the wall was almost mocking me. It felt like time had stretched itself to twice the length. Katelyn was sitting in the hospital all healthy and happy, waiting for me, and I was stuck learning about what a child needs. I pictured her face all smiley and warm with those eyes that sucked up every word I said. It was impossible to describe how relieved I was that she was OK again. I didn't know what I would do without her.

Then the day ended. I ran out of the building so fast that heads turned. I saw the tram ahead pulling into the stop so I sprinted faster in hopes of catching it before it left. But then I saw someone familiar walk out and I stopped. Her black hair swayed as the tram departed and she just stood there at the stop, waiting. I continued to walk towards her slowly until her face became clearer. *Mother?*

It was strange to see her outside school because I knew just how busy she was all the time. It was a nice surprise.

"Hello Mother, what are you doing here?" I ran up next to her.

She didn't say a word but her face said it all. Her eyes were red and her face was the most serious and sombre I had ever seen. My smile melted off my face.

"Mother, what's wrong? *Mother?*"

"It's Katelyn," she said and I could hear the strain in her voice.

"What?" My heart did a flip. "Did she have a relapse?"

"No."

"Then what? Mother, please talk to me."

"She, she…" Mother could barely get the words out.

"She what?!" I was practically screaming.

"She's dead, Ava. She's dead."

Chapter Eight

Katelyn, Six Hours Earlier

"Bye, Ava bear," I called out as Ava shut the door behind her.

I looked over at my best friend through the glass door. She stood there with her fingers pressed against it then she gave a little wave. "Bye Kay." I couldn't hear her but I knew what she said.

Then she left and I slumped back in my bed and stared at the ceiling. I loved Ava so much, I hoped she knew that. I turned to stare out of the window at the street and the people passing by. Each of them had somewhere to be, somewhere to go; I had nowhere.

Then I mentally hit myself for sounding so selfish. It wasn't like me. Never in my life had I questioned my purpose and my responsibilities – that was Ava. Ava always wanted more, I saw it in her eyes. For her, this life just wasn't good enough. But I had learnt to accept it; it wasn't as if I could change it.

That reminded me of that one night in the forest when Lexi and I were arguing over if the Bubble had a purpose or not. I knew it did because everything in the city had a purpose. That was what it was founded on – purpose. But Lexi pointed out that we had just proven the reasons for the Bubble false by leaving it. And that was when Ava said that maybe they never told us the real reason because they were keeping it from us. And it all clicked.

Our city was designed to be as perfect as possible and even though we all made an oath to be true, that just wasn't an option. Ava made it all clear to me that maybe our elders stretched the truth a bit to keep us safe. They knew what it was like before and they knew that the best way to protect us was to hide us from what turned the world so black in the first place. That way it would never happen again.

I knew I would never tell Ava as she wouldn't understand. I had come to realise that this was something every woman figured out at one point or another and accepted for herself. It all went against everything I believed in – that staying true and honest would never turn you wrong. But what if sometimes the best thing for people was to not know at all?

"Katelyn?" The nurse peered through the door. "Are you ready for your test?"

"Sure, Claire."

"OK, I'll go and get the doctor." She walked out and shut the door behind her.

I leant over to look out of the window again at all the people. Something inside me was changing and I could feel it. Obviously there was literally someone inside me growing but that wasn't what I meant. Being stuck in the tiny room so long had messed with my brain. I found myself getting angry and upset and acting completely out of character.

It all seemed to come out with Ava more than anyone else. I used to always make sure I heard her and listened to her every word, but in the past few months I found that I was fading.

Ava was always such an interesting person to listen to, when she wasn't joking around, because she always said the most out-of-the-box things. It amazed me what went on in her head, so much creativity and questioning of everything. The funniest part was that she would always shrug it off and not embrace how intelligent she was. One day she would see.

But recently I didn't want to hear her truly; it almost made me envious of her. She had such a free mind and a free heart and I was trapped. And that made me angry with myself for thinking so selfishly. I was doing my duty and my part for the community and everyone was so grateful. I just felt like I was carrying too much pressure.

The Council members would often stand outside my door and whisper and point. This was everything to them and I just didn't want to screw up.

But what I often thought about was my lapse of judgment just days earlier. What possessed me to want to leave the Bubble? If something had happened to me, like it almost did, then I would have let everyone down. I was so fixed on the idea of doing something for me instead of for everyone else that I let down my guard and I almost got myself killed.

"Hello Katelyn, how are you feeling today?"

I looked up as the doctor walked in. "Better than ever, Karen."

"Good to hear. Now, what should we start with?"

"Maybe the scan?"

"All right, let me go and get my scanner, I'll be right back." She walked out and propped the door open behind her.

I noticed all the people milling around doing their tasks. Then I spotted Ava's mother standing by the coffee machine outside my room.

"Hi Donna," I called to her but she didn't hear me. "Donna?" Still no answer.

I crawled out of bed and walked over to the doorway. I was about to call out to her again when I saw she was talking to someone through a portable intercom, reserved for Council members only. Slowly I turned to walk back to my bed when I heard her say, "What do you mean you made a mistake, Sylvia?"

I froze.

"Sylvia, how could you do something like that and not have seen it sooner?" Pause. "You what!? Are you telling me you knew all this time and didn't say anything?"

What was she talking about?

"That wasn't a risk you should have taken. Lives are on the line."

Lives? I hoped she didn't mean mine.

"So why are you telling me four months in?"

Oh no.

"You think that's what her symptoms are from? This virus?"

Virus? Oh, please no.

"Well, what is there I could do about it now? Don't you think it's a bit late to tell me that?"

Please don't say it's too late.

"What's going to happen to the other girls, huh? Won't they all get it? How are we meant to fix this?"

Others? Not Ava, she's next.

"Don't tell me you don't know, Sylvia, you're celebrated as the smartest person to walk the earth. You'd better find a solution."

If Sylvia Carter was clueless then I could only expect the worst.

"We don't have that kind of time. They're going to get too old." Pause. "Fine, I trust you, but you'd better figure something out. What about Katelyn?"

Me?

"What's going to happen to her?" Donna ran her hand through her hair. "Just tell me, Sylvia." She paced for a second then froze, her face paling. "You can't be serious."

I felt my heart lurch.

"There has to be something we can do. Don't tell me you don't know! Figure something out!"

I jumped. Never had I heard Donna yell, she was always so collected.

"Mark my words, Sylvia, if anything happens to that girl…"

Oh please no.

"Figure something out." She ended the call and leant against the wall.

I couldn't move. My whole body was shaking from the inside out. What was going to happen to me?

"Katelyn, I'm sorry I took so long," the doctor said as she walked in. "Why are you out of bed?"

I stayed fixed where I was. Motionless.

"Doctor Karen?" said Donna, peering round the door.

"Yes?"

"Could I have a word?"

"Of course."

"Morning, Katelyn," said Donna, smiling at me but I saw that it was all a mask.

I couldn't get words out so I just stared at her.

"OK," she said and walked out with the doctor behind her.

I was so confused that I began to fear the worst. Slowly I walked over to my bed and curled up in the sheets. I buried my head under the blanket and prayed that it would all go away. I must have misunderstood; there was no way Sylvia Carter would make a mistake. I was fine. Everything was fine.

Then I fell asleep.

"Katelyn, it's time for lunch."

I slowly prised open my eyes. The nurse was peering down at me, carrying a tray. It smelt heavenly so I sat up and took it from her. "Thanks, Claire."

"The doctor saw you were asleep so she decided it would be best to do the tests later." There was something in her face that was off.

"Are you OK, Claire?"

"Yes, of course I am," she said, forcing a smile but I saw something in her eyes looked pained.

"Oh good."

She gave another quick smile and headed for the door. "We'll do the tests after you've eaten."

"OK, thank you."

She left and I immediately began devouring my lunch. I felt well rested and calm. But then I remembered why I had fallen asleep.

I dropped the bread in my hand and it fell to the floor.

Donna talking to Sylvia Carter. Something about a virus. Not enough time. No solution. Katelyn. What would happen to her?

What was going to happen to me?

I assured myself it was nothing and continued eating. Donna of all people could control a situation.

"Katelyn, are you ready for those tests?" Doctor Karen came in through the door.

I looked down at my plate. "I think so."

"Yes, you fell asleep earlier," she said as she pulled out her scanner. "I thought it would be good to let you rest."

"Thank you, I feel a lot better after that."

"Good to hear. Now lie down."

She lifted the tray on to the table and I lay down on the bed, staring at the colourful ceiling. Then the doctor pressed several buttons on her scanner and placed it over my head. The little blue light turned on and it ran slowly from my forehead down to my toes, making little beeps along the way. After three rounds, Doctor Karen removed it from my head and said, "Well done, I'll just go and check these out and we'll do the rest of the tests."

"OK."

I sat up and looked back out of the window. It was so bright outside and I could just feel the sun coming through the panes of glass, even though the Bubble only let in part of the sun's light. Apparently, it looked like a fiery circle in the sky. I had never seen it.

Gradually, I lifted the covers and walked over to the window. I pressed my hands against the glass and sighed.

Then I felt it again. A wave washed over my body covering every inch of it in a sensation of shivers. I felt cold. Then it passed and I waited to see if it would stop. But it didn't.

A jolt licked up my spine and I tensed then fell to the ground in pain. I clawed at the window, trying to pull myself back up, but the stabbing sensation surged through every inch of me, leaving my whole body numb. *Please stop.*

I breathed in and out heavily and tried to crawl over to the door but suddenly my stomach lurched and all the air left me. Clutching my hands to my stomach, I curled up into a ball on the floor and tried desperately to inhale. My lungs were burning and I knew they were far too weak.

With every last scrap of energy in me, I threw my upper body at the window and forced it open. I leant my head out and tried so hard to breathe in but nothing worked. Then the world turned fuzzy and my head felt light enough to float away. I sank on to the floor that suddenly felt so comforting and let myself drift.

"Katelyn!" The voice sounded muffled and distant.

"What's wrong?" It sounded like Donna.

"Her tests. That virus that we thought had disappeared actually multiplied."

I heard footsteps and two blurry faces appeared over me. They looked scared.

"Katelyn!"

"Listen to me! Stay with me!"

Their voices were fading away.

"Fight it Katelyn! We're getting you help!"

I tried to hold on to the voice and ride it back but I couldn't. It was like something was grabbing at my foot and pulling me down and I couldn't hold on. Then there was this bright white light filling my vision. I heard sounds and felt twitches in my body as I was lifted up. It was no use.

The light became so bright yet I wanted to go to it. It was calm and peaceful and there were no expectations or responsibilities.

Then I saw Ava. She was looking down at me smiling and saying, "I love you Kay."

"I love you too, Ava bear," I tried to say but there were no words.

I saw Mother and Donna and Lexi and Bri and Jade and some strange man, all smiling down at me. "Bye Katelyn," they said.

"Bye."

And then it all went black.

Chapter Nine

Ava, Five Hours Later

No, it wasn't happening. I just stared at my mother in shock.

"Ava, say something!" Mother was shaking me.

My trance faded. "She's alive, she's fine, I know it, I saw her," I stuttered.

"Oh Ava." Mother took a step towards me.

"Don't touch me," I snapped and slapped her hand away.

"Please Ava, listen."

"Listen to what? Your lies?"

"Ava, it's the truth."

"No, no, you're lying!" I screamed.

People walking around us froze.

"Ava, let me explain."

"What is there to explain? You can't say anything to make it better!"

Mother grabbed me by the shoulders. "She wasn't ready. Her body just wasn't right for this."

I shrugged her off. "Don't lie to me! She was fine!"

"We all thought she was getting better, but she... she..."

"Why? Why?!"

"There was nothing they could do."

My breathing was heavy and I couldn't feel any part of my body. The world was crumbling down and I was standing right under the landslide.

"I need to see her."

"No Ava, you can't."

"Why not?" I cried.

Mother's eyes welled with tears. "You wouldn't be able to live with that image in your head."

I pictured Katelyn lying in her bed peacefully sleeping and me waiting for her to wake up. Mother was right; I couldn't even live with my own imagination.

"Please tell me I'm dreaming."

"Oh Ava, I'm so sorry." Mother held her arms out to me and I fell into them and cried.

Tears just ran down my cheeks like it was a race. My heart was beating so loud I could hear it ringing in my ears. Everything was blurred. Nothing made sense. I was holding on to Mother so hard but I was alone.

I saw Katelyn's face and she let out this hearty laugh and her hair fell back and danced in the sun.

Suddenly my knees stopped working and I crumpled to the ground, still clinging on to my mother. She went down with me and we sat on the pavement and I wailed until my eyes refused to give up any more water. I felt people gathering around us and passing us by.

Once I had emptied my sorrow out of my body, I just collapsed and lay in Mother's arms on the roadside outside my school until she dragged me to my feet and we left.

At home I didn't stop to put away my coat or eat. I just ran straight for my room and collapsed on my bed with my head buried in the pillows. My eyes were sore yet I managed to let out another two hours' worth of tears. Then I saw Mother's light go out down the hallway and I turned mine off too and curled up under the covers.

But I wasn't lucky enough to fall into a deep sleep. As hard as I tried it was like I was trapped with my thoughts. So I stayed in my bed, wearing shoes and all, and thought about Katelyn.

I saw her face so clearly. She was smiling at me as I finished an entire cake single-handedly. She was wagging her finger at me from the desk in front as I ran into class late. She was giggling as I joked about motherhood classes. She was singing with her guitar as the audience gazed at her in awe. She was staring at me with curiosity as I talked in the forest. And she was always listening. Not just with her ears but with her eyes.

It broke my heart that I would never see her face again or hear her laugh or sing or talk. I wanted so badly to go back and not have left for school that day. If I had stayed...

What? It wouldn't have made a difference, I was no doctor. That almost made it hurt more, to know that I couldn't have helped her. She was alone. And I was alone too.

Katelyn would never be able to give me her words of wisdom or explain them. She would never be able to accompany me on any crazy or wild adventure I devised. She would never be able to graduate or have her children.

Her daughter. She must have died too. There was no way they could have saved a four-month-old foetus. We would never be able to raise our children together or our grandchildren, like we planned. We wouldn't grow old together or die together.

Losing her hurt so much I never thought I would make it. I imagined myself growing old in that spot on my bed in the same clothes and slowly dying there. Fading.

Did it hurt? When she died of course. Where did she go? I wondered if she was somewhere else or if she just vanished altogether. I imagined her looking at me from her new home and crying out to me, *Ava I'm OK!* But I would never hear those words. She was gone. And so was I.

The next morning I woke to voices. Light poured into my vision and I held my hand over my eyes to block it. Slowly I sat up but it only made my head hurt. My throat was dry, my eyes sore, my head ached, and my heart was broken. As I rolled out of bed, I noticed I was still wearing my jacket and shoes. I groaned and threw them across the room then slumped to the floor with my head in my hands.

Then I heard the voices again, floating up the staircase. It sounded like yelling so I quietly crept down the stairs and hovered at the top, looking down at the kitchen.

"How dare you!"

"Stop yelling at me please."

"Don't you talk back to me!"

I walked down a couple of extra steps until I had a good view of the people standing at the counter. Mother was sitting at the table, fully dressed and groomed. She looked immaculate and back to her usual collected self. The other person was pacing around the kitchen, screaming at the top of her lungs. I saw blonde hair and my stomach lurched. It was Jennifer.

"You should have known, Donna."

"Well, I didn't. No one could have known, she just had a problem that didn't enable her to carry children."

"And no one realised that!?"

"Jenny, please keep your voice down, Ava's asleep."

"Well, at least your daughter is only asleep, mine is dead!" She let out a sob.

"Jenny, please calm down and we can talk."

"No, I will not calm down!"

I was shocked. The Jennifer Rose I knew was the sweetest woman and she would never have yelled or lost her temper. Katelyn once told me they never screamed at each other, their disagreements were always resolved quickly.

"This is all your fault!"

"How is this my fault?"

"You signed her up for this! You should've known this stupid method would never have worked."

"It's all we've got. And it works perfectly, Katelyn just wasn't right."

"My daughter was perfect."

"That's not what I'm saying…"

"And now she's gone and never coming back. How could you do this to me?"

"Jenny, please…"

"I am your best friend! Correction – *was*."

"It could have been anyone, don't take this personally."

"Stop treating me like I'm stupid! Donna, you always think you're so much better than everyone else. Well, guess what, you're not!"

"Jenny, I never said…"

"Don't Jenny me!"

"Jennifer, I'm so dreadfully sorry for your loss. Katelyn was like a second daughter to me and I wish it weren't true, but it is."

"Yes, well, that's just the thing. She was like a second daughter to you because you still have another. Well, Katelyn was all I had and now she's gone." She began to cry and she placed her head in her hands.

"Jenny, you have me," Mother said and walked over to her.

"No, I don't!" She brushed her off. "How can I ever look you in the eye again after what you did?"

"Don't blame this on me, Jenny."

"Oh, but I do."

I leant in closer to try and hear more of what they were saying when I tripped and my foot landed hard on the step below. Their heads snapped up to look at me.

"Oh Ava," Mother began.

"At least one of you looks like they actually cried," said Jennifer as she snatched her purse off the counter and marched towards the door.

"Jenny, wait," Mother said and ran after her.

"I would say I'll see you around, but I won't. Goodbye Donna," Jennifer said. Then she turned and swiftly walked out, slamming the door behind her.

And just like that, both of the Roses had walked out of our lives.

Mother walked back into the kitchen and sat at the counter. She sighed and propped her head on her hand. I walked down the stairs, rubbing my sore ankle.

"I'm sorry, Mother," I said and went over and hugged her tight.

"No Ava, it's not your fault at all. I'm sorry you had to see that," she replied and held me tight back.

"I just wish it would all go away."

"Me too Ava, me too."

And even though my mother sounded strong as a rock, she too was broken because I knew what it was like to lose a best friend. And it definitely wasn't easy.

A few days later they held a small ceremony for Katelyn. It was called the goodbye ceremony and everyone that died got one. Only two, now three people had ever died in the community though, so I barely remembered the other ones. Everyone was gathered in the park, all sitting in rows of chairs by a small removable stage.

I walked up the aisle to try and find a seat when I saw Bri doing the same thing. She was wearing a peach dress that I recognised from Jade's birthday earlier in the year. She looked over and saw me. The two of us just stared at each other for a moment. Everything sounded so silent that I could hear the air flowing around me. Then she held up her skirt and started running over across the grass. I did the same until we met and without saying a word she wrapped her arms around me and I didn't let go of her for what felt like years.

She pulled back to look at my face. "Hi."

"Hi."

We stood there in silence.

"I'm sorry, Ava."

I forced back the tears. "So am I Bri, so am I."

"Ava! Bri!"

Both of us turned to find the voice that called us. I saw Lexi standing at the other side of the park waving at us. Jade stood beside her, staring at the ground. They started to run over to us.

"Hi," Lexi said as she reached us. "How have you both been? I've missed you all."

"I've missed you too, Lexi," Bri said and gave her a quick hug, then Jade. "And you, Jade."

Jade just nodded in response.

"How are you, Ava?" Lexi asked.

"How do you think?" I snapped.

Her smile fell and everyone went silent. Out of the corner of my eye I saw Lexi fidgeting with the ruffles on her dress and poking the dirt with her shoe.

Bri stared from Lexi to me then back to Lexi with a concerned expression. "Should we go sit?"

Lexi's head remained fixed on the ground as she said, "Yeah, that sounds like a good idea."

The four of us manoeuvred our way awkwardly to sit in a row near the front and it pained me to think that Katelyn wasn't with us. I looked around and saw hundreds of people, our entire community, sitting in the spare white chairs to honour my dear friend's memory. Some of them looked sad, some utterly depressed, some heartbroken, some wistful, and almost all were crying.

I spotted many familiar faces and it was like being at the Election or a Liberation Day celebration. Out of the corner of my eye I saw Jennifer Rose sitting alone in the front row, the only woman who had had a daughter and lost her. It was obvious that she was trying desperately to pull herself together, but it wouldn't last another moment.

"Welcome everyone." The entire crowd looked up to see my mother speaking into the microphone at the front of the stage. "Today we are all gathered to honour a life, and one very special one at that. Katelyn Rose was a hardworking member of our community, like every one of you, but she was also more than that. Katelyn was lively, bright, funny, charming, caring, honest, sweet, generous and completely gorgeous. She was a talented musician as I'm sure you all know, a fabulous student, a creative thinker, an amazing listener, a wonderful daughter and a caring friend." Mother nodded at me and I had to look away to keep from crying my eyes out.

"And to top it all, Katelyn Rose was one of the bravest people I have ever met. When our community called on her to take on an incredible responsibility, she didn't even hesitate to accept. She carried out her duty with pride and honour and for that we all owe her our overwhelming gratitude.

"And it was while performing her contribution to our community that she passed." There was a stir in the crowd. "Her doctors promise that it was painless and peaceful. She is on her way to brighter things now and even though we have no right to ask any more of her, I know that she will always look down at us as our guardian. We shall miss you, Katelyn Rose."

Several sobs erupted from the gathering of people and I saw Jennifer Rose completely doubled over with emotion. My heart ached for her and for the person that should have filled the empty seat beside me.

Mother continued, "Now I shall also announce that the Repopulation Phase will go on as planned using the same procedure."

I gasped and threw my hand over my mouth. *But Mother knew I was next…*

"I understand that many of you are probably assuming that we would alter the procedure, but after recent analysis it has been concluded that Katelyn passed due to her body being incompatible for carrying a child."

… so was I the new experiment?

"However, no one was aware of this so there was nothing the doctors could have done to save her."

Would they be able to save me?

"We will be conducting more thorough tests from now on but I can assure you all that Katelyn Rose had an extremely rare condition, like the one that our talented song writer Naomi Tyler passed from."

Hearing the mention of one of Katelyn's idols made my insides bunch up and I flashed back to Katelyn singing her favourite song during the Election, her voice like honey.

"The Council will provide more details later in the week about the procedure. But now we must pause to commemorate Katelyn Rose's bravery and wonderful life."

Mother walked to the other end of the stage and collected a tablet from the lone chair. She brought it back over to the centre of the stage. "Now the other members of the Council and I will read aloud some of the anonymous commemorations that members of our community have made about Katelyn."

She stepped aside and a different Council member walked forward. "'Katelyn was a charming person to talk to, I will miss her visiting my store.' 'Katelyn Rose had an incredible take on everything and we shall miss her presence in the classroom.' 'My heart goes out to Jennifer Rose, I am terribly sorry for your loss.' 'Goodbye Katelyn darling. Safe travels to you.'"

The commemorations continued like that for a while, each with a different thoughtful comment on Katelyn's life. The Council members rotated so they read about ten, then switched. A few of the comments were memories.

One member read, "'Once I was having trouble with my intercom so Katelyn came over from next door and helped me out. She then stayed and talked to me for hours, she brightened up my day.'"

Another read, "'I'll never forget the time that she and the young Miss Hart did their little routine on stage. It was a wonderful performance all round.'"

That one almost made me cry, but I didn't. The one I did cry at went like this:

'Katelyn was my friend. No, she was more than that, she was the person that listened when I wanted to talk, that spoke when I was too shy, that surprised me on my birthday, and that made every minute I was with her special. I love you Katelyn.'

I looked over at Bri who was staring at her lap. A tear rolled down her cheek and fell on to her pale palm. She brushed it aside and looked back up at the stage. Soon my own eyes were watering and I felt the waterfall pour down my face. I was so choked up that I almost missed as they read out mine.

Sylvia Carter was the one who read it, "'I have too many memories of Katelyn to give them all and they are all too special to choose one. I once told her I loved her because she said the deepest things, but they were so deep that I didn't understand them, and when I asked what they meant she always said that if I figured it out for myself it was better for me. But the truth is that I loved her for many more reasons, too many to say them all. I loved that when she sang everyone would stop to listen. I loved that for her everyone and everything else came before her own needs. I loved that she knew me so well it was like she knew me better than I knew myself. I loved that she trusted me no matter how insane I sounded. I loved that she didn't just laugh with her voice but with her heart. I loved that her eyes were so honest that she didn't even need to speak for me to know what she was thinking. The one thing I never got to say to her was goodbye. And that's what I love the most. We'll never say goodbye. She'll be here forever.'"

There was a silence. Sylvia Carter seemed so astounded by what she just read that she couldn't continue. I saw Mother staring at me from across the crowd, she looked so sad. Even my friends were staring at me. My face seemed to burn and I tried desperately to distract myself. Then Bri reached over and squeezed my hand, just like Katelyn did so many times. She smiled at me.

"Um, continuing…" Sylvia cleared her throat and read out the next one and the next.

Then, some four or five hundred commemorations later, Mother took the stage one final time. "Now would each of you please go and choose one flower from around the park, any one you like, and then bring it and put in the giant vase at the foot of the stage. It will then be put in the city square outside the Town Hall for the next week to honour Katelyn. After you put in your flower you may leave or stay and chat with friends, and everyone has the day off today. Thank you."

Everyone stood to gather flowers and I saw the Council members do the same.

"Should we go?" Lexi asked.

"Sure." I nodded and the four of us stood and walked over to the flower displays.

There were hundreds of different ones and the entire city was buzzing around the sections looking for their favourites. Some people chose quickly, instantly picking a beautiful plant and making their way back to the vase. Others took their time to enjoy the flowers along the way. I noticed some women having trouble deciding which one was the best.

We all walked down the path between the overflowing collections. Jade stopped and slowly plucked out a dark red flower. The petals were folded inwards and it hadn't bloomed yet.

I knew what she was thinking: Katelyn died too young to shine. Therefore she chose a flower that hadn't bloomed. But what Jade didn't know was that Katelyn had shone so hard the sun was jealous.

"I'm going to put this in. I'll meet you all back at the stage."

"OK."

She ran off and the three of us continued looking. Lexi walked over to the bright yellow daffodils which matched her dress and admired them all, eventually choosing the best one.

"What do you think, Ava?" She looked at me expectantly.

"Katelyn would have loved it."

She smiled. "Good."

Bri came over and said, "I found mine." She held out a small blue flower with five blue petals and a yellow centre.

"It's beautiful, what is it?" I asked.

"A forget-me-not."

I flinched inside.

"So what did you get?"

"I haven't found one yet."

"There are some nice ones over there," said Lexi, pointing at a bright coloured section where several people were milling around.

I scanned the park and saw a smaller section by the edge with barely anyone there and said, "I think I'll go this way."

"OK, we'll wait for you here."

"Thanks." I turned and walked over to the section I had spotted.

As I passed other people walking back to the vase, I noticed a lot of roses. Typical – her name was Katelyn Rose so clearly a rose made sense. Truth be told, nothing reminded me more of Katelyn than a light pink rose, gentle and fair. But it was the kind of flower that people chose if they didn't know her well. *Let me get a rose for the Rose girl.* But I wanted a unique flower, because that's what Katelyn was to me.

After five minutes of walking, I reached the small gathering of flowers by the end of the park. Everyone had left that area and I was left alone to admire the flowers. Not many people came to this section because it was too far away for them. But it was far more beautiful. The plaque in the ground read *Rare Exotic Flowers: these flowers have been preserved from different countries before they were destroyed.* Perfect.

I circled the section several times to breathe in the fresh scents of each type. Then I found the one I wanted. It was small, like Kay, but it burst into a huge bloom. The petals were almost a golden colour and they curled at the ends like a ruffle. The centre was light pink and it gently faded as it stretched further out. As the wind brushed the gentle flower it glowed and I could just see Katelyn in it.

Carefully, I pulled it from the ground and walked back over to Lexi and Bri. "Ready to go to the vase?" I asked.

"Did you find a flower?"

"Here." I held it up.

The two of them gasped and said, "It looks just like her."

"You mean because it's gold and she had blonde hair?" I raised my eyebrows.

"No," Bri said and looked up, "I can see her laughing when it sways. It looks like her heart."

I felt something warm and soft inside seep through me. "You're right Bri, it does."

We all walked back to the vase, which by then was almost full of flowers. It was a jaw-dropping display of colour. Katelyn would have loved it. Together we put in our flowers. I placed mine in the heart of the vase and even though it was shadowed by the bright and vibrant flowers surrounding it, I could still see it shining through.

"There you are," said Jade as she joined us by the vase.

"Sorry, we went to the further part of the park," Bri explained.

"No, it's fine. Do you want to sit?" She pointed at the empty row at the back of the collection of chairs.

"Sure."

We all went and sat down and I noticed most people were all talking at the front by the stage. There was barely anyone around us.

"That was really nice," Bri said.

"Yeah, I didn't remember what these were like," I said, pulling at the hem of my light blue dress.

"It's strange to think that we'll all get one too," Lexi said.

"Yeah."

We all sat there silently searching for words.

Finally I broke the silence, "I'm scared."

They all looked at me. "About the procedure?"

"Yes."

"I am too," Bri agreed, "it just doesn't feel right."

"How do we know it won't happen to us too?" Jade added.

"And I go next. At least if it doesn't work again you all will know and they'll have to change it. But as for me, I'll be dead."

"Don't say that," Bri said and put her arm around my shoulders.

"And it's not like we have a choice," Lexi declared, throwing her arms in the air.

"I hate all of this responsibility," Jade grunted.

"Maybe that's what killed Katelyn." They all turned to me. "It was just too much."

Everyone digested the idea for a second. I had seen the signs. She cringed as the nurses over-pampered her and wouldn't do anything except stare out of the stupid window. Feelings of hopelessness and the pressures wore her out.

"Ava's right, how crazy is it that a seventeen-year-old girl has to hold the responsibility of the survival of the human race?"

"No one checked beforehand that she was 'compatible'?"

"It's like they believe so strongly in their method working that they refuse to try anything else."

"What if there is nothing else to try?"

"Then what's worse: no more people after we die or killing off all the ones they have left?"

"If it doesn't work, eventually they have to accept it."

"Yeah, and preferably before I become the next failed attempt."

"Ava, could you talk to your mother?"

"I could try."

"Sometimes I wish we could just run away from all of this," Bri sighed.

I turned to her and something clicked. "What if we could?" I asked.

"What do you mean?"

I grinned slowly, suddenly filled with a sense of hope.

"Oh no, not the…"

"Let's go back to the forest!" I exclaimed.

"No Ava, it's too dangerous," Bri tried to reason with me.

"Besides, we can't go without Katelyn," Lexi added, staring down at her lap.

I sighed and slumped back in my chair. "I just want out," I said wearily.

"Forever?"

"No, just a temporary escape to clear my head." It was only as I said it that I realised just how much I wanted one.

"Clear it somewhere else," Jade said and ruffled my hair.

"I just thought that maybe we'd all feel a little more comfortable about going into this if we had some space from our everyday lives. I know I would."

"But what if we get eaten?" Bri asked.

"Then we don't have to get the surgery."

"What if next time we go the Bubble stays shut?" said Jade and crossed her arms.

"Then we don't have to get the surgery," I sighed. "Listen, I just don't want to die without going back one more time."

"Even without Katelyn?"

I looked at Bri and said, "Even without Katelyn."

Lexi sighed, "I guess it could be OK."

"Last time we went, Lexi, you were having so much fun I thought you might never leave," I said and laughed remembering her darting through the trees screaming.

"It was sort of fun…"

"Yeah, well, I fell asleep," Jade recalled.

"It was like two in the morning," I said, still laughing.

"Three," she corrected.

"Fine, we can go later. Does that work, Jade?"

"Hmm… I guess."

"So let's meet at the edge of the Bubble by that little tree at seven?"

"Then our mothers will know we left."

"We can say we went to the show," I suggested.

"But then we'd have to be home by nine," Lexi stated.

"So we can say we're going to the show and dinner."

"Wait, but everyone has the day off," Jade reminded us and sat forward. "We need a better excuse."

"Nothing with sleepwalking!"

"Fine, how about…"

"No, Jade!" we all shouted.

"But I'm the best storyteller."

"I can't believe we're lying," Bri said with a shudder.

"Who said anything about lying?" Jade asked, leaning forward. "Remember what I always say: it's storytelling. A lie means there are malevolent motivations involved, storytelling doesn't. And everyone needs to tell a story or two in order to exercise their creativity."

I thought back to Mother telling everyone that Katelyn was fine when she wasn't. "It's alright Bri. This one's for our own good."

"If you insist."

"Let's just say that we all want to go and catch up so it will be a while."

"Sounds good."

"Also I think we should honour Katelyn," Bri suggested.

"What do you mean?"

"We each bring an item that reminds us of her, then we put them in the forest."

"That's a nice idea," said Lexi and reached over and squeezed Bri's hand.

"OK so it's settled," I confirmed to the group. "Tonight at seven?"

"Tonight at seven."

Chapter Ten

Ava, A Few Hours Later

Seven came and I found myself crouching by the bushes at the edge of the city. It was dark and the Bubble wall radiated a clear glow, only just visible from the inside. Strangely, it was colder sitting near the Bubble and I had to rub my hands together to keep warm.

Then I heard whispering coming from the other side of the hedge. I gripped the trunk of the lone tree and pulled myself up. The top of the hedge was slightly higher than me so I just had to wait and see who came.

"Are we at the right place?" a voice asked.

"I'm pretty sure," another voice replied.

Then two hands stretched through the hedge and a head popped out. "Yep, I can see the tree," said Lexi as she crawled through. "Ava?"

"Over here, Lex."

She turned and jumped. "Ava, what are you doing behind the tree? You scared me."

"Sorry," I said and walked out from the shadows.

"A little help?" asked Jade who had one foot poking out of the hedge but was struggling to get the rest of her body through.

"Here." Lexi leant over and pulled her through.

Jade dusted off her shoulders. "Thanks."

Bri snuck through a moment later. "Is Ava here?"

"Hi Bri." I waved.

"Oh hey. So should we go?"

"Did you bring the light-up tablets?"

"Sure did," said Lexi and held up a small square tablet and flicked it on.

The bright light shone straight into my eyes. "Whoa, turn that off."

"Oh sorry." She flicked it off and the light disappeared.

"We don't want anyone in those houses to see the light."

"But there are no back windows."

"Do you really want to take that risk?"

"No." She shoved the tablet back in her pocket.

"Do you have the stuff for Katelyn?" Bri asked.

"Yeah," I said and rubbed the little plastic chip in my pocket. "Should we go?"

"Sure."

"Let's get to it."

"One second," I said and reached over behind the tree and grabbed the large piece of bark. "We need this."

"Not to get out we don't."

"But how do you propose we get back in?"

They thought for a moment then Lexi widened her eyes with understanding and said, "Clever, Ava."

"Aren't I just?"

"Come on, you first Bri."

We took turns running through the Bubble and experiencing the momentary feeling of flying. I placed the bark on the grass saying, "Don't want to carry it all the way."

"Makes sense."

After we had gathered ourselves together, we all headed towards the thicket of trees and hiked uphill until we had put a fair amount of distance between the Bubble and us.

"Is it OK to switch on the tablets?"

I looked back towards where we came from and said, "I think so."

"Thank goodness, I was worried I would trip over a tree or something," Lexi said and reached into her pocket and pulled out four tablets. "Here." She passed them around.

"Speak for yourself, I've tripped over the entire forest by now," Jade complained as she took her tablet from Lexi.

"How do they turn on?" asked Bri as she held hers up.

"Like this," said Lexi as she reached over and pressed the button on the side.

The light was even brighter in the dark of the forest. "Geez Bri, shine it somewhere else would you?"

"Sorry Ava," she said and pointed it at the ground.

"Anyone else think it's really cold out here?" Jade shivered slightly.

"Yeah, I was thinking that," I said and pulled down my sleeves. "Any ideas why?"

"Maybe trees radiate cold."

"I don't think that's it, Jade."

"Let's keep going, I think it's past that fallen building," said Lexi and shone her tablet at a ruin.

We continued walking for a while until the ruins were behind us and it was only trees and shrubs. Before, I had little idea of what our surroundings were, but the tablets meant that I saw all the little details. Curves on the tree trunks, water settling on the moss, dirt smeared across the rocks. It was strange yet intriguing at the same time.

"Here it is," Lexi called out.

"How do you know?" I asked.

She shone her tablet at a tree and I realised why. Dangling from the lowest branch was a little pink ribbon. It was frayed at the edges and slightly duller in colour but it was the same ribbon.

I fell to my knees and burst into tears.

"Oh Ava." Someone ran over and hugged me. "It's OK."

I wanted to stop, but someone had jammed the stop button in my eyes and the flood came out. Katelyn danced around in my memory, yet I felt her fading. I realised that as time passed, her memory became more distant, and that's what hurt the most.

"Come on, Ava." I felt arms lifting me up and sitting me down on something cold.

"I'm sorry, it's just…"

"You don't need to apologise," said Bri as she wiped my eyes with her hand. "Do you still want to have the ceremony?"

I sucked up my tears. "Of course, let's do it now."

Bracing one hand on the surface I was sitting on, I stood. Bri, taking that as a sign, ran over and opened her bag. She combed through it then walked back over as we all huddled around her.

"So let's all put our memorabilia in the pouch. Who wants to start?"

"I will," said Lexi and reached into her pocket and pulled out a short thin item.

"Is that a tablet pen?"

"I haven't seen one of those in years."

Lexi laughed. "This was from back when we needed them for writing on tablets in school."

"Look at us, all grown up, able to use our fingers like adults," I joked.

"So what's it from?"

"Katelyn was sitting in front of me in class and the teacher asked us to write something or other, and I realised I forgot my pen. So I tapped on her shoulder, this must have been five years ago, and I asked if she had one I could borrow, and this is it." She held it up. "And that's how we met. Been friends ever since."

"That's nice," said Bri with a smile. "Here, put it in the bag."

Lexi did as instructed. "Bye Katelyn."

"I'll go next," said Jade and extracted a thin tablet from her pocket.

"Your light-up tablet?"

"No, this is an electric document."

"Of what?"

"When we went to the archives for Bri's birthday ages ago, Katelyn was trying to get me to visit the stupid music section. She gave me this brochure and said I'd enjoy it. I told her she was wasting her breath. I actually found this lying under a pile of stuff a few days ago so I went to see it. She was right, it was amazing."

"I remember that," Bri said.

"Well, here it is, proof that Katelyn was an incredible crazy mind-reader," she said and dropped it in the bag.

"So here's mine," I said and took out the plastic chip from my pocket.

"Hey, what's that?" Jade asked and leant in to look at it.

"This is a guitar pick. Katelyn dropped it before we left my house for Bri's birthday, so I guess it's the same age as Jade's brochure. We slept out in the backyard the night before and I guess she must have dropped it in the grass when she left. I found it the next night. It was the one she used at our show, you know at the Election."

"That's a great memory, Ava."

"Yep, Ava's dance moves are certainly memorable."

"Don't make me show them to you, Jade."

"Oh please, not the dancing!" she said sarcastically. "Anything but that!"

I did a little jump in the air and clicked my heels. "Prepare to face your doom."

"All right you two, no dance wars here. Put your item in the bag, Ava," Lexi said and pointed at the pouch.

I kissed the little piece of plastic. "Here you go, Kay." It fell into the bag.

"Here, hold this," said Bri and handed me the pouch and ran over to her bag. She came back carrying something in her hands.

"What you got there, Bri?"

"Forget-me-nots." She held up the bunch of little blue flowers.

"From the goodbye ceremony?"

"Yeah, I saved some. Here's to Katelyn, someone we will never forget."

"Hear hear!" we cheered as she dropped them in the pouch and sealed it.

"I also brought this," Bri said and ran back to her bag and came over with a very thin tablet. She switched it on to show a photo of Katelyn. "It's an electronic photo."

"I recognise this," Lexi recalled.

"You took this photo, Lexi."

"I did, didn't I?"

"Oh yeah," I said as I suddenly remembered. "We were at the park and Lexi just got her new camera so we were taking photos."

"That's it," said Bri, nodding.

The photo showed Katelyn with a daisy chain in her hair and her head tilted back laughing. She looked beautiful.

"Wasn't Ava dancing around behind the camera?" Jade asked.

"Oh, now I remember! We were having a dance-off, Jade."

"That's ironic."

"And Lexi was trying to take pictures."

"That's right – Katelyn was laughing at your Ava-special-flip-trip-turn-fall-over-on-your-face-kazam."

"I did not fall on my face."

"You did too."

"How'd you get the photo, Bri?" Lexi asked as she turned to her.

"I asked you to put it on an electronic photo tablet for me, so you did, and here it is."

"What are you going to do with it?"

She held up the pouch and attached the photo to the front. "I put a clip on it."

"But that photo is from years ago."

"I know, and I have tons of photos of her in the Centre, but I just thought that this one really captured how I'll always remember Katelyn – laughing."

"She had a great laugh," I said and smiled to myself as I heard it drifting through the trees.

"She did." A lone tear slid down Bri's cheek and silently landed at her feet.

We all stood there for a moment to listen to Katelyn laugh. The gentle sound wafted in the breeze and tickled my soul.

Then her voice faded from my head. "Should we hang the pouch?"

"Uh, sure," Bri said as she snapped back to reality. "Over there?" She pointed at the ribbon tree.

"That sounds like a good idea."

We all walked over and Bri hung the pouch on the branch next to the ribbon. I took a moment to remember Katelyn in all her glory – hair streaming behind her, laughter in the air, eyes so kind and warm.

Then I heard something. A rustling noise came from the bushes behind me. I spun round. "Did anyone hear that?"

"The rustling noise?"

"I heard it too."

"It came from the bushes."

"What do you think it is?"

"We should go."

"Yeah, it's probably the wild animal."

The others all turned to go and collect their things. I stayed rooted to the spot. The sound came again.

"Hurry Ava, let's go."

"Hold on one second," I said and crept slowly towards the source of the sound.

"Ava, what are you doing?"

At that moment I wasn't really thinking straight at all. Something inside me just said walk.

"Ava, don't go there, it might be an animal."

I kept walking, each slow footstep made a crunch as the fallen leaves were trampled. I didn't hesitate a second. After another step I reached the bush. Carefully, I placed my hand on the leaves and pushed them aside.

Then I saw two eyes.

I jumped back, startled. It was hard to see in the dark, but they were a beautiful golden green colour and they stared back at me with curiosity.

"What is it?"

"Ava, please come back."

I looked into the eyes, trying to decipher what they belonged to. Then they disappeared. Without thinking, I stepped through the bush just as the creature took off running. I ran after it, following the sound of movement.

"Ava, come back!"

I kept going after it and I heard it running faster. I reached out to grab at it, but just as I did, my foot caught on a root and I fell hard on to the ground. My hands clutched dirt and I tasted it in my mouth.

The running stopped and the animal turned and walked back over to me. I could hear it panting directly above me. It was tall.

I spat out the dirt in my mouth and sat up, searching for my light-up tablet on the ground. The footsteps grew louder as it came closer and closer. My heart was pounding as I began to claw frantically at the dirt for my tablet. Soon I felt its smooth texture amongst the dirt and I flicked it on and shone it directly at the creature.

It shied away from the light, covering its eyes with its hands. It took a moment for my own eyes to adjust to the light, but when they did I was shocked.

Before me stood a human, not an animal, yet it was the strangest girl I had ever laid eyes on. She was tall, far taller than me, and her shoulders were broader than most. She had very short hair and thick muscles on her arms, legs and stomach. I noticed she was shirtless and I gasped, scooting backwards.

I heard the others yelling in the distance. She gave me a strange look, most likely similar to the one I was giving her. I shone the light at her face; her jaw was square and covered in little dots. It was the most bizarre person I had ever seen.

"Who are you?" I asked it.

"Are you OK?" she asked as she took a step forward and I jumped backwards. The girl froze.

Her voice sounded so deep, almost like…

Then it hit me. It wasn't a girl at all. It was a boy.

"Are you OK?" It started walking closer.

"Stay back!" I cried and crawled away from it.

"Ava, what's wrong?" Lexi came running up behind me

"It's a… a… b-boy," I stammered.

"A what?"

The others came running over.

"It's a boy!" I screeched.

They looked at it for a second then we all screamed in unison and everyone took off, running away from it. I struggled to my feet, still keeping the tablet trained on it.

"Wait." It grabbed my arm as I stumbled to my feet. "Who are you?"

I froze and stared at him for a moment. He looked back at me with total curiosity. Then I slapped his arm away, turned and ran.

I kept running after the screams of the others and the flashing lights. My feet were burning so hard I thought they might fall off. I turned to look over my shoulder but he clearly wasn't following me. I only ran faster.

Once at the Bubble, we each ran through under the bark until we were back inside. We didn't stop moving until we were all the way back to the tram stop, running through the doors and falling into our seats, panting. It left the stop and I finally paused to breathe.

"What was that?" Jade asked through pants.

"Was that really a boy?" Bri whispered.

"I think so." I couldn't believe what I was saying. The concept hadn't really hit me until then. Suddenly the image of the towering figure in the darkness was pounding in my mind, clogging any other thoughts. I felt faint with terror over what could have happened.

"I thought they were extinct!" Jade whispered harshly.

"Apparently not."

"Why are we whispering when there's no one here?" Lexi asked just as the doors opened and two women walked in.

"That's why."

"Let's go back to my house," Bri suggested.

"Good idea."

Once we reached Bri's house, the four of us bolted through the door and up the stairs.

"You girls are back early, I thought you would be out late," said Georgina O'Connell as she walked into the hallway.

We all stopped.

"Well, Ava had a little tumble in the mud," Bri said and pointed at me, and I noticed how dirty I was.

"The mud?"

"We were at the park, remember?"

"Oh yes, of course. Well, you girls go on up and I'll bring cookies."

"No thanks, Mother, we're not hungry." Bri began to run up the stairs again, dragging me behind her.

"Speak for yourself," I whispered to her as we ran over to her room.

She slammed the door and we all flopped on to the bed.

"OK, what happened back there?"

"Well, I was chasing it then I fell so it turned and came back. So naturally I assumed it was going to eat me or something and shone the tablet in its face. Then it said something and I realised it was a man because it had such a deep voice."

"What if it was a deep-voiced girl?"

"It looked like a man, it was really tall and just looked different. Also he was shirtless, I've never ever seen a person shirtless, it was embarrassing."

"So it was a barbaric human," Jade declared.

"Well, no, but he obviously wasn't from around here, no one ever walks around shirtless."

"What if he was taking a shower?"

"In what?"

"Good point."

"But men are extinct, it must have been something else," Lexi stated.

"It was a man!"

Bri threw her hand over my mouth. "My mother will hear you."

"Sorry," I mumbled through her hand.

"But there's no way," Lexi continued.

"We have to tell the Council," Bri said and removed her hand.

"We can't do that," I argued.

"Why not?"

"Because, what would they do?"

"I don't know, get rid of it?" Jade threw her hands in the air.

"Listen, I know you all think he poses a threat to the city but he doesn't."

"And how do you know that? Did you have a cup of tea with him?"

"He didn't know what I was either. He looked at me like I look at broccoli when I'm expecting cake. Like this." I tilted my head to the side and widened my eyes in shock.

"How does that make him OK?"

I was asking myself the same question. Inside I was terrified and completely shaken by the whole experience. I'd never been more afraid in my life. But with all things like this, it made me wonder. And wondering for me was never-ending; I had been bitten by a curiosity that I couldn't shake. I answered Jade's question, "If he didn't know what I was, then he won't know about the city or the Movement."

"I don't know, Ava." Bri bit her lip.

"The Council are already super stressed with Katelyn and everything, this would only make things worse."

Everyone glanced at each other worriedly.

"Fine. We'll keep it secret," Lexi sighed.

"But we have to promise to keep it between the four of us only," I insisted.

"All right, promise," everyone agreed and we all shook on it.

"Let's also all promise never to go back there," Bri added.

"Yeah," everyone said and nodded.

"I can't promise that," I said and they all turned to look at me.

"What? Why not?"

"Because I want to go back."

They all stared at me in shock for a second. Then, all at once, they started yelling at me about how I was out of my mind and going to get killed. We were all yelling back and forth over the top of each other, so loud I couldn't tell what anyone was saying. Then Bri burst into tears. She began sobbing hysterically and we all turned to stare at her.

"Bri, what's wrong?" I asked.

She calmed down and rubbed her eyes. "Oh Ava, please don't go back."

Everyone looked at me. "Is that why you're upset?"

"It's just," she sniffled, "when we lost Katelyn it was just so hard and it was only recently, so the wounds are still fresh. I just... I just don't want to lose you too. That would break my heart."

I imagined Bri wailing hysterically as she sat at my goodbye ceremony and everyone trying to comfort her while she cried out her sorrow. I saw her sitting in her room staring out of the window like Katelyn did and losing herself, slowly withering away.

"Oh Bri," I said and wrapped my arms around her and rocked her gently. "I promise nothing will ever happen to me."

"That's not good enough, you need to swear to me that you'll never go back. Ever. Swear?"

I hesitated a moment, watching my hopes of learning more about the boy and his forest fade. "Swear."

"Thank you, Ava," she said and held me tight. "Trust me, it's for your own good."

"You better be right."

After Bri had calmed down and assured us that she was all right, we all went back home. As I walked through the door, I heard someone milling around in the kitchen.

"Mother?"

"Oh Ava." I heard shuffling from the other room. "I thought you would be out late."

"Change of plans," I said and threw my jacket on the chair and walked into the kitchen just as she shoved some of her tablets into her bag. "What's all this?"

She looked around as if noticing the mess around her for the first time. "Oh this? It's just some work."

"What's it about?" I sat down in the seat across from her at the table.

"Uh…"

I looked down and saw open an electronic document titled *Revised Reproduction Centre Schedule*, "Oh," I said.

"I'm sorry but it has to be addressed."

"No no, I get it… um… it's just."

"Just what, honey?"

"Well, I was actually wanting to ask you about that. Am I still next?"

"Of course." Mother went back to reviewing her documents.

"Oh. So do I get the same surgery and all?"

"Well, it will be similar, but we've decided to adjust it for every person so we can accommodate."

"Do I go in on my birthday?"

Mother looked up at me. "Actually no, things have changed a bit you see. You'll probably be called in a month or so, but I can give you an actual date later."

"A month?" I gaped at her.

"Don't look so surprised, we need to monitor you separately without there being too many other people to deal with."

"But that's so soon."

Mother placed her hand on mine. "You'll be ready."

"I'm just a bit worried, that's all."

"Oh sweetheart, there's nothing to be worried about," Mother said and smiled at me calmly. "The Council are working round the clock on this."

"Why? Is there something wrong?"

"Oh no, of course not, it's just that we want to take extra precautions this time."

"There's no chance that I would…"

"No," she interrupted, "none at all. Ava, you will be absolutely fine, I promise you that. And the best part is that I'm going to be a grandmother!"

"I forgot about that."

"You have no idea how happy that makes me."

It was strange to think that I was going to be carrying a tiny little person inside me that I would call my child.

"Is there a way to know what it'll look like or be like?"

Mother thought for a second before speaking. "Each one is designed to suit the personality of the mother and grandmother and the lifestyle it will receive. However, Sylvia doesn't decide exactly what it's like, she just alters a few things to make sure there won't be complications."

"Complications? Like what?"

"Like… say the child was very dependent and always wanted her mother and grandmother around, and we were both on the Council – that just wouldn't work. That kind of thing."

"Isn't it weird to decide what a person is like?"

"It's much more logical if you think about it. Why not avoid problems if you have the capability to?"

"I suppose. Will I know what it'll look like?"

"That's most likely random, but any child of yours will be beautiful."

"Oh Mother," I said and nudged her playfully.

"Of course, she may not get our signature Hart black ringlets and periwinkle blue eyes."

"Your hair is straight," I said and twisted a lock in my hand.

She sighed, "Wasn't always."

We sat there for a moment and I stared at her in admiration. "Well, I'm off to bed. Night, Mother."

"Goodnight, darling," she said and reached over and kissed my cheek. "See you in the morning."

Except I didn't see her the next morning. All I saw was a message that she had to run and would be out late. For the next few days all I got were messages that work was just too chaotic and I would have to find my own dinner or go over to the O'Connells. It later occurred to me that Mother was so preoccupied that she didn't notice I was covered in dirt.

The few times I did see her, she was too stressed to talk or too tired after her long day.

"Are you OK?" I would ask.

"Of course," she would reply before hurrying off to her room to sleep.

But most times she didn't even sleep; I saw her light still on under the door and it didn't turn off until much later, sometimes not at all.

"Mother, you've been acting stressed, is everything OK?"

"Oh, is that what you think? It's so nice to see you so concerned, but honestly I'm just very tired, been having a lot of late nights. I promise everything is all good."

"If you insist."

This continued for several days, me asking her how everything was, her denying any problems. The other important thing circling around in my head was about the forest. I would think about the boy I saw and suddenly my mind would fill up with questions to ask him. I imagined sitting down with him to chat, carrying some sort of weapon as protection of course, and asking him who he was.

Then I would convince myself that the only way to get answers was to go back. But every time I stood to gather my stuff, I saw Bri crying her heart out at the thought of me being killed by a wild boy. So I would sit back down and try to talk myself out of it.

One night I had a dream about Katelyn and woke with a start. After pulling myself together, I saw it was practically five in the morning, but I couldn't fall asleep again, so I went down to the kitchen to get some food.

The significance of that morning though was during my return from my early-morning snack. I was passing Mother's room when I heard her say, "I know Ava doesn't get exceptions because she's my daughter."

I froze and inched closer, trying to hear more. She must have been talking on the portable intercom, which only Council members received.

"But her being my daughter makes me see clearly that we cannot rush into this without fixing the bug first."

Bug?

"Sylvia's on it but I want to give her a few more months… Yes, I know that we have limited time."

Limited time for what?

"We need to think about the others. What good is it if we lose them all? How will we look then, Margaret?"

That name sounded familiar… where had I heard it?

"Maybe we should look for an alternative… OK, fine I get it, not enough time."

Then I remembered overhearing a similar conversation at the Centre with a woman named Margaret. The Council were all talking about something to do with test results and time. I couldn't remember great details, but it obviously wasn't good.

"OK, I'll see you in the office. Bye." I heard her moving around, so I ran back to my room and shut the door behind me.

Suddenly I felt nervous. Thoughts of what she could have been talking about infiltrated my mind like poison. *Was it about the surgery? Did it involve me? Why was there limited time? Why was the conversation so secret? Was it related to the other conversation I overheard?*

The main thought that kept passing through my mind however was: *Was my life on the line?*

That small incident had firmed my decision and suddenly I saw that I really only had one option. So I changed clothes and gathered all the necessary belongings into my little brown bag. After I heard the door shut behind Mother as she darted out for an early morning yet again, I snuck down the stairs and quietly left the house. And before I knew it, I found myself on the tram headed towards the edge of the city, and hopefully the answers.

Chapter Eleven

Ava, Half An Hour Later

I stared at the Bubble wall like a challenge. After checking over my shoulder and checking over my nerves, I jumped through to the other side. I steadied myself and placed my piece of bark on the grass next to the Bubble.

"You can do this, Ava," I assured myself and began walking into the forest. It was very different when I could see everything, unlike before at night. The colours stood out the most – vibrant greens and browns with different shades of colour on the plants. It was so much more beautiful than that silly image on Katelyn's window…

Katelyn.

I had to be strong, so I forced myself onwards through the thicket until I had passed the ruins and was left to wander through trees alone. I only prayed I was heading the right way. Occasionally, rustling would sound from the bushes and I would stop and wait for him to come out.

"Hello?" I would call towards the noise. But there was always no answer, so I would continue.

After walking for ages, the noises started becoming more frequent, a rustle here, a snap there. Paranoia began to seize me and I started to walk faster and faster until I was running. I kept running past trees and dodging unidentified objects until finally I tripped over one. It was bound to happen. Luckily I threw my hands out in front of me so my face didn't smash into the large rock protruding from the dirt. But when I sat up I noticed a large gash on my left palm and a bit of blood seeping out of it.

"Ouch," I said and tried to wipe it away, but it only made it messier. "Oh well."

I gathered myself and continued walking until I reached the clearing. The tiny pouch and ribbon dangling from a tree branch was my sign and I slumped on to the log to catch my breath.

Then it occurred to me that maybe I wasn't doing the right thing. What if I did die? Then Bri would be so crushed. Not just Bri, but everyone – my mother, my friends. It would ruin everything; I was supposed to get surgery in a few weeks. I considered turning back while I had the chance, but I caught myself. I had come so far.

I stood and put my hands to my mouth. "Hello! Anyone there! Please come, I want to talk!" I yelled out towards the trees. Then I sat and waited for him to come.

It took about ten minutes, but soon I heard rustling in the bushes in front of me. I reached down and grabbed a large stick off the ground and held it firmly in my good hand. My heart was pounding and I had to fight to keep my breath steady as I walked over to the noise, branch poised in front of me. I pushed the leaves aside and there he was.

He looked completely different in the light. I could see that his hair was actually a light golden brown, which matched perfectly with his deep golden green eyes. He seemed tall, but not as strikingly so as several nights before, and he was covered in thick muscles. He also looked much darker than he seemed before, almost Lexi's colour, but I noticed a thin line of white on his hips poking out from under his tattered shorts.

His gaze too surprised me; it was firm, like he was taking in all of his surroundings, but he looked at me with such intense amazement, I felt my cheeks burning.

"I've seen you before," he said with the deepest voice I'd ever heard. "Who are you?"

At the sound of his voice something twitched inside me; it was a feeling I'd never experienced before and originated deep in my gut. He took a step towards me and I held up my branch at him.

He held his hands up and backed away. "What, were you planning to attack me with that?!" he chuckled.

Hearing him laugh made my stomach twist again and I prodded the air with my weapon of defence.

"Whoa, calm down, I won't hurt you," he said gently.

"How can I trust you?" I asked.

"Cross my heart," he said and made a crossing motion over his left shoulder.

He talked like a normal person, with perfect English, so I felt a bit surer that he wasn't a crazy wild man.

"So are you going to put down the intimidating weapon then?" he asked with a grin.

Slowly I lowered it and said, "I want to talk."

"About what?"

"Come sit," I said and beckoned him over towards the clearing and we sat side by side on the log.

"Who are you?" I asked him.

"I asked first."

"My name is Ava Hart."

"I'm Derron."

"Just Derron?"

"Just Derron."

"Why no last name?"

He looked puzzled for a moment. "Well, that's what everyone calls me."

"There are more of you?" I was beginning to analyse my escape plan if necessary.

"Yes, I live in the Village over there," he said and pointed out towards the trees.

"How did you survive out here?"

He thought for a moment then said, "Well, four men brought us here almost seventeen years ago, when we were all babies, and set up the Village. Then they died of diseases when we were young so I guess we just learnt how to fend for ourselves."

"So there's an entire city of you?"

"What's a city?"

"It's like a large community with buildings and people and businesses," I said, gesturing with my hands. "You know, a city."

"So like a village?"

"I don't know, I've never been to a village."

"Where are you from?" he asked, looking at me and I was sure he was trying to analyse me too.

"The city. There are only women there though."

"Women? So you are a girl then?"

"Yeah, you've never seen a girl before, have you?"

"No, I've heard about them but I thought they were myths."

"Where I'm from they told us that men went extinct many years back so seeing you is strange to me. How did you survive The Great Wars?"

"The what?"

I realised that he had no idea about my city or how we thought of men as vile corruptors. It was probably best that it remained that way.

"Never mind. How many of you are there?"

He counted on his fingers. "Six including me."

"You know maths?"

"Maths?"

"I guess you don't. How do you know how to count?"

"Cain taught us."

"Who's Cain?"

"The eldest in the Village. He remembers things from before we came here."

"Like what?"

"He doesn't say much. Mostly things like how to speak English, get food and social courtesies and stuff. Otherwise, we all would have died."

"Lucky you... why don't you wear a shirt?"

"A what?" He looked down at himself. "Why would I do that?"

"Because it's the civilised thing to do."

"But it's not practical."

"Why not?"

"It would be covered in sweat and dirt within minutes."

"But, but..."

"Why, does that make you uncomfortable?"

"I-I…" I knew exactly why. But for some reason I couldn't form the words. All I could do was stare at the strange boy before me, with this sensation of being uncomfortably intrigued. "It's just strange."

He smiled and said, "You're strange."

"Says the person that lives in the forest."

He laughed and looked out towards the trees then back at me. "Oh, you're bleeding," he said and reached over and grabbed my hand. He inspected the rapidly bleeding cut gently. "Let me take you back to the Village to fix this."

"No, I think I'm fine," I said and pulled my hand back.

"You're not. That's how the men died – infected wounds," he said and shrugged his shoulders, "but if you want to die…"

I saw Bri crying at my ceremony. "Fine," I said, "take me to your Village."

"Here." He stood and held his hand out to me. "Take my hand."

I hesitated for a moment, looking at his dirt-covered palm. His eyes were honest though, so I gave him my good hand. He stared down at it for a moment then smiled, somehow causing me to shy away, my face flushing as I did so. Then he led me through the trees. His movements were swift and exact, dodging every tree perfectly and leaving me to fight to keep up. He never stopped to get his bearings, just kept going like he knew the place cold.

As we walked, I began to feel even more nervous about being in a city of all men. They were the root of pure evil and couldn't possibly do anything except bring upon destruction. But there was something about Derron that made me feel safe; I knew he wouldn't let them hurt me. But I realised that I had left my merciless weapon back at the clearing, so he had better stick to my expectations.

"Here we are," he said and pushed aside some branches to reveal a larger clearing.

It was not at all what I was expecting. What he called buildings were actually little huts made of large pieces of tree trunks with scruffy nets covering the doorways. There was a large pile of wood in the middle of the clearing which was black at the ends, and several smaller similar piles scattered around. At one end of the clearing was a large box made of more chopped wood, with all sorts of things sticking out of it. There were sharp spears, ropes, leaves, berries and bottles. It seemed so primitive, but at the same time so developed for having been left alone in a forest with nothing.

"This is…"

"Amazing, right?" he finished for me. "Here, let me fix your hand."

Derron led me over to a small hut and held aside the net for me to walk through. It was dark inside, but I could see many different bottles with liquids and herbs.

"Here, you can sit there," he said and pointed to the leaf bed on the floor.

"Thanks." I sat on the barely comfortable seating.

He walked over to the collection and pulled out a container with a clear liquid and a bandage. "Hold out your hand."

I did as instructed and he poured the water-like substance on my cut. It stung like crazy. "Ouch!" I yelled and snatched my hand away. "What is that?"

"I don't know, but it prevents infection."

"It hurts too, did you know that?"

"Believe me, I know," he said with a grin and put the liquid back. "Give me your hand."

He took it and wiped the dirt away with his own hand, then took the bandage and wrapped it tightly around my palm. His hands felt rough and laboured, yet his touch was gentle.

"Thank you," I said and looked into his eyes.

"No problem," he replied and smiled back at me, and his eyes seemed to sparkle as he did so. Golden flakes swimming in a sea of emerald. I then noticed he was still gently holding my hand, his thumb brushing against the fresh bandage.

He seemed to realise too and cleared his throat. "So how about a tour?"

I didn't think there was much to see, but he seemed so eager. "Sure."

"Great, this way."

The two of us left the little hut and he took me over to the other ones. "These are our rooms; we have to share so there are two people in each. But someone is always on night watch so sometimes you get lucky and get the place to yourself."

"Night watch?"

"You know, someone sits outside and guards the Village in case wild animals come."

"So, they are real!"

"You've never seen an animal?" He looked stunned.

"I've seen pictures."

"What are pictures?"

It was my turn to look stunned. "It's when you capture a moment so that you can see it again, like a drawing except it's the real thing."

"That's the strangest thing I've ever heard of." He looked utterly amazed. "Oh, so as I was saying, the hut we were in before is the place where we keep all the medicine, and when someone gets sick they have to stay in there until they get better."

"Why's that?"

"So they don't get the rest of us sick too."

"In my city people never get ill any more or die from sickness."

His eyes widened. "That's amazing! How do you do it? Could you teach us?"

"Um… I don't know exactly, it's like something they give every child when they're born so that they are immune to everything. It was invented long before The Great Wars."

"Could you get some for us?"

"I don't even know what it is."

"Oh." He looked disappointed. "Well, that would change everything." He continued walking.

I had to run after him to keep up. "How so?"

"Well, there were twelve of us at the start, but six died because of diseases. They were only babies and the men were much older, but that's our biggest fear."

"Wow, we have very different fears in my city. Actually, now that I think about it, we don't fear that much at all."

"You're lucky. Now here is the storage box," he said and pointed at the large handmade box full of random things. "We keep weapons and food in here."

"Weapons?" I imagined an army of men attacking our city and tearing it to pieces.

"To fend off animals."

"Oh, right."

"Hey Derron!"

We both turned round to see two boys walking over from the trees waving.

"You can meet the others," Derron exclaimed and began running towards them.

"Yay…" I walked after him.

Derron reached the others and they all started doing this strange hugging-like thing except one of them had the boy's head under his arm and was rubbing his head with his fist and they were all shouting. Eventually they stopped just as I caught up with them and said, "Hi."

The two boys froze. "What's that?"

"This is Ava, she's from the city." Derron nudged me closer to the group. "She's not going to attack us, I promise."

"He looks funny."

"Funny?" I raised my eyebrows.

"Ava is a girl, Owen."

"Cain, I thought you said girls were myths," said the boy who thought I looked funny, as he turned to the other.

"Well, I haven't seen one since I was seven, I thought they were all gone."

"I thought men went extinct, but I guess I was wrong," I pointed at Derron as proof.

"Ava, this is Cain," Derron said, pointing at the taller one, "and this is Owen." He pointed at the one who called me funny looking.

"Pleasure to meet you, Ava," Owen said and gave a little bow.

"Where did you come from?" Cain asked, his face completely serious.

"The city, there are only women where I'm from. It's called Emiscyra."

He looked at me hard, inspecting me, no doubt. "How did you find us?"

"I was in the forest and I saw Derron so I came back."

"Cain, I was putting out the fires when I heard her calling," Derron explained, "so I went down to the Old Village and there she was, heavily armed of course." He winked at me.

"How can we trust you?" Cain said and narrowed his eyes at me.

"How can *I* trust you?" I asked, narrowing my eyes back.

We had a stare down, each of us refusing to answer.

"Come on Cain, she looks nice," Owen said and elbowed Cain.

"Yeah Cain, please?" Derron asked the statue-like figure.

He looked at me seriously for a second. "Fine, I'm sure she means no harm. I'm sorry, I just want to make sure my brothers are protected."

"Cain's a big softy," said Owen with a wink. "Don't be fooled by the straight face."

"And we owe him everything," Derron added. "He was nine when the men died, whereas we were three, so he taught us all we know. Isn't that right, Owen?"

"Yeah yeah, thank you, Lord Cain."

"Don't you mock your lord," Cain said in a booming voice, "or I shall unleash my wrath!" He jumped on Owen and the two of them started yelling again.

"What are they doing?" I asked Derron.

"Um… I don't know. I can't really explain; it's just something we do." He grabbed the two of them by the neck. "Boys, we do have a guest here."

They all looked up at me and smiled, saying apologetically, "Sorry Ava."

"It's fine," I said, laughing.

"Come on, let's take you to meet the rest of us." Cain took off through the trees with Owen trailing him.

"Should we follow them?" I turned to Derron.

"No, they're going to get the others."

"Oh."

"Don't worry, I'm sure they'll like you."

A minute later, Owen, Cain, and three other boys came running from the thick trees into the middle of the Village, yelping. They were all shirtless.

"So this is the girl," one of them said as he ran over.

"Ava, this is Mason," Derron introduced me.

"Hi Ava, welcome to the Village."

"And this is Kevin," Derron said, pointing at a shorter boy with light blonde hair.

"Hi," said Kevin and waved at me.

"And this is Jared," said Derron as he pointed at the last boy who was leaning against the hut.

"Cain, I thought you told us that girls weren't real," said Jared to the eldest.

"Well, I was wrong."

"So we're just going to let her in?"

"Jared, she's right here," said Derron, motioning to me.

"I know," he replied, rolling his eyes.

"Ignore him, he's a jerk," Cain said matter of factly.

"That's better than what he normally calls me," Jared remarked.

"Are you going to stay with us?" Mason asked.

They all turned to me expectantly. "Um no, I just came to visit," I replied.

"Well, you're welcome any time," Cain said.

"Thanks."

"All right boys, let's go and get some dinner," Cain announced. "Derron, you stay here with Ava, make sure she gets home in one piece."

"Sure thing."

The other five of them took off and grabbed all sorts of items out of the wooden box, then ran out towards the trees, yelping again.

"Why do they yell so much?" I asked Derron as we stood in the middle of the deserted Village.

He scratched the back of his neck and replied, "It's just what we do. Come, let's go to the hill." He began walking towards the far end of the Village.

He walked so fast I was out of breath trying to stay at his pace. It was extraordinary to see him navigate his way around flawlessly when to me it all looked like the same thing.

"Haven't we passed this tree before?" I asked.

"No," he said, laughing. "We're almost there."

Eventually, we reached a much larger clearing and the bottom of a somewhat steep hill.

"This is the hill," he said, stretching out his arms.

I looked out at the trees that seemed to stretch on forever. "This is incredible," I said and stumbled a little.

Derron rushed over to steady me. "Careful, it's hard to balance though." He placed one hand on my waist and the other on my arm as I regained balance. I could feel the warmth of his breath on my neck and shivered slightly. Then I looked up. "Oh my gosh!" I screamed.

"What? What is it?"

"Look!" I pointed up at the sky. "There, those white things."

"You mean the clouds?"

"I've never seen the sky before." I said and sat down on the grass.

"Are you telling me that you've spent your entire life staring at the ground?" he asked as he sat down next to me.

"No, in my city there's a Bubble covering it, so it only projects light and dark."

"So you've never seen a cloud?"

"No... they're amazing."

He pointed at one. "See how that looks like a tree, that one on the left."

"Oh yeah, and that one looks like a person standing upside down," I said, indicating the little white spot.

"That's the cool thing about clouds, they're all different."

"That's what my friends always tell me is my favourite thing."

"Clouds?"

"No. Difference."

"I like that every time you wake up, the day is going to be completely different from the last one."

"Same! Or like how even when you've been going to the same restaurant for your whole life, there's always something new to try."

"Restaurants are where you rest right?"

"No, you eat there."

"There's a special place just to eat?!"

"Yeah," I said, laughing.

"You must take me to this restaurant."

I imagined sitting at the table with Derron, eating away, and all the other women hiding under their tables terrified, "Maybe some day."

He smiled at me just as the sun hit his face and his eyes seemed to glow.

"I've never seen the sun either," I said.

"I'd show you, but it's hidden behind that cloud," he said, pointing at a cloud with a glowing light bursting from behind it. "But you can't look directly at it or it'll burn your eyes."

"Burn them?!"

"Yeah, you should be careful."

I quickly turned away from the glowing cloud. "So where were you before you came to the Village?"

"Well, I don't know," he said, looking puzzled. "Cain said that the four men brought us to the Old Village but we eventually moved here."

"Where's the Old Village?"

"It's that place that you and your friends go to; you hung a bag from the tree."

"That was Katelyn's."

"Who is she?"

"My best friend." I looked out across the trees. "She died."

"I'm so sorry, Ava. I would have loved to have met her."

"You would have liked her."

We sat in silence for a moment. "One of the babies that died was my brother. I never knew him really because we were so young."

"That must still hurt you."

"I just felt responsible."

"You're not." I put my hand on his shoulder.

"I know that now," he said and picked at the grass.

I looked into Derron's eyes and saw Katelyn. He reminded me so much of her – his laugh, his smile, the way he listened to every word I said. Her memories seemed clearer around him; I could practically see her sitting with us.

"I should head home," I announced and stood up.

"I'll take you," he said and stood too.

"I don't think that's a great idea."

"Let me walk you back to the Old Village at least."

I sighed, "Sure."

We made our way down the hill and he took me on the shortcut through the trees straight to the Old Village.

"Will you come back?" asked Derron.

I looked around at the trees. "Yeah, I'll be back after school tomorrow. So in the afternoon."

"I'll meet you here."

We just stood there for a moment. Then I reached over and hugged him.

"What are you doing?" he asked.

"It's called a hug." I pulled back. "In my city we do it to greet someone, to comfort someone, as a sign of friendship, or to say goodbye."

"What was that one?"

"A sign of friendship. It means I trust you."

He smiled at me shyly then hugged me back. "I trust you too."

"So what do you want to do after school today?" Lexi leant over and asked me from her desk.

"I can't, I promised my mother that I would help her with this work project thing," I began, putting my tablets into my bag.

"You sure? We could go get some food maybe."

"I'm really sorry, Lexi," I said as I zipped up the bag and stood to leave. "Maybe tomorrow."

"OK…"

"Bye," I said and ran out of the door and headed towards the tram.

Before I knew it, I was at the Bubble, then outside the Bubble, then at the Old Village, calling out to Derron, "Derron! It's Ava!"

I sat and waited for him until I heard that deep voice, which was much more striking after being around women all day, sound from above me, "Hey there."

My head snapped up and there he was, covered in dirt and standing on the branch of a tall tree, grinning. I had the strangest feeling in the pit of my stomach again, but I pushed it aside. "How did you get up there?" I asked in amazement.

"I climbed it." He swung around the trunk and jumped down from branch to branch until he landed on the ground. "Would you like to try?"

"Try climbing? Oh no, I think I'll stick to the ground."

"Come on," he said as he walked over to me, "it's amazing."

I sighed, "Fine, teach me to climb, forest boy."

He grinned from ear to ear. "Here, this way." He grabbed my hand and pulled me over to a tree. "I'll lift you, then you grab that branch, see that one there," he said and pointed to one.

"Yeah."

"Well, grab that, then use it to pull yourself up and put your feet on that branch," he said, pointing at a lower one. "Then stand there and I'll come and get you, OK?"

"OK," I replied. I could feel my hands shaking slightly.

"Don't be nervous, I'll catch you if you fall," he said reassuringly and placed his hands on my waist to hoist me up.

"Fall?"

He lifted me into the air and I was so caught off guard that I almost missed the branch I had to catch. Thankfully, my reflexes kicked in and my hand gripped at the rough bark. With as much force as I could muster, I pulled myself up until my feet reached the lower branch and I stood there waiting. "Derron I did it!" I exclaimed excitedly and looked down, but he was gone. "Derron?"

"Right here." He appeared right beside me and I almost fell off.

"Hold on there. Sorry, I didn't mean to scare you," he said and steadied me on the little branch.

"Don't you know that it's rude to sneak up on people like that?" I teased.

He laughed. "Come on."

Derron guided me up the rest of the tree, making sure I put my foot in the right place and my hands on the right branch. He also caught me all of the three times I almost fell off. Eventually we reached the top and every stumble was suddenly worth it.

"This is amazing!" I exclaimed.

"Isn't it just?"

The view was even better than on top of the hill because we were above the treetops and could see everything. The colours just danced across the landscape – I had never seen anything more alive before. There were spires poking out here and there, most likely ruins, and I could see a thin bubble in the middle of the forest. It was hard to make out, because it was camouflaged as more forest from the outside, but I could still see my little city and it was much closer than I had thought. I cried out in delight because I knew no one could hear me, and I just let the wind rush right through me.

I would have stayed forever if Derron had not suggested that we go back to the Village. So we climbed back down and made our way there.

"Hey, Ava's back!" one of them yelled and suddenly I was surrounded by them.

"Hi, Ava."

"We missed you."

"Want to help us clean up the fires?"

"Move out of the way, I want to talk to her."

"No, I'm talking to her."

"Welcome back, Ava." I looked up to see Cain emerge from the group. "Give her some space, boys."

"How come you always call the shots, Cain?" said one of them.

He raised his eyebrows and they all darted off.

"So, Derron, how about we take Ava hunting with us today?"

"If she wants – do you?" he asked me.

"What do you hunt for?"

"Food, but we don't have to take you animal hunting, the others can do that."

I thought for a moment before answering, "Sure."

"Great," said Cain and turned to the others. "Boys, we're going hunting."

They whooped and all ran over to the wooden box to get things out.

"Here, this way," said Derron. He led me over to the box and grabbed a sack and a net.

The seven of us headed into the thick forest, the boys were all yelling and cheering and jumping from tree to tree. Soon they all stopped and split up. Some went over and began to chop down trees for wood, others went out to get animals, and Derron led me over to a bush.

"This is where we get the berries. These ones are good," he said, pointing at one bush. "These are bad," he said and pointed at another.

"How can you tell the difference?"

"We have been out here for almost seventeen years now," he said as he reached over and began collecting.

"That's impressive though," I replied and plucked some of the berries too.

"What can I say? It's a gift," he said, winking at me.

We gathered all the berries together and filled almost the entire sack with them. It occurred to me that they had to fight for their food, competing with animals too, whereas mine was handed to me, most times in the form of cake. The Council had made it so city robots would go outside the Bubble and farm for us, then bring crops back and prepare them to be sold. I once thought it seemed like the only way to do it, but I soon figured that some people didn't even have the option.

"Let's move down to the river," Cain announced and everyone gathered their things and followed him further into the trees.

"River?" I turned to Derron.

"You'll see," he said and led me where the others went until we were all standing above a giant pool of water.

"This is... it's... it's..." I said in amazement

"I'm guessing you've never seen a river before."

"No."

It was a flowing ribbon of water, the most beautiful colour blue, and it wound through the grass, splashing as it hit against the rocks.

"This is where we fish," Derron explained.

"Fish?"

"You know, the little animal that lives in the water, you can eat it."

"You eat the animals?"

"Otherwise we'd die."

"Oh… can you show me?"

"My pleasure," he said and turned to one of the boys to borrow his spear. "First you need to roll up your trousers so they don't get wet." He reached over and rolled up the right leg of my trousers, tickling my skin as he did so. I giggled and he looked up at me and smiled with those gorgeous eyes. I bit my lip and tried not to get lost in them forever. Then, as he went to lift my left leg, he purposely tickled just above my ankle and I laughed and tried to brush him off. "Stop it! That tickles!"

Eventually he stopped, stood, and handed me the spear off the ground. "Now we wade in the water and try and spear the fish as they come by."

"Piece of cake."

We began to walk into the river and I was shocked that it only came up to my ankles. The cool water tickled my toes as we waited for the fish to swim by.

"There they are."

I looked down and saw the strangest creatures drifting in the water. They were all slimy and scaly with no arms or legs. I jumped and asked, "Will they hurt me?"

"No, they're safe, now spear them."

I threw my spear in the water, but it landed in the dirt and the fish all drifted away.

"You do know that the best way to catch them is with the sharp side pointing at them, right?" said Derron and pointed at the end of my spear. It was backwards.

I flipped it round. "I was just practising."

"Of course you were."

After another couple of misses, it became apparent that practice time was over. Derron was laughing at my failed attempts.

"This is no laughing matter."

"How about we move to a different spot?"

The two of us waded back to the edge and walked along the river to a spot above deeper water and held the net in the waves to trap the fish.

"Here, you try," said Derron and handed me the net.

I reached over to throw the net in, but lost my footing and felt the ground give way beneath me. I tumbled into the river and entered with a splash. The water swallowed me down and it was a surprisingly refreshing feeling. Except it was so cold that my body froze for a second, paralysed by it.

I could hear the boys laughing from above me, but soon they stopped.

"Where'd she go?"

"Why hasn't she come back up?"

My head was screaming at my body to move but I couldn't feel anything. I struggled to move my numb body until I finally forced my hands free and managed to get my legs to kick as I propelled myself up out of the water and emerged, taking in a huge breath. The boys cheered and I smiled at them, shivering as I gave a little wave. But of course I forgot that I didn't know how to swim. I was having trouble staying above water, and kept dipping under, then back up, then under again. I thrashed my arms about and tried to use my legs to push me upwards, but I kept sinking back down.

Then there was a splash next to me and I felt two arms grab my shoulders and pull me back towards the edge. They flung me on to the side and I suddenly felt terribly cold, shaking all over as the air pricked me like tiny needles. I saw Derron's face above me, rubbing my arms to keep me warm. "Hang in there, Ava," he said and lifted me up and wrapped his arms around my frozen body. He breathed warm air on my neck as his body slowly thawed mine.

There was still the sound of cheering around me, but I felt so tired I couldn't move.

"Well done, Ava!"

"Nice swimming there."

Many more faces appeared around me looking down.

"And congratulations on your first fish catch," Owen said.

"What fish catch?" I winced.

He extracted a slimy little thing from my trouser leg and held it in the air. Everyone laughed including me, even though I was surprised where my energy to laugh came from.

"Here, let's get you back to the Village before you freeze," Derron said as he lifted me up and carried me all the way back.

When we reached the Village, someone gave me a piece of cloth to wear while my clothes dried, and Derron and I went and sat on the hill.

"Where did you get all this cloth?"

"Kevin is really good at weaving it. He gathers it from some plant or other."

"Well, thank you."

"Don't thank me, thank Kevin."

"No, I meant for the river, I forgot to mention that I've never swum before."

"Yeah, well, there's not much you can do about that!"

"I've never really known more than I've been taught. That applies for other things than swimming."

"I know what you mean. Sometimes I wonder what there is out there that no one ever told me."

"That's partly why I came out here in the first place, to see if there was something more."

"Maybe I should do the same thing."

"Maybe."

"I like seeing you, Ava, you're different."

"That's what Katelyn always said. And I like seeing you too," I said and looked up into his caring eyes.

"Hopefully we'll see more of each other then."

I thought about my upcoming surgery and sitting in the Centre for nine months straight. "Yeah… I hope so."

Chapter Twelve

Ava, A Few Weeks Later

After that, I saw Derron almost every day after school. Well, not almost, I was pretty sure I saw him every single afternoon following our meeting. He showed me his home and asked to see mine. It broke my heart that I couldn't ever take him to my house or to my favourite places to hang out. So I pushed all of that aside and tried to enjoy the times we spent outside of my world.

I liked spending time with him for many reasons, mainly because he was fun and caring and eager to share his thoughts with me. But over time I realised more and more that he just reminded me so vividly of Katelyn that it was like she was still there. Sometimes I would catch him laughing and it was like I was listening to her, except her voice wasn't as deep. Or he would say something and I would gasp because it was such a Katelyn thing to say. But more than that, he listened like she did to every single word I was saying with such intense understanding. And the best part of it all was that it didn't make me miss her too much or mourn her more, it only made her come back to life.

Of course Derron was most certainly not Katelyn. We connected on levels that Katelyn and I never did. We always found the same things funny, like Owen slipping face first into the mud or how only one certain plant would make me sneeze uncontrollably. The two of us would always reach the same conclusion at the same time. Like when Cain would ask what we felt like doing that afternoon, we would both instantly agree on one thing or the other. Sometimes he would do something that I would find absurd and he would just laugh when I told him he looked ridiculous. And not like an *I was insane* kind of laugh; like a *we were from such different worlds yet we still seemed to fit like a hand in a glove* laugh. And he made me feel special. Like whatever I said made perfect sense, and I could do no wrong.

"You know you're beautiful, right?" he once asked me on the hill.

I turned to him in surprise. "I'm what?"

"The most beautiful person I know," he said and reached over and tucked a strand of my hair behind my ear. "Because there's not a moment that goes by when you don't fail to amaze me."

"And that makes me beautiful – how?"

"Beautiful inside and out… get more beautiful and Owen might get jealous."

I laughed and asked, "Derron, why didn't I meet you sooner?"

I also spent some time with the rest of the boys and it shocked me that they were nothing at all like what I had been taught. I wondered if it was because they were younger than the ones that destroyed the planet, or because they had grown up away from bad influences, or because there were fewer of them. I so badly wanted to ask Mother, but that would have been the end of my late afternoon forest gatherings for sure.

One afternoon I was on my way back from the Village and I got lost. It was bound to happen at some point, but at the time I was sure I would never make it back home. I wandered through the trees trying to find the glow of the Bubble, which could be seen better later in the day. After walking for almost an hour, I stopped to rest on the ground.

I rested my head in my hands and thought through my options until I decided to shout for Derron to come and get me. I looked up, about to call out, when I heard a loud crunching noise from behind me. My head spun round to see something shiny rolling through the trees, them parting as it passed. I quickly hid myself behind a bush, heart racing, and waited to see what it was.

Finally, it got close enough for me to see that it was a large silver machine, almost my size, with wheels helping it move. There were different things poking out of it on the sides and all sorts of buttons and controls, but it basically looked like a giant container. I marvelled at it as it passed, crunching the earth and twigs beneath it with a loud sound. Not very discreet.

I watched as it moved and noticed it was carrying pieces of trees in it. There were also doors on the side labelled *Minerals*, *Crops* and *Metals*. It was like the machine was collecting something. Then I saw it. The tiny little plaque nailed on to the front. It was hard to read but I knew it was the crest of Emiscyra. The script golden E intertwined by deep green vines, to represent growth.

It was clearly a city robot; therefore it would lead me to the city. I waited until it was quite a bit ahead of me before I leapt out from my hiding spot and crept behind it through the trees.

It navigated its way through the forest until it reached the clearing and the Bubble. I waited under the shelter of the trees as it passed through the Bubble wall without hesitation. So it let robots through, but not people. Maybe it was just sensitive to a certain body heat emitted by animals and people.

I stayed in my spot for a while until I felt the coast was clear, then I ripped a piece of bark off the tree and ran downhill through the Bubble wall, holding the bark above me. When I reached the other side it was nothing like what I was expecting. The entire place was covered in huge buildings, bigger than anything I'd ever seen. There were robots milling around and dropping off their collected items at the appropriate places. I snuck over to the back of one building, being careful not to be seen, and peered through the window. Inside were smaller robots, all busy preparing things on conveyer belts. In the room I was looking at they were making clothes.

I must have been at the factories, which were what they were called. Apparently, robots farmed outside the Bubble and collected things, sometimes from far parts of the land, and brought them to be assembled into our everyday needs, like furniture, clothes and food. It was on such a huge scale though that I was stunned. There must have been thousands of robots all programmed for different jobs.

I knew I was on the other side of the city, so I would have to find a way to get back home without being caught. So I snuck along the back of the building until I reached the corner. I then checked around it and continued walking until I reached an alley between two buildings, which I hid in. I saw the exit up ahead and was about to emerge when two large robots ran past me. I slammed myself against the side wall as they passed.

One of them stopped, I heard it scanning, and a red light shone on the ground near my feet. I scooted away, but it kept scanning the ground, approaching my hiding spot. I held my breath and waited. The light inched closer and closer, each centimetre making my skin crawl. My breath came out ragged and I tried as hard as I could to flatten myself further. Then it stopped, just millimetres from my feet. I held my breath. Finally it beeped and flashed green then retracted and I heard the robots move on.

I took that as my chance to run for the exit, but as I passed into open space I saw a building with several large doors on it and several robots entering and exiting from them. Above each door there was a label. They read *Collectors, Long Distance Collectors, Assemblers, Checkers, Analysers* and *Security.*

Security? That was the only door that was closed. I didn't have time to analyse it further, because I heard robots coming in the distance. I reached the door on the fence which stretched around all of the many huge buildings, but it was locked and it didn't budge when I yanked at it. I spotted an iris scanner on the side and bent down so it had a clear view of my eye. The light scanned me and beeped:

"Goodbye, Donna Hart."

There was a click sound and the door unlocked. I threw it open and ran until I was as far away from it as possible.

The strangest part was that when I turned round it looked like office buildings from the front and the fence covered the large open floor where the robots roamed. It didn't look nearly as intense as it had from inside. I wondered why.

"Mother, I'm home!" I yelled up the stairs as I walked through the door.

No answer.

"Mother?" I began walking upstairs to her room. "Mother, are you on the phone or something?"

When I walked in there was no one there, of course, and the entire floor was covered in clothes. The place was a mess: bed unmade, clothes dangling all over the place like they'd been tossed out of the wardrobe in a rush. Mother must have had trouble finding one of her suits again when she was late for a Council meeting.

I sighed and began making the bed for her. It wasn't the first time that had happened and most times she didn't even notice when I cleaned up for her, but I knew it would take off a tiny bit of the stress that seemed to overwhelm her life. After I had tucked in her covers, I picked up all the clothes off the floor and folded them as neatly as I could. Balancing a mountain of clothes in one hand, I tried to open the wardrobe door with the other. As I manoeuvred the clothes on to the shelf and pushed them into place, something fell off the top shelf.

Reaching down to pick it up, I realised it was paper. For a moment I thought back to that leaflet I brought home so many months before, but it wasn't that. It was a small white scrap lying on the ground. It was such a shock to see paper outside of the archives that I didn't want to pick it up for fear that it would combust in my hands.

Cautiously, I bent over and picked up the tiny scrap and flipped it over to reveal a photo. I sat down on the bed and looked at it. There was a woman with dark black hair lying on a hospital bed wearing the kind of gown that Katelyn wore. In her arms was a tiny little baby with clenched fists and its eyes tight shut. Its face was all red and puffy too and it had a full head of black hair. The most surprising part of the photo was that there was a man there too, with his arms around the woman, looking down at the little baby. Both of their faces were full of such love and affection that I almost jumped. The woman only had eyes for the man, and in those eyes was nothing but pure love – it was clear even through the tiny scrap of paper. And I knew who it was all too well.

The woman was my mother, except far younger, and I was the baby. I realised then just how much I looked like her – not just our hair and eyes but every other feature as well. The same flick at the end of our noses, the same wrinkle in our eyes when we smile. I also realised something far more important. That man was my father.

And my mother was looking at him like he was the centre of her world. She loved him. And she lied to me.

I had always been taught that women needed men for children. That was it. But I had just realised that women could love men too, like the way I loved my mother or my best friend. And men could love too, like the way my father looked at me like I was his everything, as ugly as I looked in that photo.

Mother told me he was evil, her exact words were, "Your father was pure evil, just like the rest of them." I remembered so clearly her reciting these words as if she had said them so many times over and over again that she actually believed them. Why did she lie to me?

I felt so betrayed by her that my heart felt like one of those fish that Derron speared. They had all lied to me, to everyone. Almost half of our city knew that men and women loved each other and probably loved one themselves, and the rest of us were manipulated to believe that they did nothing right. What gave them the right to decide what I thought about men?

Anger ripped through me and tears began welling up inside me. All this time I was right. I was right about everything. I shoved the photo into my pocket and stormed out of the door.

Within a flash I was at the Old Village.

"Derron! Derron, it's me!"

"Why are you back so late?"

I looked up to see him jump down from one of the trees, his face barely visible in the dark shadows.

"I-I-I just missed you, that's all." I threw my arms around him and buried my face in his chest.

He rubbed my head. "Are you all right?"

"Yeah I'm fine," I said and wiped the tears from my face.

"Do you want to go to the hill and talk?"

I nodded my head.

"Come on." He put his arm around my shoulders and walked me up to his favourite spot. "So," he said as the two of us sat down side by side, "what happened?"

"It's just I…" I looked up at the sky and gasped.

"What is it?"

"What are those?!" I pointed at the sky, which was covered in millions of tiny white lights.

"Ah, those are stars."

"Stars…" I marvelled at the beautiful array of white dots and how they glittered against the dark sky.

"Sometimes you see shooting stars, that's when one flies across the sky."

I remembered standing in my backyard months before and seeing a flash of light beyond the Bubble. "I think I saw one once. It was like a flash of light."

"Yeah that was probably it, or it could have been lightning."

"What's that?"

"During a storm you see this flash of light strike the ground followed by this boom sound called thunder. We always hope one doesn't hit the trees near us."

"What would happen then?"

"It might catch fire."

"You can make fire without a digital fireplace?"

He laughed. "It's like no one ever told you about all the best parts of life. You have all these things that duplicate natural occurrences, but you've never experienced the real deal. How do you live like that?"

I sighed, "How do you pine for something when you don't even know it exists?"

We sat there in silence for a moment.

"Did you know that men and women could love each other?" I turned to him.

He thought for a second. "Well, I didn't even know that women were real," he said with a smile, "until I met you. Actually Cain once told us that women were said to be able to make men fall in love with them. He described it once as 'a beautiful spell'."

"Beautiful, huh?"

"He said that it was different from the way we all loved each other as brothers, it was like there was a special type of love that you could only share with a soul mate or something like that. He said that it pulled at every nerve in your body but was incredible."

"How did he know about it?"

"One of the men told him before he died. But Cain only repeated it to me and Kevin, he said the others wouldn't understand."

"Well, it sounds amazing and it kills me to think that I would never have known about it."

"But now you do." He smiled with his eyes, just like he had done so many times before.

"And no one in my city will ever be able to experience it!" I threw my hands in the air. "It's like they kept it from us so that we wouldn't feel like we were missing out. How could they do something like that?"

"Well, I would say the same thing about my Village, but I can't."

I raised my eyebrows. "Go on."

"Because I've experienced it," he said as he reached over and held my hand, "with you."

Suddenly everything vanished and all that was left was Derron and his golden green eyes that poured into my soul and made all the heartache go away.

"Even though I only figured it out now," I said as I twined my fingers with his, "I think I love you too."

It was like I knew all along, there was no mystery, it was part of me. And I knew that he understood too, because without saying another word he leant down and kissed me. But it was not like when Mother kissed my forehead or when Katelyn gave me a smooch on the cheek; it was like flying and floating at the same time. Like all the millions of stars around us just lit up ten times brighter.

Then I knew why they never told us about love, because having to give up something as wonderful as the way I felt when

Derron kissed me would have been like giving up breathing. I suddenly felt pity for all the women who knew that love and had to give it up when the men left. At the time I'm sure that men's treachery overshadowed any idea of love, but I wondered if the women missed it.

So Derron and I stayed on that hill, alone in the world, until the sun rose the next morning. I felt the light tickle my cheek and I rubbed my eyes open, memories of the night before filling my mind.

"Derron, wake up," I said gently and stroked his arm.

He stirred. "Where are we?"

"On the hill."

He yawned and sat up, taking in the day. "Were we here all night?"

"I think so."

"Funny, I don't remember falling asleep." He turned to me and smiled. "I remember something else." He put his arm around my shoulders and hugged me close.

I laughed. "How come we only found out about this now?"

"I don't know, maybe it was for a reason."

"Do you believe that everything happens for a reason?" I asked as I laid my head on his shoulder.

"I don't know, I only just found out that I barely knew anything."

"Don't worry, I'll teach you all there is to know about digital fireplaces and electronic documents."

"Why, thank you."

We just sat there and watched the colours of the sky change and fade. Then I remembered.

"Mother!"

"What?"

"Oh Derron, I'm sorry, I have to leave, my mother will be waiting for me. No, she'll be freaking out." I got up and started gathering my things.

"Can I walk you?"

I picked up my jacket off the ground, wondering how it got there. "To the Old Village."

"Sure, give me one second," he said and got up too.

I checked to see if Mother's photo was still in my pocket, which it wasn't, and I had to search through the grass to find it. Finally I saw it poking out and snatched it.

"Ready to go?" I asked him.

"Yeah, come."

The two of us walked to the Old Village as quickly as possible, but when we finally got there, I didn't want to leave.

"I wish I could just stay here forever."

"Ava, I wish you could too," he said and took my hands in his, "but we both know you can't."

I ran my hand through his hair. "I'll be back soon."

"I know you will."

I reached up and hugged him to me, wishing I didn't have to let go. "I'll miss you," I whispered into his shoulder.

"I'll miss you more."

"That's impossible."

He let out a laugh. "Don't get me started."

"Well, I have to go. Bye Derron."

"Bye Ava."

Even though I knew that Mother would be waiting for me, I still couldn't help but dawdle. I strolled down the street humming to myself, and for the life of me I couldn't wipe the smile off my face. Actually, when I thought about it, what were the chances that Mother even realised I was gone?

So I took my time opening the door and strolling down the hallway to the kitchen when I froze. The sappy grin on my face fell and landed on the tile floor with a splat. My heart caught in my chest as I just stared at the figure before me: Mother all dressed and freshened up with a look that could kill.

"Welcome back, Ava."

"M-mother why are you up so early?"

"This is the time I normally leave, Ava. But truth be told I have actually been up since four a.m. yesterday." Her voice was like sharp icicles, every word bit at my skin. "Do you know why?"

"I can't imagine."

"Well, I came home from work yesterday, early in fact, and my daughter was nowhere to be found."

"I stayed over at Lexi's house. I'm sorry I forgot to tell you." I walked over to the fridge.

"Oh well, that makes sense. I did actually personally visit the O'Connell's and the Samuels' and the Naumann's homes at one this morning after my daughter never turned up."

I gulped.

"You want to know what every single one of those girls told me?"

Not really.

"They said that they haven't seen you in weeks, except for school, and even then you're in your own world. Just what world exactly is that, Ava?"

I kept my mouth shut.

"What world is it?" Mother yelled, causing me to jump.

I spun round to face her and said, "I've just had a lot on my mind."

She stood up and walked over to me. "Ava, you need to rest. Your surgery is days away."

"What, do you want me to sit in my room all day?" I could hear my voice rising.

"This is not the time to be keeping secrets from me, you need to talk to me."

"Talk to you!? You're never here!" I stepped away.

"I am always here for you."

"No, you're not! When have you been home for dinner in the past week? When have you said good morning to me before I left for school?"

"Ava, I know I have been busy with work, but you can always come to me."

"No, I can't! Even when I do try to talk to you, you never hear me!"

"Don't talk to me like that! I am your mother."

"So what? That doesn't change anything! If you were my mother, you would be here when I need you!"

"I am here!"

"No, every time I try to give you my opinion or try to make you see things my way you always find a way to spin it on its head."

"What?! I do not."

I stormed into the living room. "You are always manipulating me into doing what you want! Like when I wanted to specialise in pre-Movement history you convinced me that politics was a better choice."

She came rushing in after me. "And did you listen? No!"

"But that's not my point! You just can't stand me not doing everything exactly like you!"

"Where is this coming from?"

I didn't know where it was coming from. All I knew was that I was enraged.

"And you have been lying to me, to everyone, for years!"

"Just like you lied to me about where you were last night?!"

"Why don't you tell everyone the truth about men, huh?"

"The what?!"

"They did more than oppress and hate and destroy and you know it!"

Mother looked at me like I slapped her. "Where did you get such horrific ideas? Men were evil and nothing less!"

"What's your proof?!"

"Look around you!" She gestured her arms in a circle. "Our world was almost destroyed because all men wanted was power and money and land."

"That's a lie! Stop lying to me! I am much older and smarter than you think and I know that men were more than that – some were, but not all."

"Where are these crazy ideas coming from?"

"This." I reached into my pocket and pulled out the photo.

Mother gasped and snatched it from my hands, looking at it closely.

"You loved him! You told the entire community that all men were evil when you were in love with one yourself!"

There was a heavy silence hovering as Mother's glare burnt a hole through the photo. Her face turned red and her knuckles white. Then she erupted.

"HOW DARE YOU!" Mother exploded. "How dare you jump to conclusions! And go through my private things!"

Her rage threw me slightly. "Actually, I was cleaning up your pig sty of a room. But you never seem to notice!"

"And how dare you try to justify men when they almost cost you everything!" She barely heard me. "Brave women fought for you to be alive and this is how you repay them?!"

Suddenly my anger melted into immense sadness. "Why did you hide so much from me, Mother? About my father?"

"What about him?" She began to simmer down.

"You said he was evil."

"That's because…"

"Don't even say it!" I was practically crying. "Just look me in the eyes and tell me that the one person you loved more than me was nothing but a life-sucking demon!" I imagined myself saying that about Derron and knew I never would.

Mother just glared at me, her cheeks aflame.

"And what about Katelyn, Mother? Did you lie about her too?!"

"Is that what this is? Are you still angry about Katelyn? Ava, I know you are in pain but…"

"Don't pretend you know what this feels like."

"Ava, this is not how you should be letting out your pain."

"I'm not! I want to know the truth! How did she die?"

"Ava…"

"How did she die?!" The idea that there was something more was only really settling in at that moment. "She didn't have a body problem, did she? Because I know that you tried to cover up her being ill and you wouldn't have done that without a reason. You always have a reason." I thought back to what Katelyn said that night in the forest: "The city never does anything without a reason."

"Katelyn couldn't be helped, there was nothing we could do."

"You have found a way to cure people of every single disease known to woman except how to have a baby?!"

"Sylvia Carter knows what she's doing."

"Yeah well, *you* might think so, but she doesn't have me convinced yet."

"Ava," said Mother and sat down on the sofa behind her, "we can't bring her back."

"This isn't about that!" I calmed down and said solemnly, "I don't want to have the surgery."

"You what?"

"I'm not going to do it."

"Ava, I'm sorry but there is no discussion in the matter."

"See, that's it again! You give me no freedom to make my own calls in life!"

"Because I am your mother and have been around far longer than you. I know best."

"But you don't!"

"Don't speak to me like that!" she snapped and stood up sharply.

"Then don't speak to *me* like that! You forced me to see the world the way you see it; why can't I have the freedom to see it my way!"

"Because you don't understand! And you never will!"

"Try me."

"It's not that simple."

"Then make it simple! I'm tired of this back and forth pretending!"

"Pretending of what?!"

"That you actually care about me!"

Mother stared at me, shocked. "What did you say?"

"You don't love me! You love what you want me to be!"

"Ava, of course I love you."

"How can I believe you again when all you do is lie?!"

"Stop thinking so two-dimensionally, it's pathetic."

"See!" Tears were brimming in my eyes and I felt so alone. "You can't believe that my thoughts might have significance!"

"You are making all of this out of nothing."

I let out a furious scream. "Why can't you see me?! Look at me!" I pleaded. "Stop trying to make excuses for me thinking the way I do!"

Mother stood there in silence, then gathered herself. "You, young lady, are not leaving this house, do you hear me? I will walk you to school and pick you up afterwards, apart from that you remain here. End of discussion."

"Oh, but this is not the end of the discussion."

"This is way out of line, you need to rest. Go to your room, Ava Richardson."

"What did you just call me?"

We both stared at each other. Apparently Mother was out of explanations. "Just go to your room, Ava."

I stormed over to the staircase and thudded up each step, spinning round when I reached the top. Mother was standing at the bottom with her arms folded, watching me.

"You know what?" I sneered. "I blame you for Katelyn." Then I turned and ran into my room, slamming the door behind me on the conversation and my mother.

Chapter Thirteen

Ava, The Next Morning

My door stayed shut all day with me hidden inside. I heard Mother shuffling around outside, getting ready for work and leaving. Right then, I was so thankful that it was a weekend, otherwise I would have had to bear riding the tram to school in either utter silence or a non-stop lecture from my mother. I didn't know which would have been worse.

I stayed in my room all day, hidden under the covers, while Mother probably busied herself with the immense task of preparing my surgery. Every time I thought about it, the whole thing made me sick to my stomach. Once I thought about it so hard that I actually was sick, luckily I made it to the bathroom on time. No one ever got sick, so I knew that my gut was probably warning me.

I spent the day wrestling with all the feelings inside me about what I knew and what I didn't know and what I wanted to learn. Eventually, I became so fed up with the nagging in my gut that I decided to leave. As soon as Mother returned from work and her lights switched off, I waited another half hour then bolted out of bed, fully dressed, and climbed out of my window. Our house had a random ledge poking out of it that allowed me to rest my feet on it before climbing on to the lower window to jump to the ground. Katelyn and I mastered it years ago.

Then I ran, as discreetly as possible, until I found myself dodging trees and passing the Old Village. I followed the route Derron always took me on until I reached the Village. Owen was standing outside guarding, and practically falling asleep, while the others were away in their huts.

When he heard me coming, Owen sat up and yelled out, "Wake up boys! Ava's here!"

Some of them began to emerge from their huts, yawning. I was exhausted but I kept running once I saw Derron come out from the hut with Cain.

"Ava, why are you here so late?" he asked as I ran over to him panting.

"I-I-I…" then I burst into tears.

Water just poured from my eyes and I couldn't contain my sobs. All the boys stepped back like I was sprouting a second head and stood there uncomfortably.

"Uh, is she OK?"

"Yeah, I got her." Derron put his arm around my shoulders and walked me to the hill. "You all go back to sleep," he called from over his shoulder.

When we reached the hill and sat down, he turned to me and asked, "So what's wrong?"

By then the crying had stopped. "I had a fight with my mother."

"I'm sorry, do you want to talk about it?"

"You know I had to sneak out to get here? She forbade me from leaving, what is that?" I was practically laughing.

"Sounds like it was bad."

"Beyond bad."

"Do you want to tell me what it was about?"

"That's the thing," I said and picked at the grass, "I have to tell you the truth about my city."

"Will I like this truth?" He didn't sound worried at all.

"Well, I don't know." I knew there wasn't much point in debating it so I just jumped right in. "Basically my city was created a long time ago, actually right around when I was born so not that long ago, by a group of women. Except there were men before and now there aren't."

"I already knew that though."

"Here's the thing… the women kicked out the men because they felt that they were irresponsible."

He laughed. "Irresponsible – how?"

"They felt that men were the reason the planet almost died, because they were poor decision makers with clouded judgment and that kind of stuff."

"Well yes, pretty much all of us boys are a bit loopy in the head, except Cain, but I am talking to a girl who thought that rain came from a magical waterfall in the sky!"

I punched him on the shoulder playfully. "Not the point."

"OK, OK, continue."

"So they hate men, like they teach us in school that they are 'the root of all evil' and that's why I almost flipped out when I saw you."

"'Cause you thought I would what?"

"Kill me or something."

"I would never kill you," he said and held my hands between his.

"Well, I know that now, silly. But my mother always told me that men never did anything good, but after meeting you and the others I know that was a lie. I just want to know the whole truth, and no one will tell me."

"You think I might know?"

"Well, anyone at this point with some idea of how this all happened and why it was covered up would be helpful."

He thought to himself momentarily, then said, "I think I know who might have answers for you. Come, let's go back to the Village."

He pulled me to my feet. "Thanks," I said.

"I think it's about time you got your answers."

The two of us walked down to the Village to find Cain sitting at the lit fire poking it with a stick. He looked up as we approached, like he was expecting us.

"Cain, Ava has a few questions that we think you might have the answers to."

He looked closely at me for a second and said, "Sit."

I did as I was told.

"So you want to know how we got here, am I right?"

"How did you…"

"Ava, you have curiosity dripping out of your ears," he interrupted. "I had a feeling you would want to know. I just want to make sure it's for the right reasons."

"Right reasons?"

"You're not going to betray us by telling your people where we are so they can slaughter us?"

"What? No, of course not Cain. I'm just sick of not knowing anything."

"If she was going to do that, she would have done it already," Derron said and sat down beside me at the fire.

"You're right, but I'm sure Ava understands why I'm cautious."

I stared at his face from behind the flames and said, "So you know."

"Actually, I remember. I was seven when we left your city."

"You came from my city?"

"No, it's more complicated than that. I sometimes hear you speak of The Great Wars – well, I remember them."

"What are The Great Wars?" Derron asked.

"It was a time when everyone was fighting each other, before you were born. It was complete chaos, everything broke down and the only concern was one's own life."

"That's how they founded my city," I added. "Because everyone had such powerful weapons that they almost killed the entire human race, so my city was founded by women who wanted to preserve our species."

"So, what Ava was taught was that all men were cruel destructive people – am I right?" Cain asked.

"Yeah."

"They blamed the destruction on men, an entire gender, because they thought that they would be better off without them."

"Isn't that a bit rash?" Derron asked and raised his eyebrows.

Cain sighed, "That's what happened."

"So, how did you get here then?" I asked Cain from across the fire.

"Well, I once lived in your city, except it was called something different back then."

"What?"

"London."

"That's a strange name," Derron said.

Cain rolled his eyes. "Anyway, there was a group of women, like you said, and they gathered together more of them until they had enough to start a movement. One of them was extremely bright and she developed ways to keep them all safe from missiles and things like that."

"Sylvia Carter."

"What?"

"That's the woman you're talking about, she made the Bubble around our city so nothing can get in."

"Yeah, that's it, something about a shield. So anyway, I was living with my mother then and we were neighbours to a couple that knew about what was happening. At first, we all thought that it was our ticket to survival, so we did everything we could to help them. I remember my mother letting the women have their meetings in our basement.

"And they were successful; they isolated a part of the city and were almost at their goal when one day they announced that all the men would have to leave, or they would be removed by force.

"Luckily, before this all happened, our neighbour's wife told us about that decision and said that we needed to leave to find refuge before they kicked us out. So our neighbour gathered together all his friends and their sons and planned for us to leave. He took some boys like me and Derron and Derron's brother, even though our fathers weren't coming. Mine was dead anyway, but our neighbour was like a father to me.

"So the four men and the eight boys all planned to find refuge in another city and then send for the mothers and daughters. I had to say goodbye to my mother and our neighbour had to say goodbye to the wife he loved so much and to his newborn daughter.

"Then we left. This was near the end of the Wars, so almost everyone was gone. We walked for miles, reaching town after town, but no one was there. We never found a town.

"The men decided to go back to our city to see if the women would let us back in, but it was surrounded by a huge shield and we couldn't penetrate it. So we created the Old Village nearby, in case they might reconsider. They never did, so we moved further and further into the forest.

"The hardest part was that all the boys were babies. Imagine four men and me, trying to build a village in all kinds of messed up weather, with seven crying babies."

"Cain, I had no idea," said Derron and he looked so sad.

"I didn't really tell the others, because I knew they wouldn't understand at such a young age."

"What happened after that?" I asked, feeling so many different emotions run through me.

"We were about to move further into the forest when all the men caught this disease from something they ate, I don't really remember. And they all died, just like that. Before they died, though, my neighbour told me about what happened so I could tell the others one day. He told me everything he knew about the Wars, the Movement, the city and life. So when he died, I was able to feed us and keep us alive until they became old enough to understand how to do all this." He gestured around him.

"Thank you," Derron said to Cain, "for everything."

"Don't worry, it was all worth it," said Cain and smiled from behind the dancing flames. "Just remember you owe me for every time I had to change your nappy!"

Derron laughed. "I don't even want to know what you had to use for nappies!"

"You're right, you don't."

The two of them laughed and I felt a warmth rise in me like that of the fire. "Why did you never tell the others all this?"

"Because at that time I was angry, and once I cooled down I realised that they would be angry too when I told them. I knew that they would seek revenge, which would only end in chaos," Cain stated as he got up and walked round to Derron. "Derron over here, though," he said and locked his arm around his neck and ruffled his hair, "is actually smart. He wouldn't do anything stupid, well not anything that I know of."

Derron shoved him off saying, "Glad to know you think so highly of me."

"Don't flatter yourself," said Cain and sat back down at the fire.

"None of this explains why they lied about men being terrible people though," I said.

"Well, Ava, I think you prove why they lied," Cain suggested.

"And how's that?"

"Once you found out the truth, you wanted to change things, am I right? You're thinking *we should let the men back in!*"

"Well, of course!"

"And that's exactly what they don't want."

"You know, no one dies in Ava's city," Derron said. "How come they die out here?"

"I told you, we have a cure for everything," I explained, "but people have died before."

"Really?" Cain asked. "I guess I thought you all lived forever."

"No, my best friend died."

"I'm sorry."

"Another woman died too, she was really old though. You see most people above forty fled because they were afraid of the changes the women in the Movement suggested. So my whole city is made up of fairly young women, none of them really die. Oh, but there was this one woman called Naomi Drake who was quite young and wrote music who died of a genetic illness."

"Did you say Drake?" Cain said and looked at me with a shocked expression.

"Yeah, Naomi Drake."

"There was a man who was one of the four called Damian Drake. He wanted to send for his wife to join us, but he never did, and one day the men were out hunting when they found her. She had escaped, but starved in the forest because she never found us."

"Why didn't she just go back? It's not that far."

"Could you show us where it is?"

"How?"

"Come," said Cain and stood and walked over to a tall tree. "Derron says he taught you to climb, could you point it out?"

"Sure." I looked up and the tree seemed so high that I felt queasy for a second.

Derron helped me position myself and instructed me on the climb, following closely behind me. I forbade myself from looking down, knowing that it would only scare me more. I just had to trust that Derron would catch me if I fell. So I kept going, almost falling several times, until I reached the top. I let out a cry of joy just as Derron reached me. Cain appeared at the top of the tree next to us and asked, "So where is it?"

I scanned the forest carefully, knowing it was easier to see at night, but it was almost invisible. Finally I saw a ring of no trees and knew the Bubble must have been in the middle. "There!" I pointed at it. "In the middle of that ring of clearing."

"That?" Cain sounded surprised. "But it's so close."

"That's what I'm saying."

"But you can barely see it," Derron exclaimed. "Why hide it?"

Then it hit me. "I think I know, can we climb down?"

"Sure."

The three of us made it back down to the bottom, me almost falling several times.

"Cain said that a woman by the name of Drake escaped and died out here. And I wondered why she couldn't just go back. But the thing is that the Bubble doesn't let people back through, it only lets them out."

"But how do you get back in?"

"I have my ways… but the point is that I think they try to hide it and don't make it easy for people to get back through, but simple to get out, not because they want to keep people trapped inside, but because they don't want anyone that leaves to be able to speak of what they find."

"Then why let them out in the first place?" Derron asked.

"I don't know."

"Maybe because they don't want curious people in the city at all," Cain suggested, looking at me. "If you're the kind of person who wants to go outside, then you're most likely a threat to them, so you may as well stay outside."

"So they lied about her death?" I was shocked.

"Probably."

"So they tell everyone that she had a genetic disease, but really she left the city and they never tried to go and find her."

"Guess not."

"What kind of barbaric people are we?" I felt ashamed of my community.

"Don't think of it like that," said Derron, trying to comfort me.

"How else should I think of it? How do I know they didn't do this to other people?" I turned to Cain. "What were the other men's names?"

"Rose, Andrews and Richardson, my neighbour."

"Rose?"

"Yeah."

"That's Katelyn's surname."

"You know his wife?"

"His daughter, she was my friend that died."

"Well, I'm sure she was a wonderful person, because I know her father was."

One of the other names sounded familiar to me and I tried to remember where I'd heard it. "What were the two other names again?"

"Andrews and Richardson."

"Where have I heard that before?" I thought out loud.

"Maybe you know their families. Andrews was Jared's father, he wasn't married actually and Richardson was..."

"I've got it!" I exclaimed.

"You do?" Derron asked.

"When I had that fight with my mother she called me Ava Richardson and when I asked her why she shrugged it off."

"What's your mother's name?"

"Donna."

Cain laughed. "I guess she must have changed her name."

"Wait – what?"

He smiled at me. "Turns out we were neighbours once upon a time."

"Are you saying that…?"

"Your father was a wonderful person, I loved him like my own."

"My-my-my what?"

"Ava," Derron said and put his hands on my shoulders, "I think your father was the man that organised our escape."

"But that would mean that…" I could barely get out the words. "That my mother planned to join him."

I suddenly felt so dizzy that I sank to the ground. I just stared at the fire.

"Are you OK?"

"She was against them leaving."

"She told him to leave to protect him, she saved all our lives," said Cain as he came and sat beside me.

"But she lied to me."

"What do you mean?" said Derron and sat on the other side.

"She loved him and she told me that he was nothing but evil. How dare she expect me to always tell *her* the truth!"

"Ava, let's go back to the hill," said Derron as he took my hand and helped me stand.

"Thank you, Cain."

"Anything for Harold's daughter," replied Cain. He winked and walked back over to his hut.

Derron and I strolled up to the hill, hand in hand, and we both lay on the grass to watch the stars. It was a gorgeous night, practically perfect.

"I'm just so angry." I broke the silence.

"With your mother?"

"With everyone! It's like they decided what we should think."

"In a way."

"And they just left the men to fend for themselves! It's like they didn't think that maybe they could have figured out a way to make it work. I mean not all of them were insane like the people that started the Wars."

"True."

"But never mind that, they still never told us any of that. What if I wanted to come up with my own opinion? No, can't do that. I have to think the same thing as everyone else. And my mother yells at *me* for thinking two-dimensionally!"

"You should be allowed to come up with your own opinion."

"Right! It's like they just stripped away our freedom."

"Kind of."

"And what about my mother? How hypocritical is she?! *Men are bad, Ava,* but it turns out Mother is the reason six of them are still out there!"

"Thank you, Donna."

"Of course, I'm super happy about that because otherwise I never would have met you, and I couldn't imagine life without you, Derron, but it's beside the point."

"I couldn't imagine life without you either."

"She just… ugh! She drives me crazy! And I'll never be able to shove it in her face that she's a lying, life-sucking maniac because I have to keep you a secret."

"Well, I wouldn't say life-sucking…"

"And now I'm going to have to just pretend like everything's fine when really it's not! And another thing…"

"Another thing?"

"Katelyn's mother did the same thing! So maybe all of them sent their husbands and sons away! What if the entire city is pretending?! Then what?!"

"Ava…"

"What?! Oh sorry, I didn't mean to snap."

"It's OK."

"Have I been ranting?"

"A bit."

"I'm sorry."

"It's OK. Come here," he said gently as he wrapped his arms around me and held me close to him. "Everything's going to be OK."

"You sure about that?" I asked into his shoulder.

"Positive."

"Derron, thank goodness I have you. You always know what to say."

"Call it a gift."

I laughed and then leant back so I was facing the sky again. "What do you think about all this?"

He let out a deep breath and said, "Well, I disagree with you slightly."

"Oh really?"

"Yeah, I completely understand why you're angry, but if you think about it, they just did it to protect you."

"No, they did it to control us."

"Not in their eyes. Sure they kicked us out, they didn't have to do that but they did, and you know why?"

I shook my head.

"Because they wanted to keep you safe. You said they created the city so that the human race would stay alive. Well, to me that sounds like trying to protect it."

"But their methods…"

"Were all out of love. I know some things were wrong, but imagine if all the girls your age thought the way you did – they would be furious. Then what?"

"I don't know."

"Then the system that those women worked so hard to create would break down and they wouldn't be able to maintain that fabulous lifestyle you all have."

"It's far from fabulous."

"Not really, anything you want is simply handed to you; you don't have to pray that you'll have food the next morning, or that fire won't strike and burn down your home as you sleep."

"Well, you can do whatever you want with your time and believe what you want and think what you want. No one tells you how to behave."

"You think I could just say anything I wanted to the others and they would be like 'Oh, sure Derron, that's cool'? Sometimes we all have different ideas on how to do things. It's not always easy."

"That doesn't justify my mother lying to me, that's our number one value in Emiscyra – honesty."

"Your mother was just doing her job, Ava. I'm sure she didn't create the rules. She was just doing what she had to in order to keep you all safe."

"I guess…" I sat up and ran my hands through my hair.

He sat up too and put his arm around my shoulders. "Feeling any better now?"

"Sort of, but I can't stop thinking about this surgery I have to get."

"What's a surgery?"

"It's like an operation where they open you up and fix things, or in this case possibly ruin things."

"Ruin?"

I turned to face him. "You need men to have children and we don't have any, so they came up with a different way for us to have them through this surgery thing. I'm not really sure how it works, but it does, and then you have a baby."

"So, you have to have one even if you don't want it?"

"Well, of course I want it, everyone does. It's having someone who you are responsible for shaping into an individual human being. Plus it's an honour."

"Then why are you worried about it?"

I sighed, "Because that's how my friend Katelyn died. She had the surgery and four months later she was gone. They said her body wasn't right for it, but then I overheard this call that my mother made and she was talking about there being a bug and not having enough time to fix it."

"So you think it will kill you?"

I let out a deep exhale. "Yeah, that's what I'm afraid of."

He sat there in silence, absorbing what I just said then asked, "Is it for sure?"

"No, they tell me it will work but…"

"You don't believe them?"

"Not in the slightest."

Derron lay there, silently processing. I was impressed by how calmly he was handling the news. He was the one person that was always strong and always true, the one person I could hold on to when I was not.

"But my mother is the Leader of the Council, so as her daughter, it would be a scandal if I refused to do it."

"So, then you have no choice."

"You think I should just go along with it?"

He rolled over to face me. "I think you need to stand by your mother as your city's Leader. That doesn't mean I want you to do it."

"Even if it works, I still have to stay there for nine months while I'm pregnant, and then I probably won't have very many opportunities to leave when I have a child to look after."

"So you're saying that…"

"We might not see each other for a while."

"How long is a while?"

"Maybe a couple of years."

"A couple of years!" he sat up.

"That's what I'm saying." I sat up with him. "I just can't figure a way out of it, I can talk to my mother but… who knows what she'll say."

"No, you need to do this, so don't change everything just for me."

"But you're more important to me than any of this, can't you see that? Maybe I could run away, I don't think Cain would mind if I lived with you all and I could learn to hunt and make fires and…"

"Ava," he interrupted me and took my hands in his, "we both know that's not an option."

"But…"

He bent down and kissed me. "We'll find a way to see each other."

"What if we don't?"

"We will, I promise."

I wrapped my arms around him. "I hope you're right."

"Let me walk you back to the Old Village."

And the two of us walked all the way there, as slowly as we could manage. In the past few days I had felt closer to Derron than before, yet suddenly I was forced to give him up and pretend he never existed. I wanted so badly to just run away and go anywhere else that would allow me to be with him. As we walked hand in hand, I wanted him to be the one sitting in the waiting room with me, like I was with Katelyn.

When we reached the tree with the little pink ribbon - all frayed at the edges, dangling from a low branch, low enough for a little person to reach - I wished I could freeze time.

Derron ran his finger over the lines on my palm. "Well, I guess you have to go now."

"Yeah, I guess I do." I stared as his finger delicately drew patterns on my pale palm.

We stood there silently waiting, and hoping that it wasn't the end.

Then Derron clutched my hand to his heart and looked down at me. "I'll miss you Ava," he said quietly.

In the dark it was hard to tell, but I could see the sadness in Derron's eyes. "Not as much as I'll miss you," I said and wiped away the tears that were forming in my vision.

He tilted my chin up to look at him. "Impossible," he said and smiled sadly.

"Don't you get me started now."

The two of us laughed half-heartedly, but it didn't make the situation any easier than it was. So I just reached over and hugged him as tightly as I could, as if that would keep him with me forever.

Finally, as I pulled away he asked, "Was that a comfort hug or an *I trust you* hug?"

"It was a goodbye hug."

"Ava," he said and ran his hand down my cheek, "I promise that I will find a way to see you again."

"You better." I leant in and kissed him one last time, feeling his heart beating in time with mine. Then I pulled back so our faces were almost touching. "Goodbye Derron," I whispered.

And then he was gone.

Chapter Fourteen

Ava, One Hour Later

I tried to talk myself out of the surgery and tired myself doing so, but it was useless. I knew that going through with it would mean losing Derron, as hard as I tried to pretend it wouldn't. Because, even though there was a small chance that I would find an opportunity to escape to the forest, I wouldn't be able to do it. Mainly because I would find it too hard to see him and then be forced to say goodbye, but also because Derron had taught me that I had to be strong and honour my community. Of course I didn't like things they did, but that was no reason to disgrace them. And I wouldn't be able to do that to my daughter, leaving to another world for an escape. I never wanted her to feel like she wasn't enough for me; I wanted her to believe that she was the centre of my world.

Not to mention that it was far too dangerous. One day a city robot or maybe even a person would catch me leaving and would follow me, giving away the location of the Village and sending something to destroy it. Then I would have lost Derron for good out of my own selfish need to be with him.

And then I realised that as deep as my love for Derron was, even though we had only shared a few weeks of precious time together, I had to let him go. It made me understand how hard it must have been for Mother – to choose the women over my father. I imagined her sending him away, knowing that it was the only way to keep him safe, even if she never saw him again, and then growing older and wanting anything to come and block out her pain. Even if it meant telling herself that he wasn't what she remembered, that he was worse than that.

I knew then that I had no choice but to go through with my decision. So I climbed back up through my window, changed my clothes and went to the bathroom to rinse my face. I looked at the girl in the mirror and wondered *was she making the right choice?*

I hoped so as I made my way downstairs to find Mother sitting at the kitchen counter, coffee in hand. "My, you're up early. Did you sleep well?" she asked.

I grabbed a mug and filled it then sat down across from her. "Mother?"

"Yes, dear?"

"I wanted to apologise for the way I acted. It was immature and unreasonable, and if I had something on my mind I should have just talked to you about it instead of attacking you. I'm sorry, it won't happen again."

"Oh Ava." Mother reached over and grabbed my hand. "I'm sorry too, I shouldn't have yelled at you when you were only trying to tell me how you were feeling. I'll try and be here for you more, OK?"

"That would be nice. And Mother?"

"Yes?"

"There's another thing." I swallowed hard. "I'm ready to go through with the surgery."

"Oh darling, that's excellent!"

And before I knew it, I found myself at the bottom of the glass steps of the Reproduction Centre. It seemed to sparkle like a shard of ice, yet I was sure it couldn't be as cold in there as I was inside. I flashed back to standing in the exact same spot with Katelyn, except I was alone with no one squeezing my hand.

"I guess it's now or never," I sighed to myself.

I began to walk up the thin glass steps and through the doors until I was back in the unbearably familiar whitewashed walls of the reception. Louise was at her place with her light blue uniform, flipping through something or other on a tablet. I recognised some other familiar nurses milling around, they turned and looked at me curiously as I entered. Suddenly, I understood how Katelyn felt; I was the new experiment.

"Ava!" Mother walked over to me with open arms.

"Hi, Mother."

"Oh, welcome. You know Sylvia, right darling?" She indicated the woman standing beside her.

Silver grey hair, sharp green eyes and that sneeringly cold smile. "How could I forget?" I replied coolly.

"Pleasure to see you again, Ava." Sylvia's voice sounded just as icy as I remembered. "If I'm not mistaken, wasn't the last time I saw you when you were up on stage doing your little show?"

"Yes, it was. Except Katelyn was with me that time. Now she's not." I glared at her long and hard.

She glared back smugly then almost grinned. "Well, we'd better get going, hadn't we?"

"Come, let's all go to the waiting room to discuss," said Mother as she began walking down the hallway. "If I remember correctly, it has a wonderful view of Yosemite."

"Niagara Falls."

Mother stopped and turned round. "I'm sorry?"

"It was Niagara Falls."

"Oh, right," said Mother. She continued walking and began blabbing about something or other.

My mind was on Derron whom I hadn't seen in a week for fear I wouldn't be able to leave. His smile in my mind helped me make it into the waiting room without falling over or fainting.

"Here we are, please sit," said Mother.

I did, feeling a major sense of déjà vu.

"Now the procedure will be similar to before if you remember it."

"I do."

"Well, there are a few different parts to the surgery, but it's basically the same thing. You will also have to remain here in the facility for the nine months of your pregnancy; however you will be allowed outside as long as you are supervised. Your schedule has changed slightly, but overall it's a similar combination of healthy diet, exercise, sleep and brain stimulation. Now the nurse should be on her way soon." Mother peered down at her watch then looked up and said, "Ah, there she is, perfect timing."

"Hi, my name is Claire and I will be helping you prep for surgery."

I looked up at her and recognised her face. "I don't know if you remember me, I'm Ava."

"Oh," she said and looked sad for a moment. "Yes, I remember you. Are you ready?"

"I guess."

"Ah, this is so exciting!" Mother chirped. "We'll come and see you when you're done, sweetheart."

"OK." I stood to leave.

Mother grabbed my hand. "Good luck, darling," she said and smiled.

"Thanks."

"Yes, good luck," added Sylvia and sat back in her chair calmly.

"Let's just hope it works, right? I mean it is your head on the line." I grinned sarcastically.

She gave me a calculating glare, like I was utterly fascinating to her.

"Shall we go?" the nurse asked.

"But of course," I said as I shot Sylvia a last cold smile and walked off behind the nurse. She led me down the hallway until we reached a small room at the end. "You can sit here," she said. "I just have to go and get the tests. Oh, and can you put on this gown while I'm gone?" She reached over and handed me a thin blue gown, like the one Katelyn wore.

"Sure."

"OK, I'll be right back." And she walked back out.

I sighed and inspected the room as I put on the thin gown. The whole place was fairly small with a bunch of shelves and different medical tools on them. Of course, it was rather neat, but it just felt so cramped. The only place to sit was on the little bed, so I didn't know how easy it would be for someone to perform a surgery.

"Here we go." The nurse walked back in with several unidentifiable things in her hand. "So, I'm going to need to take a few samples first."

"Samples?"

She extracted a little device, which looked like an electronic pen, from her collection. "Now open your mouth."

I didn't see much point in arguing so I did as asked. Little did I know she planned to stick it in my mouth, causing me to almost spit it out.

"Oh don't worry, this is just collecting a saliva sample."

"A what?" I tried to say, without moving my mouth.

"That should be enough," she said as she removed the treacherous device and inspected it. "Blood next?"

"Blood?!"

She reached into her pile of torture weapons and took out another pen-like device. "Hold out your arm."

I hesitated.

"It's fine. All I have to do is give you a little prick. Trust me, you're lucky. In my day they had to stick this huge thing in for several minutes."

Slowly I gave her my hand and in one swift motion she stuck the device in the bend of my arm and removed it again.

"Are you sure you did it? I couldn't feel anything," I said as I took my arm and inspected it for marks.

"That's how it works, Sylvia Carter invented it."

"Of course she did." I rolled my eyes.

"Now we're almost done, I just need one more sample."

"Of what…?"

She handed me a plastic cup. "The bathroom is through that door."

I turned to find a door behind me which I hadn't even realised was there. "Wait, you want me to…?"

She nodded her head.

"Oh… OK…" I got up and did as instructed, perplexed as I was.

After I returned she took all my beautiful bodily fluids and put them on a tray. "I'll just send these up to the lab," she said and smiled as if there were flowers in her hands instead. "Oh, you can go through that door on the right to wait for the doctor."

"There's another door?" I looked over my shoulder to see a door labelled *Operating Room.* "I guess there is."

"Good luck," she said and then she was gone.

I went over to the operating room door and opened it slowly, unsure of what to expect. It was very brightly lit and far bigger than the testing room. In the middle was a huge bed with several chairs and tables, full of more medical things, around it. I shut the door behind me and walked over to the bed, assuming it was my seat.

As I lay down and stared at the bright lights above me, I thought about Katelyn doing the exact same thing. Except the difference between the two of us was that people had slightly lower expectations of her. I knew that she always felt the pressure was too much, but really all people expected of her was to have a successful pregnancy and a healthy child. She was sure that the procedure was safe, she was honoured as the first brave girl, and the entire community was behind her.

What did I have? I had the pressure to live. If I died, then my entire community would probably go extinct. Sure that was the same with Katelyn, but she didn't have any idea. In her wildest dreams, death would never have crossed her mind as an option. I had to live every day of those nine months hoping I would make it to see the next one.

And people were too afraid of it going wrong to be excited for me. How many women would hug my friends in the street?

Or come and visit me to congratulate me on the honour? It wasn't an honour any more, it was a burden. And I had the task of carrying it on behalf of the entire human race. Lucky me.

"Hello Ava, I'm Doctor Karen," she said as she walked over and shook my hand. "I think we've met though."

"Yes we have."

"I just want you to know that we did everything we could."

"I'm sure you did." I attempted a smile but it didn't do much.

"So," she said and took out her tablet, "your tests are running in the lab, but first, I just need to run a few more tests myself."

"As many as you need," I said and tilted my head back to stare at the brightly lit ceiling.

The doctor fiddled around with several devices before selecting one and scanning me with it. She then proceeded to scan me with another one, and another, and another, until I was pretty sure I had fallen asleep.

I was woken by the nurse scampering in carrying a tablet. "Doctor, you need to look at this," she said anxiously.

"One second," said the doctor. She smiled at me then walked over to the nurse. "What is it?"

The nurse pointed at the tablet then handed it to her. The doctor scanned it several times with wide eyes then gasped and flung her hand over her mouth. "No…" She gaped at me then turned back to the tablet. "Run it again."

"Yes, Doctor." The nurse grabbed the tablet and ran out of the door.

"Is everything OK, Doctor?" I asked and sat up.

"Of course, dear. Let me just finish with these tests," she said as she grabbed another device and scanned me with it.

Then the nurse bolted through the door at top speed. "The lab says that the results are accurate," she panted and handed the tablet back to the doctor.

"What?" The doctor gasped and stared at me like I was a wild animal.

I shied away and asked, "Is everything OK?"

"Wait there," said the doctor, then the two of them ran out of the door.

I sighed and sat up in the bed feeling slightly nervous, but more just irritated. I picked myself up and walked over to the door to the waiting room. Through the glass hole in it, I could see the doctor conversing with my mother. Doctor Karen appeared to be speaking extremely quickly with an astonished look on her face the whole time. Mother just nodded her head until the doctor reached over and whispered something in her ear. Mother gasped and stepped back slightly, then regained her original calm composure and said something back.

Doctor Karen held up her tablet and Mother scanned it with her eyes, nodding as the doctor kept talking. Then she gasped again and put her hand over her chest, looking completely stunned. She looked up through the glass hole in the door at me with the exact same look. I rolled my eyes.

Mother turned back to the doctor and said something; the doctor nodded and walked away. By then I had stopped even trying to guess what was happening. Mother was pacing in front of the door deep in thought, then finally she turned and walked into the room.

"Does anyone care to explain why people look at me like I just grew a third arm?" I enquired.

Mother walked over and sat on the bed next to me. She sighed like she was trying to find words. "There isn't going to be a surgery today."

"What? Why not?"

She drummed her fingers on her thighs and looked around the room. "We cannot proceed with the surgery because," she said, turning and looking me in the eye, "you're already pregnant."

My jaw dropped. "What?!"

"I said, you're already…"

"I know what you said, but *how?* I thought it was impossible without the surgery!"

"Ava, did you leave the Bubble?" Mother demanded with a voice of steel.

I froze.

"Unless you snuck into the centre and gave yourself the surgery, there is only one way to get pregnant. And I know you couldn't have done it here."

My lips remained sealed tight.

"Did you find men or other people that could have been men?"

I tried desperately to think of something.

"Ava, answer me!"

"OK, yes I did," I blurted out. "I left the Bubble."

"You what?!"

"I was curious! I didn't know what I would find."

"How did you…?"

"Before Katelyn died, the five of us found a way outside just to explore and nothing happened. But when she passed away, we wanted to go back to hold a private ceremony for her, so we went back and I saw a boy."

"A boy? Like a child?" She looked disgusted.

"No, like my age."

Mother sighed, relieved. "Well, that's a bit better, continue."

"So then the others made me promise not to go back, but I…"

"But you just had to go back, didn't you?" Mother interrupted.

I sighed, "Do you want to know or not?"

"Fine, continue."

"And when I went back he was there and we talked. He told me about his home and said that there were others…"

"Others? How many?"

"Six total, all around the same age. Anyway, I got to know him better and I went back a lot."

"How often is a lot?"

I hesitated and then said, "Like every day…"

"Every day! For how long?"

"A couple of weeks."

"For goodness sake, Ava!"

"Can I just explain?"

"Fine, go on."

"All right, where was I? Oh right, so I got to know him and he was the nicest person and he was such an amazing listener and he had this incredible laugh!" Derron's face appeared in my mind. "And he was so funny and…"

"Ava, I get it."

"Sorry. So then when I found that photo and I made the connection about that kind of love… well… I kind of fell in love with him."

"After a few weeks! Ava, that's not love."

"Yes it is! I know it isn't a lot of time, but I'm being honest when I say that I would do anything for him and he would do the same for me."

"Oh dear," she said and put her head in her hands. "I thought that living in a world of just women would eliminate this problem."

"I'm sorry."

She looked at me. "But Ava, men are terrible, cruel, heartless..."

I raised my eyebrows.

She trailed off and sighed, "But I guess you know that's not all true."

"Yeah, pretty much."

"Ava," said Mother as she held my hand, "are you sure that these boys behaved appropriately?"

"Yes! They were super welcoming and friendly and Cain, the older one, answered all my questions."

"Did you say Cain?"

"Yeah, apparently he was our neighbour. He knew Father..."

"Yes, yes he did." Mother stared off into space. "There weren't any older men, were there?"

"No." I knew what her real question was. "He died."

Her head snapped back. "They told you that?"

"All of the men died. Only the boys were left."

"Oh."

"I'm sorry."

"No it's..." she said and waved her hand in the air, "it's nothing, I just..."

"Miss him?"

She looked at me with sad eyes. "No I... uh," she said, rubbing her eyes. "How did you, um, how did you even know how to conceive a child in the first place?"

"I didn't. It must have just happened without us realising what it meant. How do you do it anyway?"

Mother scratched the back of her neck and said, "Um, that's not really important seeing as it already happened, so let's just get down to business."

"Business?"

Mother let out an aggravated sigh. "I'm just so mad at myself for not protecting you better. I thought that you not knowing would have made you safer. But it actually did the opposite. Darn those animal instincts!"

"Animal instincts?"

"Never mind." She waved it off. "Now we need to discuss what action to take."

"What do you mean?"

"You can't just have it!"

"Why not?"

"I think that the only solution is to remove it and give you the surgery."

"Remove it? How can you say that?"

"Ava, listen to me, we have no choice. How are we meant to tell the entire community that men exist? That would create chaos."

"But I want to keep her..."

"It might not be a her, Ava, and that's what's even more dangerous."

"Wait, it might be a..." I looked down at my stomach in awe.

"Yes, a boy! And that's why we need to give you the real surgery."

I snapped my head up. "I want to keep it. Whatever it is."

"You can't!"

"But it's my decision!"

"No, not any more. You may think you are doing the right thing, but we need to protect our community."

"And that's exactly why I should keep it."

"What on earth does that mean?"

It suddenly came to me. "This one is more likely to survive than the fake one you would put in me."

"It's not fake…"

"Fine – the artificial one. Either way, the great Sylvia Carter must have messed up because, for some unimaginable reason, it didn't work."

"That was a fluke, this time…"

"A fluke? Can you really afford another 'fluke'?"

Mother chewed on her lip. "Ava, if it's because you're worried about… you know… then you shouldn't."

I thought about it for a second. "I'm not afraid of dying. Well, I am, but I genuinely think this will work. You can't keep doing this trial and error, lives are on the line!"

Mother sat there, deep in thought.

"Mother?"

"It would be biased to give my own daughter special privileges," she thought aloud to herself, "but this one might in fact help the community."

"What if you just don't tell anyone?"

She turned to me. "*Lie?*" she spat it out like poison in her mouth.

I tilted my head to the side. "Don't act like you haven't already."

"What?" She put her hand to her chest. "Ava, don't accuse me of doing something so…" She stopped when she saw my *I'm not buying it* face. "What are you suggesting?"

"Tell everyone I had the surgery."

"And if it's a boy?"

"Then take it as a sign."

She raised her eyebrows.

"Fine, we can deal with that when the time comes."

"And we also have to keep it a secret about these boys. That is of the utmost importance."

"So I can keep it?"

Mother sighed, "Yes, you can keep it."

"Oh, thank you Mother!" I sat up and hugged her. "You won't regret it."

"I better not. Now I'm going to tell the doctors that this is to be kept between us." She stood to leave.

"You're not going to tell Sylvia?"

"I think it's best if we don't." She smiled. "It'll be our little secret."

And it was our little secret. I spent the following days convincing everyone that I had a successful surgery and was pregnant with a healthy girl. My friends visited almost every day, which surprised me seeing as I hadn't been paying much attention to them. The Council members visited all the time and they too believed that inside me was the product of surgery. Sylvia Carter would often look at me suspiciously, but every time my test results came back positive, I would simply say to her, "Don't worry *yet* Sylvia."

Then one morning, I was sitting with Mother in my room when I announced my latest decision. "Mother, I've come to a decision."

"Yes, dear?" She looked up from her tablet.

I checked over her shoulder that the door was shut. "I want Derron to be a part of the child's life."

"Absolutely not," she said emphatically and turned back to the tablet.

"But it's his just as much as mine."

"That's irrelevant."

"But no one will know," I pleaded. "I'll just go to the forest and meet him there."

"You most certainly won't."

"Oh please, Mother, I need him."

She stared at me in shock. "It is far too dangerous for you to gallivant off into the forest alone with a baby."

"I know it so well! I promise I'll be safe."

"I said no, Ava."

We sat there in silence. Then Mother's face lit up. "Could you point it out on this map?" She held out her tablet.

There was a ring in the middle indicating our city with trees around it. The river was down at the bottom, my clue.

"It's here," I said, pointing at the rough location, between the river and the city.

"Oh," she said and looked surprised, "it's closer than I imagined."

"That's what I'm saying. Please Mother?"

She looked at me curiously for a moment. "I guess..."

"Yes!"

"As long as you are accompanied by me."

"You have a deal. Thank you, you don't know how much this means to me."

"Anything to protect your best interests, Ava."

But several days passed and Mother always seemed too busy to take me. I was growing desperate. Once I knew that I could have him back in my life, I just assumed it would happen instantly. And when it didn't I began to get nervous.

Finally, I couldn't take it any longer and devised a plan to sneak out on my own. During one of my scheduled walks out I asked if I could go with Lexi instead of the nurse. Of course they agreed, and Lexi met me outside the building, as planned.

"So you said you needed me to cover for you," she said as soon as we were out of hearing.

"I have to do something that they would never agree to. I can't tell you, Lex, but I need you to trust me, OK?"

She thought for a while before asking, "You won't do anything dangerous?"

"Dangerous? Me?"

"Don't joke with me, Ava Hart. I'll do it as long as you promise that whatever it is, it's safe."

"I swear."

"OK. What do you want me to do?"

"Walk around the city for a while and meet me at the café in an hour. Then we'll go back together."

"You better be there in an hour though as I have to leave for the school photo in the park."

"I will." The tram pulled into the stop. "I have to go. Thanks Lexi." I hugged her.

"Any time."

Within minutes I was at the Bubble and then out of it and, before I knew it, at the Old Village.

"Derron! Derron it's me!"

I waited but he didn't answer.

"Derron! Cain!"

Nothing.

I told myself that it would be more fun if I surprised him anyway. So I walked over to the Village myself. But nothing could have prepared me for what I saw when I got there.

The huts were smashed to rubble and all the fires blackened to nothing. There were all sorts of pieces of food lying on the ground and smashed bottles of medicine.

I walked through, crunching on glass as I did, in complete shock. There was no way they just left. The place had been attacked. *But by what?*

The storage box was empty with all the weapons missing. I ran to every building searching for any sign of people, calling, "Derron? Derron! Cain! Owen! Somebody!"

My heart was racing and I fought so hard to talk myself out of thinking the worst. Then I saw something catch the light. I walked over to the shining little object buried in the ground. As I got closer, it appeared to be silver, a piece of metal.

It was lodged in the earth right next to a pile of stray berries so I pulled it out from the ground. The piece of metal was blank on one side and there was dirt covering the other. I rubbed it clean with my elbow to reveal a little golden T. Then I realised what it was.

It was the plaque with the crest of Emiscyra on it. I recognised the thorny green vines all too well. There were holes in the metal where it would have been nailed to a city robot...

Oh no. Oh please no.

I took off, running further into the forest screaming, "Derron! Derron!"

Anger flooded through me because I knew that by pointing out the Village on the map I had signed the death warrants of all six of them. Mother betrayed me by sending robots to destroy them. How could she?

"Derron! Derron!"

I kept running until I heard a crunching of metal and skidded to a halt. The trees in front of me began to part and slowly one of the largest robots I'd ever seen came crawling towards me. I remained still, breathing heavily, heart racing. Then it stopped. Silence.

My heart was beating so hard I was sure that the robot could hear it. Then I saw in thick black letters on the side: *Security*. Like the closed door at the robot complex.

Before I could analyse it further, the robot flashed a blue light over me and began scanning. Every part of me stayed frozen except for my wildly pumping heart. I kept as still as I could until the light retracted. Then it flashed red.

Uh oh.

Without hesitation, the robot charged towards me at full speed. In an instant I turned and ran as fast as my legs could take me. I had to sprint while dodging every tree that obstructed my path. The robot just chopped right through them with the blades poking out of its sides.

"This is so unfair!" I cried.

I kept running until my feet were numb. Then I tripped over and scrambled through the dirt, trying to get myself up. As I looked back at the robot, I saw it unlock its blade from on top and point it at me.

Then I took off running again, terror seizing my whole body and adrenalin being the only thing strong enough to keep me moving. Then I saw the Bubble wall up ahead and took it as my escape. I suddenly realised that I wouldn't be able to make it through.

I turned and sped off the other way, back into the trees, and kept going even though my lungs were screaming. Then I reached a large rusted building and ran towards it, throwing myself through the smashed window. The robot reached me, and I backed away until I hit the wall. All I heard was a violent screeching of metal on metal as the robot tried to get closer. The window wasn't big enough so it poked its blade inside and stretched it out towards my throat.

My fingers clawed at the wall behind me but it was no use. The blade inched closer and closer until there were only centimetres between it and my neck. I tried to search for a way out but realised it was useless.

Was I going to die?

The blade was almost at me and my heart was pounding so hard I couldn't hear the metal shrieking any more. Then just as it was about to slit my throat, it stopped. There was silence.

Then it flashed green and slowly recoiled and shut down. I collapsed, breathing heavily. I was alive. My head was spinning, but I managed to sit up and crawl out of the window. That's when I saw the tiny little camera at the front of the robot pointed at me. They must have been watching.

I took the camera in my hands and ripped it off then threw it into the building I hid inside. Then I took off, running back towards the Village, still cautious of others lurking. I racked my brain desperately searching for any idea of what happened to the boys.

The blade was clean, indicating it hadn't been used to spear anyone, yet there could have been others that did. Assuming the camera was only used for the Council to sit and watch, the robot would not have had any way of telling one human from the other. It must have detected me using heat sensors, in which case the boys would have tried to find a way to mask their heat. In my head I filtered through all the ways to cool oneself down in a forest. Then it came to me. The river.

I turned and tried to navigate my way there until I heard the rushing of the cool waves. Suddenly it appeared before me, and seemed more beautiful than ever. Without rolling up my trouser legs, I waded into the water, yelling out, "Derron! Derron! Cain!"

And sure enough there they were, crouching in the water with weapons poised. I ran towards them, splashing as I did so. "Over here! It's Ava!" I called.

Some of them turned and held out their spears until they saw it was me. "Ava?" they said.

Then I saw Derron crouching at the back, looking around frantically; the sight of him almost brought me to tears.

"Derron!"

"Ava?"

Then we both ran towards each other, as fast as the water would let us, and I leapt into his arms.

"Oh, thank goodness you're alive," I said and wept into his shoulder.

"How did you…?"

"I had to find you. I'm so sorry, this is all my fault."

"Don't say that," he said and stroked back my hair, which was pretty wet from all the splashing.

"No, I told my mother because I had to, and then I told her where you lived and she sent the robots to kill you and…" I collapsed on him. "I'm so sorry."

"Ava?" Cain said and waded over.

"Oh Cain, you're alive too," I said and hugged him.

"Why did you have to tell her?" Derron asked me.

"Actually, that's why I came. I, uh, I have to tell you something."

"Is it good?"

"Very good." I took his hands. "I didn't have the surgery."

"What? Why not?" He tried to suppress his excitement.

"Because I was already pregnant." I laughed and added, "And it's yours."

"It's what?" said Cain, practically jumping out of the water.

"Wait, how is that possible?" Derron asked, looking confused and amazed.

Cain slapped his hand to his head and said, "You didn't…"

"I didn't what?"

"Never mind."

Derron turned back to me. "Wait, so you're having a baby?"

"I'm having our baby."

Cain was still smacking himself in the head, but Derron looked unbelievably happy and exclaimed, "This is amazing!"

"Hey, what's going on?" the other boys asked as they came over.

"I'm going to be a father!" Derron yelled.

"Oh boy," said Cain and rolled his eyes.

"Are you serious?" Owen asked with wide eyes.

"How does that even work?" Mason asked, turning to Cain.

"Please don't ask."

"This is worth a celebration!" Owen cheered.

Then the boys all reached over and picked me up and held me in the air, whooping.

"Whoa boys, put her down, we don't want to hurt it."

So they lowered me into the water and lifted Derron instead, cheering as they did so. He slapped them on the back, laughing. Cain just stood there gaping.

"Cain, you look like you've seen a ghost," I said and waded over to him. "Is everything OK?"

"Yeah, I'm just a little surprised that's all. Congratulations, Ava."

"Thank you. And I still don't see what's so surprising."

"Just that you two... never mind. You don't need to know."

The others came running back over and dropped Derron into the water, splashing Cain and me in the process.

"So, I need to ask you all a favour," I said as I wiped the water from my face.

"Anything for you."

"Yeah, you name it."

"I want you to come back with me to the city. I have a plan."

Chapter Fifteen

Ava, One Hour Later

"Can we go in now? Mason is sitting on my arm," Owen whined.

"Ssh! Quiet, Owen, just one more minute."

I poked my head out from the bush we were hiding in to check if anyone was coming. "All right," I said, gesturing to the others, "let's move."

Then in one swarm all seven of us jumped out of our cramped hiding spot and rushed over to the front door.

"What is it?" asked Mason and stared at the tall building in awe.

"It's our town hall. Come, the Council should be in there now," I said and bent down and held my eye over the retina scanner.

"What are you doing?" Jared asked.

"Scanning my eye. No one knows that they don't work properly though." The light turned on and started scanning.

"Don't work?"

The scanner beeped. "Yeah," I said and pushed open the doors, "they can't differentiate members of the same family."

"I still don't get it."

Cain slapped him on the back and said, "None of us do."

"All right, let's go, quietly though," I said and signalled for them to go inside.

One by one we slipped through the large wooden doors and crept down the hallway. The whole place had such a different atmosphere from when we were gathered for the Election. It felt spooky and cold, probably because of the old style architecture and dark wooden walls.

"This place gives me the creeps," Owen said, shivering.

Derron came over and squeezed my hand. "Are you sure this will work?" he whispered in my ear.

"I can only hope."

Finally we reached the end of the long and looming hallway and another set of large wooden doors with a plaque that read: *Council Headquarters.*

"This is it," I said, pointing at the plaque. "Everyone ready?"

"Yeah."

"OK."

"Ready."

"Now remember to let me do the talking, OK?"

"Sure, Ava."

"Whatever you say."

I planted both of my feet firmly in front of the doors and pushed aside any fears or nerves. Then with one swift motion, I shoved both doors aside and marched into the room.

It was not what I was expecting.

There was a large round table in the middle with all the Council members sitting around it, looking shocked at my forced entry. Around were smaller desks and thousands of screens littered around the tables and on the walls. I looked up and saw one of them playing back footage of me running through the forest being chased by the robot. The playback stopped.

"Can we help you?" one of them asked.

Everyone was staring at me expectantly.

"Ava?" Mother stood from her seat at the head. "Ava, what are you doing here?"

"Actually, it's not just me," I said, signalling at the boys. "I brought friends."

Slowly, the six of them strolled over to stand next to me, and I heard some of the members gasp.

"Hi," said Owen, waving at them and Cain had to slap his hand away.

"Are those...?"

"Yes, these are boys," I said and stood firm.

The whole room erupted into astonished cries and panic. Some of the women even got up and stood on their chairs.

"Calm down! Ladies please!" Mother shouted out.

"Donna, I thought we handled this," one of the ladies protested.

"What on earth are they doing here?"

"Donna, is that your daughter?"

"Quiet!" Mother yelled. "Ava, what do you want?"

"I want you to let them back in."

There was silence, then all the women started laughing hysterically, slapping their thighs.

"She's kidding, right?"

"No, I'm not." My voice was iron.

"Ava, you can't be serious..." Mother tried to reason with me.

"Oh, but I am."

"Young lady, aren't you meant to be resting? You are the pregnant girl, am I right?" An older-looking woman inspected me suspiciously.

"Well, I'm sorry, I didn't really have a chance because I was being chased by one of our own robots," I snapped. "And speaking of that…"

"Ava, please don't," Mother pleaded.

"Did you all know that the Repopulation Phase is a bust?"

There were a few murmurs in the group.

"That's right – the brilliant innovation that your famous Sylvia Carter here designed," I said and gave her a nod of my head. "It doesn't work!"

There was another set of whispering. So I glowered at Sylvia, but she just smiled like a pillar of ice.

"Where did you hear that, Miss Hart?" one woman asked.

"Oh, I just figured it out when they told me that my best friend died," I sneered. "Did you know that it kills people? Did she convince you that it was fixed?"

Silence.

"That's why we need them, you see. They are the only safe way to have children," I said and walked over and held Derron's hand. "And I plan to prove it."

"Donna, what is going on?"

"Ladies, I can explain."

"Can you, Mother?"

"Ava, what are you doing?" I saw the panic in her eyes.

"Yes, my dear," one of the women said and stood up. "You may think that you are wise, but everything we do here is for your own good. Why do you have to stir up trouble?"

"But you are all missing the point! These people," I said, gesturing at the boys, "are nice, generous and thoughtful and do not deserve to be tossed aside. Why can't you accept that and let them join us?"

"Ava, you haven't seen the world like we have," Mother tried to reason with me. "You don't know what they're capable of."

"They wouldn't hurt a fly."

"Then we better not tell her about the rabbit stew," Owen whispered to Cain behind me.

"Your mother's right, Ava." Sylvia stood and walked over to me. "How about you all leave and take these boys back to where they came from?"

"Make me."

Her mouth slowly curved upwards into a sinister grin as she said, "As you wish."

Suddenly the doors flung open and robots came swarming in. There were six of them in total, all marked *Security* in thick black letters. As they boomed into the room, each extended a long arm from its side and began to chase the boys, clawing at them from behind.

"What are you doing!?" I screamed.

"Just what you asked," said Sylvia and stood there smiling.

Each robot had targeted a specific boy and most of them had already caught theirs. I saw Owen and Kevin dangling from the spindly arms, kicking about frantically. My mind was racing and everything was moving so quickly, I could barely think. I saw Derron jumping over the tables as the robot chasing him began extending its arm longer and longer towards him.

"Mother, make it stop!"

"I'm sorry, Ava."

By then almost all of the boys were strapped to the sides of the robots. I saw Cain struggling to break free and the arm hitting him over the head, causing him to go limp. Something inside my gut twisted.

Derron was still dodging one and finally it grabbed at his leg and dragged him along the floor.

"No!" I ran over to him and started whacking the robot's metal arm.

Then I felt two human arms grab my waist and yank me backwards with such force that I felt dizzy. I turned to see Sylvia force my hands behind my back and shove them into something cold and metal.

The robots began filing out with the boys dangling limp on the front. I saw Derron's sandy blonde head hanging low and felt my heart bursting.

"No! Derron!" I screamed and tears poured out of my eyes.

"Come with me," ordered Sylvia and dragged me backwards.

"No!" I kicked at her. "Let me go!"

She pulled me through a back door and dragged me down a dark grey hallway which looked shockingly different from the rest of the building.

"Where are you taking them?"

She kept pulling me until we reached the end of the hallway where she kicked open the door and threw me inside. I leapt for the door just as she slammed it on my shoulder. A shooting pain flicked down my arm and up my neck and I crumbled on to the ground sobbing.

As soon as the pain subsided I looked up to see Sylvia watching me with a calculating grin through the bars of the door. I lunged at her and she laughed menacingly and sneered, "Don't even try."

The door was locked from the outside, but it was made of bars so I could see through. It was almost like a prison cell.

"What, am I your prisoner now?" I spat at her.

"Why don't you make yourself at home?"

I looked around to see a tiny grey concrete room with nothing in it at all except for a light bulb hanging from the ceiling. They obviously didn't plan to keep me there long.

"Where are you taking them?" I demanded.

She shook her finger and said, "No no no, you're better off not knowing."

I let out a raged scream, "You let me out of here now!" I pounded at the door with my body and fought to free my hands from what chained them behind my back.

Sylvia remained perfectly still, just inspecting me.

Finally I gave up and slumped on the floor, glaring back at her. "So you plan to keep me here forever then?"

"Oh no, that simply wouldn't work."

"You think you can stop me talking?"

"I don't think that you'll get many opportunities."

"What, so I'll be under confinement for the rest of my life?"

"What is it you're trying to achieve, Miss Hart?"

"Why don't you let me out of the cell and I'll show you?" I snapped.

She stood there, almost laughing to herself. "Ava Hart, you really are a little thrill seeker, aren't you? What is it you're searching for huh? Power? Defiance? Attention?"

"Answers."

She nodded. "Well, if that's what you want. When I created the artificial embryos it was a huge breakthrough. But I had to preserve them somewhere. They were all tested and perfectly usable, but then tragically a virus infected them all. I didn't catch it until it was too late to save your friend, and so I tried desperately to fix them." She shrugged her shoulders. "No use. And I realised that to make more would take years. We just don't have that time. So I figured that I would try another method I was working on, but here's the catch. For our city to prosper, we needed to get rid of a few… irregularities."

"Like what?"

"I've known that you've been sneaking outside the Bubble for quite some time. You don't think I built a shield that didn't even detect when people went in or out, do you?" She laughed to herself. "But of course you did. And when I realised that your curiosity was going to be a bit of a problem, I came up with a solution.

"I never told anyone that the new method was ready for use because I knew who girl number two was, and felt that she needed… a little special treatment."

"You know that telling me this doesn't keep it a secret, right?"

"Oh, but that's the point," she said and leant in closer. "You won't live long enough to tell."

"What?!"

"I waited to announce the new method because I wanted you to have the old one. If everyone believed that it was fixed, then even your own mother would have no problem agreeing. And now you won't survive another few days, as I gave you a very special embryo, and then when all hope is lost, I will present the new and improved reproduction method."

I sat there stunned. "Why are you doing this?"

"For the good of our community! Imagine if you had been successful in bringing the men into it, then there would have been chaos! For years I have made it my mission to protect the human race and I will not let some naïve little girl ruin it. But you'll never understand. Enjoy your time here, I'd be surprised if you even made it till tomorrow." She turned and walked away.

"You're just going to leave me here?!"

She kept walking.

"Sylvia, come back!"

And then she was gone.

It suddenly dawned on me that she had no idea that I never had the real surgery. She thought I was carrying an infected embryo, when really my child was most likely perfectly healthy. I laughed to myself that I had the upper hand. But then I remembered that the boys were probably on their way to be slaughtered and it was all my fault. The guilt struck me so hard that I felt sick with myself.

Maybe I truly had ruined everything. I smacked my shoulder against the wall in anger and tried to find a window or another door. Nothing.

I tried to stay awake but eventually it was all too much and I collapsed in exhaustion.

I remained asleep until shouting coming from the other room woke me. I sat up, feeling groggy and sore, and tried to establish where the noises were coming from. Soon I figured that people were talking outside the door to the headquarters.

Without putting too much strain on myself, I slowly dragged my limp body across the floor and as close to the door as possible.

"Let me in there, Sylvia!" a voice rang out.

I tried to hear but I only picked up words.

"You can't... crazy! Open... I am... authority... daughter..."

Mother?

Then the door slammed open with a clang and I jumped back just as Mother stormed in.

"Ava?" She looked shocked. "What have you done to her?!" She ran over to the door and reached through the bars.

"Mother, please let me out."

"Who put you in here?"

"Sylvia… where did she take them?"

"Oh honey, look at you!"

"Please get me out."

"I will, I promise," she said and stood to leave.

"Where are you going?"

"I don't have the key. I'll be back soon sweetheart, OK?"

"Hurry."

She ran out of the door back to the Council Headquarters. I sighed and leant my head on the cold metal bars. Then I saw the scanner. It was pinned to the wall outside my cell and just waiting for someone to use it.

"Wait Mother, there's a…" But she was too far away by then.

I tried to fit my head through the bars in such a way that I could get a closer look. I assumed it was an eye scanner, but there was no way I could have fitted my head through far enough to reach it. I sat back and shoved my feet through the bars and kicked at the scanner in an attempt to knock it off the wall. It remained stuck pretty firm, so I adjusted my heels on the edge and pushed on it as hard as possible until I heard a screw pop out.

"Yes!"

I slapped the thing with my heels until I found the corner without a screw and shoved my foot behind the metal and ripped another screw free. I manoeuvred one foot between the scanner and the wall and the other on the other side of the scanner and, with as much force as possible, I tore it off the wall.

The metal crashed to the floor with a bang and there was a spark of electricity from the empty spot. Then I spun round and kicked at the door, letting it swing open beautifully.

Without another pause, I jumped to my feet and leapt outside and towards the exit. There was another scanner, so I held my eye up to it and the door clicked unlocked. Just as I rushed through into the big meeting room, it struck me that the place was completely deserted.

"Where'd everybody go?"

The screen played images of the robots tearing apart the Village and the boys leaping out into the trees for shelter. I saw Derron turn for a second and my heart twisted. I knew I had to make things right. For him.

Chapter Sixteen

Ava, Twenty Minutes Later

"Attention ladies! Please all look this way at the camera!" The photographer was trying to organise the group of girls sitting on the grass. "All right, in three, two, one…"

"Wait!" I ran over and jumped in front of the camera just as it flashed. I stumbled backwards, shielding my eyes. As I regained vision, I realised that everyone was staring at me in utter shock, either in response to my appalling state, or to my presence in the first place.

"Hey, would you mind moving, miss?" The photographer sounded irritated.

"Ava Hart?" One of my teachers came forward. "What happened to you?"

Lexi stood up from amongst the crowd and ran over to me. "Geez, Ava. You said it wasn't dangerous!"

"I didn't think it was, I'm sorry."

"Are those chains?" she asked, inspecting my wrists.

"Long story, can you help unchain me?"

"Ava? Why are you covered in dirt?" asked Bri as she ran up next to us.

"Yeah, and water," Jade followed.

"Is that blood?" Lexi gasped.

"Where?"

"On your wrists!"

"Probably from the robots or the chains."

"What!?" they all shouted.

"Ladies, what is going on?" A teacher walked over.

"Oh right, I have to make an announcement to the group," I stated as Lexi tried to pick the lock on my chains.

"A what?" the teacher asked.

"Trust me, it's important."

"I can't get it!" Lexi exclaimed.

"It's fine Lex, let me talk to the group."

"Are you going to explain to us first?"

"You can all hear it," I said and gestured for her to sit.

"Ava, what are you doing?" The teacher looked completely horrified.

"Hello everyone," I said as I walked over to where the camera was stationed. "Sorry to interrupt your school photograph day, but I really need to tell you all this. I'm Ava, in case you didn't know. So you're probably all wondering why I'm covered in dirt and why I have chains on my hands and why I'm not in a hospital and stuff. Well, I have to explain to you all something very important and I don't have much time.

"A couple weeks ago I snuck outside the Bubble and went into the forests surrounding it."

Everyone gasped.

"Yes, I know, '*how did she do that?*' you all ask. Well, it doesn't matter how, the important part is that I did and I met some really amazing people. Yes, there were people outside the city. And they showed me the most incredible things and were so friendly and generous." I sighed. "The only thing is that they were boys."

Another gasp, even from the teachers.

"It was shocking because I thought they were extinct. Well, they're not! And once I got to know them I realised that they were actually just like us and completely harmless. I swear. And I thought to myself, hey, why are they excluded from our city?

"Then it hit me. Our parents don't like them. They're afraid of them because they've seen the bad sides of men. Well, *we* haven't. We haven't even been given a chance to see the good sides. And yes, there are good sides, many in fact. So I decided to try and include them in our city, because I was foolish enough to think it was that simple.

"You know what happened? The Council tried to have them murdered, destroyed their home, and almost killed me. But that's not all. Then, when I brought them here, the Council, our trusted Council, had them attacked by city robots, knocked unconscious and dragged off to who knows where, locked me in a prison cell, then ran off and left me in there to rot. And let me tell you this," my stomach growled, "I am really hungry."

There was a small laugh from the crowd.

"I know you all probably think I'm losing my mind, and I might be, but I have never been so sure about anything in my entire life. We have been lied to since the day we were born. Not just by the Council, but by our parents and anyone who has lived through the Wars. They all have this unspoken agreement, you see, that men were bad and the only way to protect us was to hide the truth. Sure they did it for our own good, but it was still unfair. We deserve to make our own opinions and decisions and think what we want. Maybe *we* are right. Sometimes people have trouble letting go of old ways and need the youngsters to help them out.

"And now my six caring friends are being taken away to be killed just for existing. So, I'm asking all of you to please help me. I believe that if we all say we want change, then they might listen. I don't know if our teachers agree, and I'm surprised that they haven't tried to drag me away for saying too much, but this is important. Don't just let these boys die."

I looked out at the crowd of girls, all sitting on the grass in their sundresses without a care in the world. They had been blissfully ignorant their whole lives, as had I until several months ago. Was it stupid of me to think that they would want to change that? I had to try.

"My friend Katelyn died believing them. She never knew that it was the virus-infected embryo they put inside of her that killed her. And they're going to put it in all of you too. This method of reproduction is doomed. Sylvia Carter herself told me and also stated outright that she had purposely put one in me so I wouldn't mess with their plans.

"They just lie and lie and lie. I was there when they said that Katelyn's test results were looking bad, but they still told you all that she was doing well. And before we knew it, there was a rotting pile of flowers in the town square."

One girl stood up. "But men are evil, why should we trust them?"

"You just answered your own question. You have been fooled into thinking that all men are evil, no matter what. You didn't make this opinion on your own! Where is your proof?"

"They almost destroyed everything!"

"Those men do not exist any more. Those few have become the generalisation for everyone. And think about this: if we are meant to be the better ones, then why are we going to oppress them the same way they once did us? This isn't about ancient conflicts, this is about us declaring that there is never just one side, and we want to know both."

"If you don't do this for me or for all those innocent boys or for Katelyn, at least do it for yourselves. Do you really want to die because the Council weren't bothered enough to let a couple of boys live with us? Because without these boys we will never be able to have more children. They are our last hope.

"Now I'm going to go find them, is anyone coming with me?"

There was silence and they all just stared at me in amazement. Then Lexi, Jade and Bri stood up.

"We're coming."

I felt tears sprouting. "Let's go then."

The four of us began walking down the street, me hobbling. At least I had my girls, I thought to myself.

"Ava, look," Bri said and tapped my shoulder.

I turned to see all of the girls getting up off the grass and walking over towards us. "Are they all…?"

"Coming? I think so." Bri smiled. "What other choice do they have but to follow crazy-insane-going-to-get-us-all-in-trouble Ava?"

I laughed. "If I had a free hand then I would hug you right now."

"Hug me later, we have work to do."

"Are you sure this is the right place?" Jade asked as we approached the robot complex.

"Pretty sure." I turned to the rest of the group of girls, and some teachers, behind me. "All right everyone! We're going to go inside and try and find the Council and the boys. Then we have to convince them to let the boys stay, and to make a few changes. Got it?"

There was a cheer from the group.

"Let's go!"

I leant over and scanned my eye on the scanner. The door clicked and I kicked it open.

"How did it open?"

"Sylvia is very bad at what she does."

We all marched through the gate and into the complex until we were in the middle of the huge group of buildings.

"What is this place?"

"Another secret."

I spotted some movement in one of the further buildings and directed the group towards it. We walked over to the door and Lexi shoved it open for me. Inside was a huge empty room with a few robots milling around.

"Let's try a different one."

We all marched over to the next building, and the next, until we found the Council all parked in the huge room, tablets in hand.

"What are you girls doing here?"

I waited until we had all filed inside and then I strolled over to the members and said, "Hello. Would anyone care to unchain me?"

"How did you…?"

"Oh this?" I said nonchalantly. "Sylvia Carter chained me and locked me in a cell, but who cares about that? We're all here about a much more important issue, right girls?"

They all cheered.

"We want to know where the boys are."

"What boys?"

"Yes, what on earth are you talking about?"

"Don't play dumb with me. We think it's about time that you all stopped lying to us. It is against the Oath."

Then it hit me.

"Of course! How come I didn't think of this earlier? I would like to make a motion to remove all members of the Council for breaking their Oath, effective immediately."

"You can't be serious!"

"Oh but I am. The Oath clearly states that 'We will be fair, we will be honest, we will be thoughtful, we will be kind, and we will be true'. I have found a direct violation of several of those."

"Like what?"

"You have not been thoughtful enough to consider the other side of these boys' stories. You have not been honest by lying to everyone about the condition of Katelyn Rose and the traits of men. You have not been kind by chaining my wrists," I held them up, "and locking me in a tiny cell. And you most certainly have not been true. Oh, and the whole virus embryo just seals the deal."

"Listen," said one of the Council members as she stepped forward, "we will not be bullied by some childish little girl."

Then the door slammed open and everyone snapped their head towards it.

"What on earth is going on?"

"Mother?" I ran over to the door to see her standing there, looking exhausted.

She walked inside. "I have been running around everywhere trying to find where my own Council went because it turns out that my daughter was locked in a cell and they didn't do anything about it! They told me she was escorted home! Then I finally come here in search of some answers and I pass by a room where six boys are lying on the floor unconscious. What is the meaning of this?"

Some of the Council members came forward to try and explain. "You see Donna, we all thought that it would be best if…"

"I don't care what you thought! This is an outrage! I am the Leader of the Council and I call the shots!"

"But Donna, you agreed that it would be best to remove the men from the forest as a simple way to solve the problem…"

"But I had no idea you would then hijack them! You do not get to make these decisions without my consent!"

"But Donna, you saw the security robots take the boys away to…"

"You said they were going to be dropped off in the forest again! What, were you planning to kill them? We all agreed that destroying their home would cause them to move further into the forest and further away from us. This is not what we agreed!"

"Donna, listen…"

"Shut up!"

Everyone gasped.

"Go Mother!" I cheered.

They all turned to me.

"Sorry."

"Ava, what are all these girls doing here?" Mother asked me.

"Actually, we were in the middle of moving to remove the Council members from the Council on direct violation of their Oath."

"I second that! And also for not following their Leader, which is in every Council member's Oath."

"Donna, be reasonable."

"Yes, this is outrageous."

"Now where is Sylvia Carter? I have a bone to pick with her." Mother began searching the crowd.

"Donna?" The Council members all looked at her with crazed eyes.

"Oh, you can leave now. I just approved your dismissal."

"But you need agreement from twenty citizens," one member protested.

"Oh do I?" Mother turned to the huge group of girls. "Who here agrees?"

Everyone raised their hands.

"Then it's settled. Goodbye Margaret – and the rest of you too."

The woman Mother referred to as Margaret came right up in her face. "We were only doing what was best for the community."

"Yes, well I guess your judgment was off then. Have a nice day, ladies."

One by one, the Council members all dumped their tablets on the ground and marched out of the door. Mother stood perfectly still and it suddenly hit me that she too had broken the Oath. In fact, in regards to being honest she was almost worse than the rest. I knew she was no saint yet there was something so sad in her eyes that comforted the nagging feeling I had that she wouldn't make any changes. Even though it was wrong for me not to move to remove her too, I knew that if anyone was going to completely reconstruct a Council, it would be Donna Hart.

I turned to Mother and asked, "But what are you going to do without a Council?"

"We'll figure something out. But now," she said as she grabbed my hands, "what do you say we go find those boys?"

"Are you serious?" My hopes soared.

"I think it's about time for some change. You're right, we need to let go. This fixed mindset has made everyone lose sense of their principles a little."

"Oh Mother!" I leapt into her arms.

She laughed. "Come on Ava, let's go."

Epilogue

Ava, A Couple of Weeks Later

"Are you nervous?" Bri whispered to me as we sat side by side in the front row.

"What me? Nervous? Never." I brushed it off.

"Then why are your hands shaking?"

I looked down and saw my palm shivering slightly on my chair. "Oh that's nothing."

Bri squeezed my hand. "Don't worry. I'm sure they'll do great."

"I hope so, Bri."

Lexi leant over from Bri's other side and whispered, "I think Jade fell asleep. Are they starting soon?"

"They should be. And how on earth did she fall asleep?"

"It's Jade."

"True, true."

"Quiet, it's starting," Bri said and pointed at the stage.

A tall regal woman with fabulous black hair glided on to the stage and held up the mic. "Welcome everyone. Today is a very important day for us all, and a significant point in our city's history, for we are welcoming not only new citizens, but also new friends, and a new perspective. I know that once our city fell into despair when judgment got clouded, even though we all believed we were doing what was right. But now I urge you all to see life with an open mind and keep our strong values and morals as our highest priority, even if they mean accepting something new or uncomfortable.

"Now I would like to thank all of you who helped us to see the light in our foolish ways, and we now know that sometimes those that have not seen the world as much as we have can act as a fresher pair of eyes. Thank you to all the un-graduates that stood up for what they believed in during our time of loss.

"Could Ava Hart, my beloved daughter and the founder of this great step in our city's development, please come forward to welcome our new citizens?"

"That's your cue," Bri said and nudged me.

"Wish me luck." I stood and walked out on to the stage as the crowd applauded.

Mother greeted me then continued, "Ava here marks the newly unveiled Integration Phase, which will take place along with the recently modified Repopulation Phase. She also marks the new Council Initiative Phase, which will redesign how the Council runs and how to include representatives from the school and local businesses to give feedback from their peers. The temporary Council is hard at work preparing all of this and our next Elections for Leaders of each subdivision will be taking place in a month's time. And to top all of that off, she marks the Re-Education Phase, which will work to teach an unbiased history and life skills lessons to all members of the community. Thank you to Ava for making all of this possible, for we wouldn't have all of this if she hadn't gone off and run into the forest when I specifically told her not to."

There was laughter from the audience as Mother shook my hand. "Thank you Ava, and we all wish you the best of luck with your pregnancy. Now will you please help me to welcome our six new citizens."

"My pleasure."

I turned over my shoulder to see the boys all walk on to the stage proudly, some of them waving, others just smiling, and all wearing shirts.

The audience cheered as they came on and formed a line.

"Now give your citizen's Oath and we shall welcome you into our city."

The boys all began in as best synchronisation as they could manage. "We, the people, promise that we will fulfil our duties to our community and support our Leader as long as he or she obeys their Oath. We will represent our city with honour. We will be fair, we will be honest, we will be thoughtful, we will be kind, and we will be true. We promise this in honour of our liberators, who fought to keep our race alive and to maintain unity. Long live the people of Emiscyra."

The crowd cheered and I walked over to the end of the line and held Derron's hand as I announced, "I now present the new citizens of Emiscyra!"

"Well done up there, Ava." A woman walked over and congratulated me.

"Oh thank you, but I owe it all to this guy here." I put my arm around Derron.

"She's far too modest," he said, smiling down at me.

"Well, congratulations to you too, young man," said the woman and tapped him on the shoulder. "Oh, and on the baby of course!" She winked at us.

We both laughed and said, "Why, thank you."

The woman walked off and I turned to Derron. "So I guess you're an official citizen now."

"I guess I am," he said and smiled as if just understanding it now. "Funny to think that only a couple weeks ago I was spearing fish and dangling off trees."

"And look at you now! All clean and not a spot of dirt!"

"Very funny," he said and wrapped his arms around my waist. "But I do recall you finding my muddy hair very..."

"Ava! Derron!" Mother waved to us from the other side of the room.

"Come on, you can tell me when we get home." I held his hand and the two of us walked over to where Mother was standing.

"Hello darling, you were fabulous," she said and pulled me into a hug. "And you too, Derron." She hugged him as well.

"Thanks Mother," he replied and grinned at me over her shoulder.

"So, any sign of Sylvia Carter?" I asked her.

"No, I'm afraid not. One minute she's all 'I have to protect the city'; next thing she's gone and run off into the forest."

"You really think she just ran away? You sure she's not hiding?"

"Where is there to hide? The city is tiny."

"Well, as long as she's gone..."

"That's what I think," said Mother with a smile.

I knew there probably wasn't much to worry about, but I was just having trouble believing Sylvia Carter was gone for good. I couldn't shake off the feeling that she was planning something. Something bad.

"Now you two go and enjoy the rest of the party and I'll see you at home."

I shrugged it off. "OK, bye Mother." As we walked over to the other boys I whispered to Derron, "I can't believe they still won't give us our own house."

"It's OK, I think your mother's just worried."

"About what?"

"Missing you," he said and smiled.

I laughed. "How come you know everything?"

"That's why you love me."

"Derron!" Owen came over and slapped him on the back. "Where'd you guys go?"

"Just socialising. Where's Cain?"

"Talking to his mother or something."

"So Ava, we're actual citizens now!" Mason said excitedly.

"Yeah, you are. I never thought this day would come." The whole thing still amazed me.

"Well, now that it has, what do you have to say?" Derron pulled me towards him.

I smiled. "Welcome home."

About the Author

Simi Prasad is an American expat living in London. Currently, she attends an international independent school and lives with her parents and sister.

She wrote *Out There* at the age of fifteen.

It is her first novel.

Lightning Source UK Ltd.
Milton Keynes UK
UKOW051410110213

206126UK00001B/1/P